Over the Edge

The Crime Writers of Canada Anthology

Edited by
Peter Sellers and Robert J. Sawyer

Pottersfield Press
Lawrencetown Beach, Nova Scotia, Canada

© Copyright 2000 by Pottersfield Press for the writers

All rights reserved. No part of this publication may be reproduced or transmitted in any form or by any means, electronic or mechanical, including photocopying, or by any information storage or retrieval system, without permission in writing from the publisher.

Canadian Cataloguing in Publication Data

    Main entry under title:

    Over the edge

    ISBN 1-895900-29-8

1. Detective and mystery stories, Canadian (English) *. 2. Canadian fiction (English) — 20th century*. 3. Sellers, Peter, 1956– II. Sawyer, Robert J. III. Crime Writers of Canada.

PS8323.D4092 1999   C813'.087208054   C99-950248-4
PR9197.35.D48092 1999

Credits:
Cover illustration: Woman with Revolver by Alex Colville. 1987. Acrylic polymer emulsion on panel. Copyright A.C. Fine Art.

Pottersfield Press gratefully acknowledges the ongoing support of the Nova Scotia Department of Tourism and Culture, Cultural Affairs Division, as well as The Canada Council for the Arts. We acknowledge the financial support of the Government of Canada through the Book Publishing Industry Development Program for our publishing activities.

Printed in Canada

Pottersfield Press
83 Leslie Road
East Lawrencetown
Nova Scotia, Canada, B3Z 1P8
To order, telephone 1-800-NIMBUS9 (1-800-646-2879)

For David Skene-Melvin

Over the Edge Copyright Information

"Licensed Guide" copyright 1992 by Eric Wright. Originally published in *Criminal Shorts*, edited by Howard Engel and Eric Wright. Reprinted by permission of the author.

"But the Corpse Can't Laugh" copyright 1999 by Mary Jane Maffini. Originally published in *Ellery Queen's Mystery Magazine*. Reprinted by permission of the author.

"Legacy" copyright 1985 by Terence M. Green. Originally published in *The Magazine of Fantasy and Science Fiction*. Reprinted by permission of the author.

"The Detective's Wife" copyright 1990 by Edward D. Hoch. Originally published in *Crosscurrents*. Reprinted by permission of the author.

"The Altdorf Syndrome" copyright 1969 by James Powell. Originally published in *Ellery Queen's Mystery Magazine*. Reprinted by permission of the author.

"Double Bogey" copyright 1992 by John North. Originally published in *Cold Blood IV*, edited by Peter Sellers. Reprinted by permission of the author.

"Generation Y" copyright 1999 by Nancy Kilpatrick.

"Trophy Hunter" copyright 1999 by Peter Sellers. Originally published in *Whistling Past the Graveyard*. Reprinted by permission of the author.

"Gifts" copyright 1999 by Rosemary Aubert.

"You See But You Do Not Observe" copyright 1995 by Robert J. Sawyer. Originally published in *Sherlock Holmes in Orbit*, edited by Mike Resnick and Martin H. Greenberg. Reprinted by permission of the author.

"Ice Bridge" copyright 1997 by Edo van Belkom. Originally published in *Northern Frights IV*, edited by Don Hutchinson. Reprinted by permission of the author.

"The Prize in the Pack" copyright 1986 by William Bankier. Originally published in *Ellery Queen's Mystery Magazine*. Reprinted by permission of the author.

"Sister Companion" copyright 1999 by Therese Greenwood.

"Keller's Therapy" copyright 1993 by Lawrence Block. Originally published in *Playboy*. Reprinted by permission of the author.

Contents

Introduction	7
Eric Wright	
Licensed Guide	9
Mary Jane Maffini	
But the Corpse Can't Laugh	17
Terence M. Green	
Legacy	36
Edward D. Hoch	
The Detective's Wife	42
James Powell	
The Altdorf Syndrome	55
John North	
Double Bogey	75
Nancy Kilpatrick	
Generation Y	97
Peter Sellers	
Trophy Hunter	105
Rosemary Aubert	
Gifts	134
Robert J. Sawyer	
You See But You Do Not Observe	140
Edo van Belkom	
Ice Bridge	158
William Bankier	
The Prize in the Pack	170
Therese Greenwood	
Sister Companion	188
Lawrence Block	
Keller's Therapy	196

Introduction

The Crime Writers of Canada was born amid the smoke and din of a midtown Toronto watering hole called Dooley's. It was 1983 and a small group — including Howard Engel and British mystery writer Tim Heald — had been summoned by the legendary Derrick Murdoch. Derrick had been the mystery book reviewer for *The Globe and Mail* for years, providing literate and insightful commentary on a genre that was still widely dismissed as inconsequential. He was also the author of such non-fiction works as *Disappearances* and the Edgar Award-nominated *The Agatha Christie Mystery*.

Derrick's idea was a professional society of writers, editors, booksellers and others who shared a common interest in crime and mystery writing. He saw opportunities for bringing members of an isolated community together for mutual support and to help promote members work to the public. Sixteen years later, Dooley's is long gone as, sadly, is Derrick Murdoch, but the Crime Writers of Canada has grown from that small group of half a dozen to more than 150, including virtually every professional crime writer in Canada. As well, the CWC boasts members in the United States, England and France.

In the spring of 1984, the CWC presented its Arthur Ellis Award for the first time. Eric Wright was the recipient, for his first Charlie Salter novel *The Night the Gods Smiled*. The Chairman's Award was presented as well — by

CWC's first Chairman Tony Aspler to Derrick Murdoch for his tremendous contributions to the genre in Canada. A year later, the award was renamed the Derrick Murdoch Award in memory of the CWC's founder.

In 1984, another significant event occurred. The CWC published its first anthology. The book was called *Fingerprints* and featured stories by sixteen members. Unlike the Arthur Ellis Awards, however, which were presented again in 1985 and every year since, there was never a follow-up CWC anthology. Until now.

Over the Edge brings you fourteen more of the best stories by members of the Crime Writers of Canada. Ten of the authors live in Canada, two are Canadians living abroad, and two are Americans who have close ties with Canada and are CWC members of long standing.

At some point, in every story of crime and mystery a character stands on the edge and looks into the abyss. These stories are about what happens to bring people to that moment; what happens in that moment, and the consequences that follow.

Invariably truths are uncovered. Sometimes they are visions of compassion and revelations of previously untapped inner strength. Other times they are dark and vicious secrets. In each of the fourteen cases presented here, however, the truths revealed are fascinating and richly rewarding.

It's been fifteen years since there was an anthology like this one. We think Derrick Murdoch would feel it was worth the wait.

Welcome to the Crime Writers of Canada's world. Come in. And follow us over the edge.

Licensed Guide

Eric Wright

Eric has won more Arthur Ellis Awards than anyone else: twice for Best Novel (*The Night the Gods Smiled* in 1984 and *A Death in the Old Country* in 1986) and twice for Best Short Story. In addition to his most famous creation, Charlie Salter of the Toronto Police, Eric has also established series about private detective Lucy Trimble and Sergeant Mel Pickett, a minor character in the Salter series brought centre stage. His most recent book, published to excellent reviews, is a memoir called *Always Give a Penny to a Blind Man* and a collection of his short stories is forthcoming. Back in the 1950s, soon after emigrating to Canada from his native England, Eric found work as a fishing guide in the north. That experience forms the vivid core of his 1994 comic novel *Moodie's Tale* and also of this sharp and evil story.

Our history teacher in grade nine was insane. He was an old man, "grizzled," I realized, when I discovered the word about that time, who wanted in his youth to be an athlete and got as far as the training camp of a professional football team. After he failed to make the cut he went into teaching — physical education and history.

He spent most of his time on the playing fields and in the gym, assisting the team coaches and generally getting in the way. He had a simple mind, and an equally simple code of life. He liked to see struggle, effort, self-discipline, the team spirit, and death in battle (he had a very distinguished war record, having fought at Ypres with the Princess Pats). His history teaching was a record of heroes and gallant failures. He couldn't stand liars, cheats, or boys who didn't look him square in the eye. We were terrified of him.

On a day in May, he left the room for a few minutes, first warning us to be totally silent. We were quiet for thirty seconds, then someone said, "He's having a quick drag in the can," and old Baker reappeared in the doorway, his face dark with fury. "Who said that?" he asked. No one spoke. He was clearly already out of control, looking to kill.

He went round the room. "Was it you?" he asked us, one at a time, and one at a time we looked him in the eye and answered, "No." All except Simpson, whose gaze wavered. Baker asked him again and Simpson denied it a second time, but now he blushed and looked away. Old Baker hit him so hard that Simpson's head bounced off the wall. (He told us later that he was deaf for two days afterwards.) "I can always tell," Baker said, looking round the room. "I can always tell."

What has this to do with the drowning of a man in a fishing camp, fifteen years later? A great deal, apparently, because even now, thirty years after the drowning, one incident always recalls the other.

# # #

They arrived one afternoon, three of them, a man named Baxter and his wife, and his business partner, Crossley. Three was an awkward number because we were set up to guide the guests in pairs: it was not possible to put three guests in one boat, and uneconomic to allocate a guide to a single guest. There was nothing else for it, though. Bailey, the camp owner, (Bailey's Circle Lake Lodge — "We fly you in, We fly you out"), assigned them to Henry Goose and me, and the following morning we waited for them on the dock to ask them how they wanted to split up.

"We'll go with Henry," Baxter said after a glance at the two of us. You could see his mind working; the Indian was bound to be the better guide.

I moved to put Crossley's bag in my boat. "No," Baxter said.

"*We'll* go with Henry. *You* take her."

His wife said nothing, simply leaned against the rail of the dock, smoking, while she waited. I picked up her bag, held the boat steady for her to get in, and checked with Henry where we should start the day.

"Grassy Narrows," Henry said.

I started the motor and headed across the lake. We would meet up at noon for shore lunch.

It took me half an hour to get to the first spot I wanted to try. As we travelled across the lake to the Narrows, Mrs. Baxter kept her eyes on the landscape without attempting to connect with me. She was a handsome woman, lean rather than slim, whose clothes were made for her, as well as being right for a day's fishing.

For the first hour with a new party you tried to assess the kind of guests they were, and then you planned the next three days. There were the familiar, chatty ones who wanted your approval at first. You had to be careful with these because they quickly became bored and could turn on you. Usually knowing very little about fishing, they measured their pleasure in terms of the number and size of fish caught. At first they were delighted to hook a two-pound walleye, but after two days a hundred five-pound fish a day wasn't enough.

At the other extreme, and much to be preferred at the end of summer, were the professional fishermen who knew that fish stopped biting sometimes, and judged you by your skill, not on the day's luck. You had to work hard for these, but they knew what you were doing and appreciated it.

Occasionally a third kind appeared, the rich sportsmen who happened to be fishing in northern Canada between shooting mountain sheep in Chile, and hunting caribou in Alaska. These people thought of themselves as *bwana* and treated you accordingly. They talked to each other about you as if you didn't understand English, or just weren't there.

These were three such guests. Alone with me, Mrs. Baxter stayed silent. I tried her with a remark when her line was in the water. "I guess those guys want to fish together," I said.

"It was my idea," she said and turned her back.

This was fine with me. Whatever she wanted I was there to provide. It was late in the season, and by this time I was tired of it; I was burned black, my hands were covered in dozens of little cuts from the spines and gills of fish I had handled, and I had told the same stories to too many guests.

She fished hard all day, stopping only when we met the others for shore lunch. Henry and I got the fire going and cooked some of the fish they had caught while our guests drank and compared notes on the fishing and on us, their guides. I didn't have to prick up my ears to hear her say I seemed to know my job. She knew I was listening, but it didn't inhibit her.

In the afternoon we fished for pike and bass, and she very quickly absorbed everything I knew, and by the end of the day could have guided me, needing only to know the name of the prey in order to go after it with the right tackle.

At supper in the guides' dining-room that night, Henry said his experience with the two men had been that of a taxi-driver. "I drove, they fished," he said. "I don't think the other guy spoke to me once."

The next day they switched. Crossley went with Henry, and I guided the Baxters. Baxter was not sure yet that he had the best, so he was trying me for a day before he let his wife or Crossley have the guide he didn't want. "I'll try Duck Lake," Henry said. "You go to the falls. I'll meet you there for shore lunch."

That suited me. Meynell Falls was actually a very steep rapids where Meynell Lake emptied into Ebb Lake, creating a big whirlpool where the fish gathered to feed on whatever came down the rapids. The pickerel here were darker for some reason, almost black and gold, and they fought like bass, which made for livelier fishing. The thing was, you couldn't anchor as you usually did for pickerel, because the water was too fast. You kept the motor going at half speed and tried to keep the boat pointed at the falls. You were usually good for a couple of minutes before the current caught the prow and swept you round in a circle to come back for another try. All three people had to cooperate closely to keep their lines clear as you circled, especially if one of them had a bite.

The Baxters could see the way it was and we did a couple of passes and caught three fish. Then, on the third pass, he threw the anchor over the side without checking with me first. The anchor was only a big piece of rock on the end of a rope tied to the back seat, and the rock was in front of Baxter on the floor of the boat. I didn't see him throw it in because I was turned around to watch to see the lines weren't crossing behind us, but I felt the boat lurch and I heard the rope twang as it went taut. I had my filleting knife handy on the seat beside me because I liked to clean the fish as soon as we caught them, otherwise you had to clean a sackful of fish at the end of the day in the camp fish hut, a stinking shed full of flies. I cut the rope just as the water started to pour over the back of the boat, and we stayed the right way up. I shut down the motor and we drifted while I scooped some of the water out of the boat, not wanting the motor to pull the stern down any further until I had lightened the boat a little. Then I started the motor and pulled over to the shore where we dried out and I explained.

"The anchor and the current pull against each other, so in fast water the current pulls down the back of the boat and we fill up. Can you swim?"

I was speaking nearly as hostilely as I felt, but Baxter didn't say anything. Nor did she. I think they saw the whole thing as my problem.

Henry appeared for shore lunch and I waited for Baxter to tell his pal, but he didn't say a word, so I helped Henry cook the lunch and we went fishing again. I said it wasn't worth going back to camp for a new anchor rope, and we would spend the afternoon trolling.

"I'd like to try this spot again," Baxter said, looking back at the rapids as we picked up for home. "Now I know how it works."

# # #

The next day Baxter went up north by himself for three days to try the Arctic char fishing at Bailey's other camp. Both men were scheduled to go, but Crossley pleaded too much sun and said he wanted to stay inside for a couple of days. While Baxter was away I took care of his wife. Best of all she liked bass fishing, so I spent most of my time paddling the shore of Duck Lake. She still said almost nothing, indicating what she wanted from me with a word or a gesture, fishing hard until mid-afternoon, then gesturing me to take her home. That suited me.

Baxter came back a day early. The weather up north was bad, and he arrived before supper. Someone told him they thought his wife and I were still out on the lake — my boat wasn't in its usual spot. Baxter decided he was hungry and went up to Crossley's cabin to see if Crossley would join him for an early supper, but his pal was along the shore, watching Bailey's carpenters put the first logs in place for some new cabins. So Baxter ate alone.

I ran into him as he was leaving the dining room. He still had his bag, and I took it off him (the guides were also bellboys if needed) and walked with him up to his cabin. On the path we ran into Crossley and Mrs. Baxter, who were on their way to supper, Crossley having called in to collect her on the way by. I left them all to tell each other the news, and put Baxter's bag inside the door of his cabin.

Two days later, Crossley drowned at Meynell Falls.

It happened like this. On the second day back, I had Mrs. Baxter to myself again, while Baxter and Crossley went off on their own, without Henry. When we had checked with them after breakfast, the two men hadn't wanted to fish, but Mrs. Baxter was keen so I took her out and Henry went into town. Then, according to Bailey, about eleven o'clock Baxter had appeared and asked if he and Crossley could use Henry's boat by themselves. Bailey hated to allow this; even experienced guides from another part of the province could get lost around the English River system, and people from New York City were not to be trusted on their own out of sight of the dock, but in the end he agreed if they just puttered around the shore line.

# # #

I had a pretty good day. Even without too many words, I could understand what Mrs. Baxter wanted now, and I was happy without a lot of chat. Around three o'clock she pulled in her line for the last time, and I took her back and tied up at the camp dock just after six. Bailey was standing on the dock, looking worried.

"You pass Baxter on the way through the Narrows?" he asked me, before I had even tied up.

Mrs. Baxter took no further notice of us, simply walked up to her cabin.

I shook my head.

"They probably ran out of gas." He dropped a full tank into my boat. "Go look for them, will you? They might have missed the channel out of Meynell when they turned around. I'll send a couple of the other boys after you as they come in."

I plugged in the full tank and headed for Ebb Lake and the falls. I found the boat as soon as I turned into the channel. It was upside down, so low in the water that only the front of the keel was showing, caught between a pair of rocks near the bank. I moved my gas tank to the front of my boat to keep the prow down and nudged closer at half speed. Baxter waved from the other shore. He was soaking wet. I pulled in to take him off and looked round for Crossley.

"He's a goner," Baxter said. His teeth were chattering. "We did all the wrong things. He threw the anchor in and the current took us and we filled up right away, and capsized. I never saw him surface."

I took him back to camp and Bailey sent for the police. Henry's brother, David Goose, found Crossley's body tangled up in some weeds in a little bay not far from the falls.

There wasn't much to investigate: Baxter hadn't even seen it happen. All he knew was that the boat turned over while he was sitting in it after he heard the splash of the anchor, and when he surfaced he was close enough to the shore to save himself, but he lost sight of the boat and never saw Crossley again. A coroner was flown in and he declared it an accidental death.

The Baxters left next day. I saw them on the dock, her leaning against the rail, smoking. She caught my eye and gave me that classic signal, the nearly imperceptible shake of the head, then Bailey hustled them on to the plane that was waiting.

He'd killed Crossley, of course, but I didn't speak up right away and then I knew I never would. The thing that made it certain was his story about the anchor. Henry didn't have an anchor: I'd borrowed his when he went to town because I still didn't have one as good as his. I had found a small rock, but it didn't always hold, so I'd wrapped a rope around it and put it in Henry's boat, just so if Henry came back he could fix himself up with some kind of anchor, but I hadn't tied it to the seat, just kind of tucked it under out of the way. The police were surprised the anchor wasn't still dragging the boat, even when it capsized, but in the end they guessed it came untied, so that was that.

I reckon Baxter threw it in, trying to capsize the boat, and when the rock disappeared, he just found another way to dump the boat.

I also knew *why* he'd killed Crossley.

The day he came back early from fishing for Arctic char, he had gone looking for Crossley in his cabin; then, not finding him, had walked on to his own cabin. With his hand on the door he had heard sounds from within, guessed what he was hearing, and turned around to go back to the dining room. Then, on his way back from supper, he had met Crossley and his wife on the way down. What Baxter had heard was his wife, giving voice at last, crying out, before I could shush her. At the time, I thought Baxter was one of the maids, come to clean the room.

So you can see why, whenever I think of Baxter, I think of that old history teacher banging Simpson's head against the wall. Even now, I still wake up feeling bad about Simpson.

But the Corpse Can't Laugh

Mary Jane Maffini

Since her first story appeared, in 1994's *Cold Blood V*, Mary Jane has established herself as a leading practitioner of the crime short story. She won the Arthur Ellis Award in 1997 for "Cotton Armour" and has become a regular contributor to *Ellery Queen's Mystery Magazine*. Co-owner of Ottawa's Prime Crime Bookshop, Mary Jane is also an editor whose most recent anthology, *Menopause is Murder*, is the third in a successful series from General Store Publishing. Mary Jane's first novel *Speak Ill of the Dead* was published in the fall of 1999. This story, reprinted from *Ellery Queen's Mystery Magazine*, demonstrates Mary Jane's gifts for quirky humour and devious plot making.

I remembered biting the ears off a pair of white chocolate Easter bunnies somewhere around three a.m. Then nothing. Morning found me with a deep thirst, a throb over my left temple, and a serious dip in my seratonin levels. Plus I felt hot, damp and sticky, trapped in a sweaty twist of sheets.

I opened one eye just a slit.

Was Harlan around? No. My brother could never resist flicking the two hundred-watt overhead lights on and off a few times when he crawled home. I had no recollection of snapping awake to a blinding flash of light, therefore Harlan was still out.

I desperately needed a hair of the dog and since dawn is never Harlan's sprightliest time, it was probably safe to go to the bathroom.

I managed to launch myself into my Dynamo scooter and turn the key. I held the left handlebar. I needed my right hand to keep my head from falling off. An empty Laura Secord box crunched as the front wheel crushed it.

I stuck my nose in Harlan's room. His bed was still tight as a fresh face lift. For sure he hadn't come home last night. Unless he'd made it to throw me off, and maybe he'd be crouched behind the shower curtain waiting to spring out wearing his clip-on fangs.

Ha ha Harlan.

Bad luck in the bathroom. Harlan must have found my stash again. No problemo. That's why I keep a secret stockpile of Toblerone in the pantry. He thinks I can't reach.

Sweat trickled between my shoulder blades. As soon as I choked down my Toblerone, I would turn on the A/C and then stick my face into the freezer side of the fridge.

I closed my eyes and motored along the fuschia hallway. Harlan picked that color, painted over Mother's silk wallpaper, knowing it would raise my core body temperature.

I made a left into the living room, which used to be my favorite spot with its pale sand walls and sweeping view of trees, lawn and ravine. Until Harlan purchased two gallons of Tangerine Tango Semi-gloss and took one wild swipe at the walls stopping over the fireplace by the edge of the oversize oil portrait of Mother and Father. A couple of orange splots speckled the gilt frame. A glob glistened on a Limoges dish.

Forget that, Harlan. I won't give in. It would take more than Tangerine Tango to drive me from my home. You can be the one to leave. If I can cope with life with these useless legs, I can cope with anything.

Harlan lay snoozing on the living room floor, his legs bent in a Fred Astaire pose. His toupée flopped a foot away, like a dead guinea pig. A Dairy Milk wrapper peeked out coyly from behind his left loafer and a lot of red gunk occupied the place where his face used to be.

Ha ha Harlan.

I wasn't falling for that. I didn't get close enough for the supposed stiff to grab my ankle.

I said. "Very funny." *A bit of ketchup squirted on your face is not enough to get rid of me.*

I kept rolling toward the kitchen.

Was it hot. Were those damn flashes going to start in the morning now? Wait. A. Minute. How many times would Harlan play the old thermostat trick before I caught on?

Sure enough. Set at 38 degrees. That'll do it. Harlan had repositioned the thermostat high on the dining room wall, over the china cabinet, out of reach from the Dynamo.

Ha ha Harlan. It will take more than that today.

I tried the barbecue fork to reach the thermostat. Too short. The broom handle was long enough but too bulky to control the buttons. Finally I taped a pencil, eraser-end up to the end of the broom handle and flicked the A/C switch.

I could count on Harlan's sense of dramatic purpose to remain in the same position until the joke was over. No point in making it easy for him. I rolled back into the living room with a bowl of Baskin-Robbins mint chocolate chip ice cream and parked. Some people chug-a-lug Prozac. Since when do synthetics compete with real chocolate?

I ate the ice cream while observing Harlan's absolute stillness and marveling at his stamina. No wonder he was so often a jump ahead of me.

Harlan had said the painter was coming at nine to finish the tangerine job.

"I'll just wait here for that painter, Harlan. Don't bother to get up."

My eye caught a peculiar metallic glint poking out under the sofa dust cover. I put down the ice cream and reached for it. Very funny. A revolver. With a strange crude metal cylinder near the top. What was that supposed to be? A homemade silencer?

Nice detail, Harlan but you're not catching me with Krazy Glue again.

I took a good look at that gun. Brown smudges smeared the butt and the trigger. Looked like Lindt's finest.

Watching a person play dead can get tedious once your ice cream's gone, so I picked up Harlan's toupée. And his favorite lighter. The one where the bathing suit falls down. "Never kid a kidder, Harlan." Not even Harlan would stay dead while his genuine human hair custom-made European hairpiece went up in smoke.

The toupée caught nicely, issuing a stream of fumes and a smell you'd rather forget. I had to admire Harlan. Not a twitch.

No points to me. Much as I hated to have Harlan out-cool me one more time, I hated the idea of having to peel Krispy Crunch bars with burnt fingers even more.

I tried blowing out the flames but the hairpiece was too hot to handle. "Ouch," I yelped and flung it onto the floor. The flames licked at the cuff of his stretch shirt and caught. Harlan didn't flinch. The room took on the acrid scent of burning flesh. No no no. I yanked up the dustcover and grabbed the silk cushions from the sofa to beat at the blaze, bumping Harlan with the Dynamo.

By the time I extinguished Harlan, it sank in. I'd always felt like killing him. Now I wouldn't have to.

I sagged back in the Dynamo and closed my eyes. I wasn't sure if the chill I felt was just shock. I could hear myself breathing, like a clogged sump pump.

Mother always said every cloud has a silver lining.

Right. Someone had done me one hell of a favor.

But who should get the thank-you?

Well, the first choice would be Buddy, Harlan's business partner in The Camelot Golf and Country Club. Then Angie, his current mistress. Surely even someone of her low tastes must be getting tired of having plastic cockroaches in her bed. And what about Jack, our nearest neighbor? He'd squandered his severance package on Harlan's useless tips on the market. Who else? Harlan had been dropped by his doctor, his dentist and his broker all of whom had bleated about legal action. I wasn't sure how Harlan headed off all those lawsuits but the word blackmail came to mind.

Yep. The list of suspects would read like the phone book. Too bad I'd be "A".

Everyone knew Harlan was bleeding the family business. Everyone knew I was fighting to regain legal control and Harlan was scheming to get me out of our family home so he could sell it. Everyone knew we hated each other.

I felt my seratonin levels dipping dangerously. I got as far as the desk drawer and pulled out a couple of Snickers hidden in a file. My hands were starting to quiver.

Ha ha Harlan. You're not going to get to me this time.

Maybe I could get off on a psychological abuse defense. No shortage of people who would corroborate that. But why should I have to defend myself? Harlan was finally satisfyingly gloriously dead and I wanted the freedom to sit back and enjoy it. I wanted to sleep without expecting ice cubes dropped into the bed. I wanted to use the toilet without finding a dock spider poised to take a jump. I wanted . . . I wanted to stop trembling.

The Snickers didn't do the trick.

Think. What next? That painter was due soon. He'd call the police. Ha Ha Harlan probably wouldn't even mind being dead knowing just how much doo-doo I'd be in.

It would be better to have Harlan out of the way before the room filled with witnesses.

# # #

One good thing about Harlan, he never trusted anybody. Correctly as it turned out. All that paranoia could come in handy. That false wall in the walk-in closet in his bedroom might be just the ticket to buy me a bit of time.

Harlan had that wall built to foil the burglars he was always expecting. That's where he kept his video equipment, cameras, coins, stock certificates, you name it. Mother's jewelry was hidden too, on a shelf six feet up. I had to ask nicely if I wanted it. Harlan kept Father's stamp collection there, at least the part he hadn't sold. The temperature was right for Father's vintage port and the 18-year-old scotch. God help any foolish break-in artist who swilled down anything in the decanters in the living room.

Of course, I got to stay right out in the open in a house with five doors in the middle of a dozen wooded acres, a sitting duck for burglars and, now, it seemed, murderers. But the joke was on Harlan. *Ha ha.*

It wasn't easy wrapping Harlan and his toupée in a moldy old sleeping bag and rigging up a travois with the broom, the mop and my travel clothesline. I used a towel to pick up the chocolately weapon. I wiped it well and tucked it in his pocket. I hoped I wouldn't blow the little five amp motor right out of the Dynamo dragging him.

The switch to open the false wall sits at the back of the fourth shelf behind Harlan's out-of-season Italian sweaters. The broom stick was still tied up in the travois so this time I attached the pencil to the yard stick. After about five longish minutes, I toggled the switch. Sure enough the wall swung.

Ha ha Harlan. I found a new use for your secret space.

The Dynamo does not have that much mobility and it took one hell of a long time tugging and yanking to get Harlan tucked in. It wasn't that easy with the mold from the sleeping bag irritating my nose. The stinky hairpiece didn't help either. Harlan was hard and wiry to begin with. Now he'd started to stiffen. I caught a sharp whack in the face with his left arm as I struggled.

Ho ho, too late, Harlan, I'm in charge now.

Using reverse, I managed to wedge him up against a stack of stamp catalogues, with what was left of his head resting on a black-bound collection of penny reds.

I toggled the wall closed and drove myself straight to the shower. It took half a tank of hot water, half a tube of Watermelon shower gel and two brushings with Sensodyne to rid myself of the smell and taste.

# # #

Afterwards I drank an entire fudge milkshake to build up those endorphins. Only then could I head back to the living room and turn my attention to the brownish, rabbit-shaped stain on the hardwood. I had an idea. I slapped down some newspaper and plunked the paint tray and the can on it.

The doorbell rang.

The painter already. I still had a bit of covering up to do. I wrestled with the first can of paint and managed to pry it open using Harlan's Swiss Army knife. The doorbell rang again before I accomplished what I wanted to.

I bet you're laughing Harlan.

The doorbell pealed a third time and, almost immediately, again. No wonder I couldn't handle that paint can, my hands were shaking.

On the fifth ring, I gave up.

I ran my tongue over my teeth in case of fudge residue, straightened my spine and called out.

"Hold your water, I'm on my way."

Pushy painter. Now I had no choice but to send him packing until I covered Harlan's traces.

But it was not a painter.

Someone soft, squishy and middle-aged looked down, looked startled, looked embarrassed, and looked away.

I'm used to it.

A real estate agent? Bastard Harlan. I felt a wave of hysteria. But Harlan can't sell the house or any property if I don't want to leave. Terms of Father's will. Not that it matters now.

"Hobart residence?" he asked.

"Who wants to know?" I said.

"May I come in?" His voice was like a double malted. No, rich, creamy chocolate syrup. Distracting. And what did he call himself?

"Did you say Detective Fudge?"

"Budge." He patted down a wayward cowlick.

"Oh." Too bad.

"May I come in?"

"What for?" I said.

"There's something I need to discuss with you."

I haven't lived with Ha Ha Harlan all my life without learning a few things. Question everything and everybody. This guy's rumpled gray suit was enough to make my spider senses tingle.

"How do I know you're the police, Detective Smudge?"

He blinked.

"Can I see your badge?"

"You know, I should have showed it to you." He felt around for the badge in several pockets until he fished out a plastic holder. I leaned forward and squinted at it. You'd think the police would know where their badges were.

Behind him, perhaps for added effect, a cruiser edged into the driveway. A uniformed officer ejected and marched crisply toward the house. If knife-edged creases were a clue, this man knew where his badge was. But maybe the joker who pulled the fast one on Harlan still wanted to play. You had to be pretty sharp to get the drop on Harlan.

"Constable Cuddihy," he said, like he had something to celebrate.

"I'll check with the station," I said, closing the door in their faces.

"Sorry," I said, opening it two minutes later. "Living out here, I never take anything on face value."

Mr. Smooth and Fudgy nodded. "You know, I don't blame you."

Mr. Confidence and Creases said, "Can't be too careful these days." Up close, he had deep circles under his eyes and cheekbones sharp enough to cut.

They followed me into the living room, awkwardly, probably unsettled by the scooter.

"Have a seat," I said, keeping my voice cheerful. "Don't mind the dust covers. We're decorating."

They sat. I parked the Dynamo on the newspaper.

A heavy dose of Spring Bouquet room freshener masked the burnt smell. Just to be on the safe side I picked up one of Harlan's cigarettes and lit it.

"So, what can I do for you?" I asked, trying not to gag on the smoke. I deposited the cigarette in the ashtray and let it work on its own.

"Hmm?" Detective Budge seemed distracted by the spectacular slash of orange on the wall.

"Like it?" I said. "My brother prefers an invigorating decor." Invigorating yes, roughly like sticking your tongue into an electrical socket. The look they gave me was worth it.

"So?" I said encouragingly. I leaned forward, flipped up the lid, tipped the paint can and poured some into the paint tray.

Detective Budge recovered himself. "Sorry to bother you so early in the morning but . . ."

"Been up for ages, trying to get ready for the painter, which my brother was supposed to do," I said. "But how rude of me. It is early. Could I offer you a cup of hot chocolate."

"Perhaps later," Detective Budge said. "We received a call someone had been shot here."

I laughed. "You're kidding."

Detective Budge's eyes widened. A couple of new cowlicks sprang up.

Constable Cuddihy's bony jaw stiffened. "Killed," he said.

Oops. Laughter. Inappropriate response.

"Does it looks like someone's been killed here?" I tried to recoup a little dignity.

The Detective gave a diffident little shrug followed by a sheepish grin. "We have to follow up on these things."

"Of course," I said, "but who . . . ?"

"Anonymous."

"Well, naturally. But who's supposed to be dead?"

They both stared at their feet. I tried to look intrigued. Finally, Detective Budge stood up and shuffled towards me. This time, he looked me straight in the eye.

"Your brother."

I shrieked and lurched forward, strategically maneuvering the Dynamo to hit the paint tray. Orange paint splashed everywhere, saturating the newspaper. "Harlan's dead?"

Detective Budge edged closer, risking a clot of orange on his suit. It was a pretty bad suit but even so. The man obviously had heart.

I moaned, "He didn't come home last night."

"You didn't call the police when he didn't come home?"

"For Harlan," I gasped. "You must be kidding."

"Pardon me?"

"He often stays out."

"He does? This is a pretty remote location, you know. You mean he leaves you alone and doesn't . . . "

He does more than that, fudge-man. He moves the phones out of my reach, and turns off the electricity at the main switch and . . .

"Wait a minute," I started hyperventilating, easy if I'm thinking about my little hell with Harlan. "What's the matter with me? It's just another joke. Ha ha!"

"Cuddihy, get a paper bag from the kitchen," Detective Budge said. "Make it snappy."

The constable clicked his heels.

"No no no," I warbled between long vibrato breaths. "That Harlan. He's pulling your leg. Gosh, I got such a fright, I think I'm going to faint."

I had my head between my legs and a great view of a bloodstain on my Phentex slipper when Constable Cuddihy goose-stepped back with a paper bag. "It's okay," I hiccuped. "Harlan scares the daylights out of me a couple of times a day."

Don't let them see that slipper.

The detective stroked my shoulder. What a light gentle touch! Cloudlike as an Aero bar.

I sat up and waved away the bag.

Detective Budge cleared his throat. "You know, we'll have to take a look around."

"Of course. Forgive me. Go ahead. Make sure you check behind the shower curtains."

They were still exchanging glances as they left the room.

I called after them, "Don't get too close to the beds. He likes to grab ankles. Made one of my friends pee on the floor once."

Detective Budge lurched back into the room, tiptoeing to avoid the tangerine puddles.

"Can I call someone for you? You seem . . . "

Hysterical? Well yes, that's the idea. "No, no one. Not a soul." I didn't have a single friend who'd been willing to set foot in Harlan's house for years.

"You know, I think . . . "

"Really, I'm fine. I'll just sit and wait for the painter. Gosh, I'll have to call someone to refinish the hardwood now."

As soon as they were out of sight, I grabbed the slipper with the bloodstain and dipped it into the nearest blob of Tangerine Tango.

All and all, I thought, that hadn't gone too badly.

# # #

"Constable Cuddihy's finished checking the grounds. Sorry to have bothered you," the detective said smoothly and fudgily.

"Don't worry about it." My voice was steady. Living with Harlan, you learn to keep your reactions secret. "I imagine you have no choice but to follow up on these things."

"Well, that's it."

"I hope Harlan's not going to be in trouble about all this … inconvenience."

"You know, if he's playing games, he sure could be."

"I suppose the sooner he shows up, the better."

"Right. He's chewing up valuable police resources."

"Dear me, would the valuable police resources like a Ferrero Rocher?" I opened a fresh package.

Detective Budge glowed. "Thank you, Mrs. Hobart."

"Miss," I said.

# # #

Of course, I'd backed myself into a corner. I had to get rid of Harlan permanently before he started to reek. Someone would notice me in my special van rolling a body into some convenient body of water. I couldn't hoist Harlan into a dumpster and anyway his fingerprints and dental records could pin the tail on that particular donkey.

The key thing was to have no one find the body.

Since the police had already searched the grounds, the septic tank seemed the perfect place. If I could figure out how to do it.

In the meantime, I kept the A/C on HIGH and gave myself a spray with mood-enhancing lily-of-the-valley fragrance. My seratonin levels stayed up. The next afternoon, I was nibbling on a nougat-filled chocolate, staring out through the rain at the section of lawn covering the septic tank and smirking to myself when Detective Budge came back.

I felt my endorphins go into overdrive. I hoped it didn't show on my face.

Detective Budge smiled like he was glad to see me too.

My skin temperature rose giving that lily-of-the-valley spray a second wind.

"Any sign of your brother?"

"He's probably waiting until the painting's finished."

"That the kind of thing he does?"

"I'm used to it."

He strolled to the picture window and looked out at the ravine and woods. "Pretty remote."

"I grew up here. I love it. Gets a little lonely now that friends don't drop in so much, that's all."

"So he just leaves you all by yourself?" He didn't say 'a helpless cripple' but I could practically see the thought bubble above his head.

"It's usually easier without him. Harlan's quite a character. Just ask his colleagues at the Club."

"Oh, we have."

"Really?"

"You know, we had a couple more calls."

"More . . . ? Gosh."

"You haven't heard anything strange?"

"Nothing but wind and rain."

"Gotta follow up. You know. Check the house and grounds again."

"Don't apologize," I said. "Take your time. It's a big place."

Detective Budge fidgeted.

"Is something wrong?" I asked. To my surprise I found I cared about the answer.

He loosened his collar. "I couldn't help but notice the bruises on your face. He doesn't . . . hurt you, does he?"

I started to say no. Stopped. Averted my eyes. Waited a beat. "Harlan has an anger control problem, especially since our parents died. He's working on it."

A muscle worked in Detective Budge's soft little jaw. "You can get help. They have counselors. Safe houses."

Of course, Harlan's never hit me. Too much evidence.

They don't have safe houses for Harlan's kind of hurting.

"I'll help you." He reached over and squeezed my hand.

God helps those who help themselves, Mother used to say. How long had it been since anyone had helped me but myself? God never noticed.

"I'll be okay." My eyes stung. That was real.

"Well, Cuddihy better get started."

"Nice that you could come along too."

"I wanted to make sure you were all right." A red flush crept up his neck.

"Gosh, the police are really taking this seriously."

"Hardly. If they were taking it seriously they wouldn't send the Loser Brigade."

"What do you mean?"

"Well, me, seventeen days from retirement, pretty well running on fumes. You know, that Cuddihy's been taken off anything serious since he shot the tires out of a gym teacher's Honda thinking a kidnapping was going on."

"Seems like a nice boy, though."

"Time bomb."

I held out the box of Black Magic. "Couple for the road?"

I would miss Detective Budge's visits. But, unless I found a way to get rid of Harlan soon, I'd probably be meeting him a lot at my trial.

He turned at the door. "Bit nippy in here. Sure you wouldn't like me to build you a fire?"

# # #

People were beginning to call. Customers. Suppliers. The Club accountant. Some shouted, some bellowed, some whined. One woman cried. But they all sang the same song of money or services owed. Talk about a downer. I could see my family legacy slipping from my fingers because of Harlan.

Then it happened. I was in the hidden closet changing a dish of baking soda. Starting to get whiffy in there. I decided to get Mother's pearls down in case they absorbed some of the odor. The yardstick and pencil did the trick. The entire case tumbled from the shelf. A wallet fell with it. I pocketed the pearls and the garnet earrings and opened the wallet. That's when I found Harlan's passport and a pair of airline tickets to Costa Rica. *Ha ha Harlan. What were you up to?*

I looked up at that shelf and spotted something else. Father's old leather case. Harlan usually kept that near his desk. It seemed worth the effort to knock it down.

Jackpot. The can was jammed with fifties and hundreds. I stopped counting at seven hundred thousand. Cool to the touch.

Sure sent my seratonin levels through the roof. I backed out and celebrated with an entire box of After Eights.

Where did Harlan get all that money?

Maybe it wasn't all good news.

Heart in mouth, I called my broker. I could practically feel the frost on the receiver. "High time you return my calls. Big mistake you've made selling those stocks in this climate. You lost a bundle. Your father must be spinning in his grave. And liquidating your IRA like that. Serve you right to pay tax on the works."

How had Harlan pulled that off? Forging a letter? Imitating my voice? Harlan could mimic anyone's voice.

He must have been busily liquidating things for months and he sure hadn't paid off any current home or Club bills. But even so, where had the rest come from? Keeping secrets for a price?

Then someone had shot him, leaving the Club on the verge of bankruptcy and me unable to pay the upkeep on the house for sure. It wasn't fair. Harlan hadn't been able to drive me out when he was alive. Would he succeed now? And worse: what if whoever killed Harlan knew about the money? What if they came back for me?

# # #

I got another seratonin blast when Detective Budge called to offer his help and support any time of the day or night. To suggest a counselor I might find helpful. He said Constable Cuddihy was also concerned.

"Thanks anyway," I said.

"Call anytime," he said. "I'll give you my pager number. Anytime."

# # #

Years of living with Ha Ha Harlan taught me you've got to plan ahead. Time to flush out the guilty party before I got flushed out myself. But at least now, I didn't feel alone in the world.

Mother always said opportunity is right under your nose. That would be my mouth. I used it to call everyone I figured he might be blackmailing and happened to mention Harlan had a date with a local reporter in the morning. At nine.

I called the Club's suppliers, Buddy, Harlan's partner, and everyone Harlan owed anything to. Called Angie, Harlan's girlfriend. Told her Harlan may have skipped but, as co-owner of the Camelot Golf and Country Club, I planned to settle his debts in cash the next morning. Nine on the dot.

One reaction confirmed my nastiest suspicions.

# # #

Detective Budge arrived just before midnight, twenty minutes after I called him. He opened the front door using the code I had given him and crept to the bedroom where I waited, with the bedside light on low. Constable Cuddihy, in jeans and a tee-shirt, was practically hopping on one foot right behind him. Very responsive considering this visit fell well beyond the call of duty.

"Did you hide your car?" I whispered.

Detective Budge nodded.

"The prowler's still around," I said.

Constable Cuddihy's eyes shone. "You can't be too careful," he said.

"I heard him a couple of minutes ago," I said, keeping my voice low. "My back is bad tonight, I can't even get into my scooter. Or the van. I didn't know what to do." Same thing I'd told him on the phone. "I'm sure he's there."

Detective Budge still looked sleepy. His cowlicks were winning the battle. The cuff of his PJs peeked out under his chinos like a small boy's.

"I haven't been straight with you," I said. "Harlan has hurt me. Maybe he's gone crazy this time. He's prowling around. I am truly afraid. You should probably have some back-up."

Constable Cuddihy whirled, his hand on his hip.

"Don't worry," Detective Budge said.

But I did worry. We were dealing with a murderer.

"It could be dangerous," I said.

"Not a problem."

"Should I have just called 9-1-1?"

"This is our case," Constable Cuddihy said, panting.

I was propped up in bed, my back to the wall. In every way.

Detective Budge sat near me. He pulled a Zero bar from his pocket and put it in my hand. "You know, you have to get to a shelter."

Constable Cuddihy perched edgily on the footstool. "I think so, too," he said. "Because . . ."

"Shhh!" I said.

The door handle gave a tiny squeak. We watched mesmerized as it turned slowly and the door creaked opened three inches. A hand reached around the corner and flicked off the overhead light.

"If that's you, Harlan," I screamed, "you'll never pull this one off."

I felt exhilarated. This could work!

Even so I damn near wet my pants when the door slammed open, smashing against the wall and the Grim Reaper leaped shrieking into the room. In the dim light, his swinging scythe had a freshly-sharpened look. The blade flashed in an arc inches in front of my face. I rolled and flattened.

"Meet your maker!" the Grim Reaper screeched, turning to swing the scythe to my corner.

This time I meant it when I screamed.

"Die die dieeee," echoed in the room.

I kept screaming when Constable Cuddihy's gun went off. The purple robes swirled as the creature leaped onto the bed, silver slashes from that scythe cutting the air.

Detective Budge was screaming too. Constable Cuddihy shrieked like an air raid warning all through the volley of shots he pumped into the swooping figure.

Then it was quiet. Except for ragged gasps from Cuddihy and a gurgling next to me on the bed. Detective Budge crumpled to the floor, clutching his chest, issuing low frightened moans.

I managed to roll close enough to turn on the bedside lamp. I leaned over the bed.

Red foam bubbled from the Grim Reaper's lips. The scythe clattered to the floor. Intelligence still flickered in those wicked eyes.

"I get the last laugh, Harlan," I whispered just as the flicker died. *Ha ha.*

# # #

Constable Cuddihy leaned against the wall, his crispness evaporated, his face turned away from the headboard saturated with Harlan's blood.

Detective Budge squeezed my hand without stopping even when he dialed. "What you must have been through all these years," he kept muttering.

"Traumatized woman," he added, at the end of the call "Severely traumatized. Send a female officer."

I was in far better shape than he. Cuddihy wept nosily.

"Never saw anything like it," he said, when he hung up.

"Harlan must have thought I'd have a heart attack. I'm surprised I didn't. Perhaps, Harlan had a brain tumor. What else would make him do such crazy things? The autopsy will tell, I'm sure." I did not mention the thought of losing the three-quarters of a million you thought you'd scooped could bring out the worst in a person. Especially a person who'd kill a perfectly innocent painter in order to set his sister up for the crime. You can't go to jail without moving out.

"You know, I don't think I'll make the seventeen days," Detective Budge said, as he assisted me onto the Dynamo. I felt his arms trembling as I held on.

"I'll help you," I said. We rolled toward the living room and the comfort of Reese's Pieces. "We can help each other."

Other officers arrived, uniformed and plain clothes. A girl with a blond ponytail turned out to be the requested female. She had a firm, capable smile.

"God, it's freezing in here," she said.

All through my statement to a pair of hollow-eyed men with notebooks, I could hear the distinct sounds of Constable Cuddihy vomiting in the powder room near the front door.

# # #

I felt bad for Constable Cuddihy. What a terrible thing to live with having shot someone, even Harlan. But as everyone said subsequently, what choice when a deranged man dressed up as death kicks open the door and slashes at you with a scythe while screaming "die"? Better Harlan than some poor gym teacher.

"It's over," Detective Budge said, stroking my shoulder as his fellow officers finished up.

"Yes," I said, "but I'm sure they'll have more questions later. Poor Constable Cuddihy."

"Would have been something sooner or later, you know. But I mean your nightmare with this man. He can't torment you any more."

I sniffled. My arms rattled in spite of myself. It would take a while to get Harlan out of this brain.

"You can't stay here . . . " I knew he meant with Harlan's blood all over my bedroom. "She needs something, a tranquilizer." He turned to the police woman.

This is my chance. Mother always said you do what you have to.

"Why don't I call your doctor?" She flicked open her mobile phone.

"No drugs," I said. "I could use a drink. A brandy."

"Sure." Detective Budge jumped to his feet.

"No! Don't touch those decanters. Harlan keeps them doctored with laxatives in case teenagers ever steal his booze."

They both blinked at me.

"Trust me. Harlan is so crazy that way. Paranoid." I didn't have to act to seem rattled. "I mean he was."

In the corner of my eye I could see pathetic little Constable Cuddihy being helped through the door.

Detective Budge gave a panicky glance at his watch. "Brandy. Well, everything's closed now. It's the middle of the night. Maybe one of the neighbors . . ."

"It's okay," the policewoman said, "I'll take care of it."

"We have lots," I said, trying to keep my voice steady. "It's in Harlan's hidden space with all his valuables. But I can't get the door open."

"Hidden space?" she said.

"Right. In back of the walk-in closet. I think you're tall enough so if you stood on the second shelf you might be able to reach the switch. The wall on the back of the cupboard swings open."

I tried not to feel for her as she marched capably toward the closet and the discovery of Harlan's second last joke.

# # #

The sun warms the cottage dock in the late afternoon, good for the bones. Detective Budge has taken well to retirement although, after a year, the steady diet of Mars bars has packed a few more pounds onto his spongy middle. He looks perfect to me although I worry about his health. The investigation is over and cleared him unequivocally. Thirty-five years of exemplary conduct shone behind him. No one ever mentioned that last seventeen days.

He tells me the female officer has gone on to a promotion.

Constable Cuddihy is not so lucky. He still wakes screaming in the night. He hopes to do better in computer programming. He says he'll stay in touch.

No one ever claimed the body in the closet. Just some poor devil Harlan picked up somewhere, hard and wiry and bald like himself. A painter maybe. That Harlan. Anything for a joke.

I reach over to the chair beside me and pat down a wayward cowlick. There was so much I could never talk about. Never mind. Mother always said you should know when to keep your mouth closed.

"How sweet it is," I say, grinning foolishly.

Detective Budge strokes my hair.

I gently deposit a couple of Hershey's Kisses between his lips.

Legacy

Terence M. Green

Achieving critical and popular success in one genre would be enough for most writers. Terry Green, however, has accomplished that in two: science fiction and crime fiction. His police procedurals *Barking Dogs* and *Blue Limbo* take place in a hardboiled Toronto of the future. In its review of Terry's most recent novel, *A Witness to Life*, *The Globe and Mail* called him, "a lyrical, contemplative writer" whose books "come alive in a way only the best fiction can." Terry has two other novels and a collection of stories to his credit. A graduate of the University of Toronto, he also holds an M.A. in Anglo-Irish Studies from University College Dublin. A retired high-school English teacher, he writes full time in Toronto where he lives with his wife and two sons. "Legacy" was originally published in 1985 in *The Magazine of Fantasy & Science Fiction*, but it remains a fresh, unique vision.

A Daniel come to judgment! yea, a Daniel!
— The Merchant of Venice (IV, I, 223)

I

It is time that I visited my father.

I do not think that he ever truly awaits my visits. But it is a son's duty, is it not? This should be a time of purging, a time of reconciliation. I feel a small measure of guilt that this has not yet occurred after the three mandatory weekly visits, and an even greater measure of remorse. Somehow, I did not think that it would be like this. What I expected, I cannot say. But certainly not this. Certainly not his acceptance. This, I must admit, has baffled me.

II

A prison or a hospital?

I think of it as the former. My father thinks of it as the latter. We are both wrong. Or, we are both right. Does it matter?

Mere semantics. The reality is the place. It exists. For my generation, it has always existed. I try to imagine what it was like before, but my mind can scarcely make the leap.

I enter by the side door. When I mentioned this to my psychocomputer, it replied coolly that I was doing this because I had not yet directly faced the issue with my father. Really, this is mere casuistry. I do this because I do it. It is a matter of convenience, of access. The computer fails to grasp the simplicity of this. Or of anything.

III

He is on the third floor, sitting in the same chair behind the glass partition. I hesitate, even though I know he cannot see me.

But I know my duty. I am his son.

The attendant — a man in a white suit and white shoes — sees me, acknowledges me, and places the earphones on my father's head, moving the electrodes into place. I nod in confirmation and seat myself at the panel on my side of the glass partition, picking up my own headset, adjusting it for comfort. Leaning forward, I switch on the microphone, preparing to speak.

This is, by law, my final visit, for this is the fourth week since my father was murdered.

And I am his son.

IV

"How does it feel?" I ask him this constantly. It is the only question that makes sense to me. This is the time for serious discourse, for questions of import. All else would be frivolity, given the circumstances. Anyone could see that.

His face is placid; his eyes remain closed. The tubes that nourish him and the circuits that monitor him dangle from his head and arms grotesquely. I know it is a miracle. But it is also a nightmare.

"It feels strange." I hear his words through my headset and nod. I have heard this from him before. *Strange*. It is the word he constantly selects. Thinking about it, one can see that it is the word that fits most perfectly. All this is, as he notes, *strange*, exquisitely so.

Our communication filters through the recording device interpolated by the authorities, according to the law. I must, eventually, ask him. But not yet. Not yet. Some time is mine. I must know him more, in however brief a time is left. This urge has grown, solidified, week to week, once it became clear what he was doing, once I understood.

I used to hate him. Now I do not know.

It is strange.

V

It was Mrs. Gorman, his neighbour, who found his body. When he failed to respond to her knocking, she peered in the small window on the top third of the door and saw him lying prone in the hall. Always a good neighbour, she was quick to respond, to do the right thing, and the authorities were duly summoned.

And because it was a case of murder most foul, unwitnessed, he was Revived, according to law, so he might name his murderer, so that justice might come to pass, before his final summons from Azriel's horn.

Even now he is fading, his thoughts disjointed, his extended time glowing but feebly. Four weeks is always the maximum; no one has been sustained longer. Perhaps someday. But not yet. Not now. Not for him.

His face is puffed from the injections, his skin harshly pink from the electrostimulation to the brain. He has died once, and will die finally quite soon. Maybe today. More likely tomorrow. But soon. There is no final escape — merely a respite, authorized and codified by the extended arm of the law, to expedite their work.

To see that justice is served.

VI

It is the heir's duty to deal with this. And I am his sole heir, the one to whom all that is his has been bequeathed. My legacy is at hand. Yet when I close my hand about it, it crumbles; when I squint my eyes to see it, it becomes transparent; when I try to give it voice, I become mute.

VII

We sit and face one another.
It is strange what I feel.

VIII

"What are you thinking about?" I ask him.

I sense his cerebral activity stirring in response, struggling against elimination.

"I think about your mother," he replies. "I think of when she was young." There is a pause. "This sustains me." There is a longer pause. "Sometimes," he adds, "I think about my father."

The silence that ensues crackles with the static between the living and the dead.

Without thinking, I ask suddenly, "Is there a heaven? A hell?" I have never asked him this. I am not sure where the thoughts came from. Now they seem impossibly rude. The chance of traumatic disappointment hovers over the answer.

"No," he says. Then: "I don't know." I feel his tremor, then sense his acquiescence. "Does it matter?"

"I thought you might know," I say. "I thought it might be clear to you."

"Many things are clear to me," he says. "The things that matter."

IX

"I must ask you, Father. The law requires it."

"I know."

Even now, though, I know what the answer will be. It will be the same. I understand this much, at any rate. He would have no reason to change it now — not after refusing to answer on the previous three encounters.

It is why I now doubt myself.

"Who killed you?" I ask.

The static reaches an unearthly crescendo, the words careening through the vapour, through electricity, through time, through infinite space. Then it is gone, and there is the unnatural clarity.

"Everyone," he answers again. "They have all killed me."

"The law wants to know," I add, pursuing my duty, for myself, for my father, and for the record. "Who is guilty?" The static rises once more, crisp, biting, then mutes to a soft stream. "Who?" I ask again.

"Time," he says. Again.

X

The answer is the same. I have heard it before. My father, even in death, will not cooperate.

I used to hate him. That is why I killed him. He knows this. Yet he will not point the finger. This, he knows, is not a matter for the law. This is between my father and me. They are mere interlopers.

Somehow, I did not think it would be like this. It is indeed strange. How could I have known? How could I have done otherwise? And how else could I have learned that I love him?

My legacy. I see it now. I see it.

Edward D. Hoch

The Detective's Wife

Edward D. Hoch

Ed is perhaps the most respected writer of short crime fiction alive. He has published more than 800 stories, and almost 50 novels, story collections and anthologies. Since May 1973, he has had a story in every issue of *Ellery Queen's Mystery Magazine*, and for twenty years he edited the annual *Year's Best Mystery and Suspense Stories*. A master of the most difficult of all crime writing challenges — the locked-room mystery — Ed won the Mystery Writers of America's Edgar Award in 1968. Ed has created more than two dozen series characters — among the best-known being Captain Leopold, the compassionate big city cop; Simon Ark, the mysterious Satan hunter; Nick Velvet, the professional thief who only steals worthless objects; and Ben Snow, the gunfighter who is often mistaken for Billy the Kid. A longtime member of the CWC, Ed is also a past president of the Mystery Writers of America. "The Detective's Wife" is a non-series story that combines rich insight with Ed's trademark meticulous plotting and injects a particularly sudden and shocking kind of violence.

When they were first married, before she realized what it would be like having a police detective for a husband, Jenny used to kid with him about his cases. Sometimes when he got home early enough for dinner he'd entertain her with accounts of the latest felonies around town. Most cases were solved by the testimony of eyewitnesses or the tips of informers, but once in a while there was the storybook crime that demanded a certain skill in the science of deduction.

It was these cases, especially, that Roger liked to explore with Jenny. He would go over the facts in careful detail; presenting what clues they'd been able to uncover, giving a brief account of suspects' testimony and alibis. If there were any. Then, invariably, he would look at her and say, "You know my methods, Watson. Who is the guilty party?"

She almost never came up with the correct solution, but that didn't seem to matter. It was a game both of them enjoyed. She was Watson to his Holmes, and, "You know my methods, Watson," became their own private joke. Once when he spoke the line in bed during their lovemaking, she broke into a fit of giggles.

That was in the early years, when life was simpler for them both. As they passed into their thirties, still childless, something changed. "There's just more crime these days," Roger told her when she questioned him about his late hours.

"You never tell me about your cases any more."

He sighed and turned away. "What's there to tell about a drug dealer who gets cut up by an Uzi? It's the same thing every day, and I get tired of talking about it."

His words made sense, she knew. Other cops, friends of theirs, had gotten burnt out. It could happen to Roger too.

But there was more. The sex between them wasn't as good or as spontaneous as it had been during those first years. Sometimes she wondered if he had found someone else. She made a special effort to interest herself in his cases, and to act as his Watson once more.

"They can't all be drug killings, Roger," she argued one night. "Tell me something interesting."

"A bartender shot to death on the west side? Is that interesting?"

"Any motive?"

"Robbery, I suppose. It was after closing time when he was alone. The cash register wasn't touched but something might have scared the killer away. Or maybe there was another motive. Some seventeen-year-old kid he refused to serve goes home and gets his father's gun. The victim must have let the killer in, so he probably knew him."

That was in February, during the eighth year of their marriage.

# # #

Jenny worked in the production department of a small advertising agency downtown. Sometimes she had lunch with the other women in the office, but more often she ate a sandwich at her desk. Occasionally, if the weather was nice, she'd venture out on a summer's day to eat her sandwich in a little park across the street where the local utility company sponsored jazz concerts on Fridays. It was here that one of the agency's artists, a bearded young man named Carl, found her on a hot August afternoon. She'd heard he was leaving soon for a better job.

"How you doing, Jenny girl? Enjoying the music?"

"It's a break from the office," she told him with a smile. "I can just take so much of ordering typesetting and engravings and printing."

He sat down beside her on the smooth stone seat. "How's hubby?"

"Roger is fine," she answered defensively. The people at work, especially the men, seemed to treat him with thinly veiled disdain because of his position with the police.

"He catch any bad guys lately?"

"A drug dealer who — "

"What about the serial killer?" Carl asked, unwrapping a candy bar and starting to munch on it. "The one who's been shooting the bartenders."

It was true that three bartenders had been slain since February, at roughly two-month intervals. One paper had spoken of a serial killer, and there was a fear that August might bring a fourth killing. She'd spoken of it to Roger once or twice, but he preferred talking about the small everyday triumphs of his job. "I don't think he's working on that," she answered, though she knew he was in charge of it.

"That's the trouble with cops." He took a bite of his Mr. Smiley Nut Cluster. "They waste their time on unimportant crimes while the big stuff gets by them."

She suddenly felt the need to defend her husband. "Roger says most crimes are solved by informers. Someone like a serial killer acts alone. No one else knows about it, so no once can inform on him."

Carl finished his candy bar and leaned back, letting the music wash over him. Jenny recognized it as an old Duke Ellington tune, one that her father had liked to play when she was growing up. "I'll have to meet Roger sometime," Carl commented. "Why don't you ever bring him around to the office parties?"

"He works a lot of nights," she answered lamely. The truth of the matter was that she tried to keep her two lives separate. Roger wouldn't like the people she worked with, and they would have little respect for him. Many of them were artistic types, who wore torn jeans to work and thought of the police as right-wing oppressors.

"Yeah," Carl said, getting to his feet. "Well, I'll see you back at the office, Jenny girl. Hope you're coming to my party."

She watched him cross the little park and enter the side door of their building. He'd left the crumpled candy wrapper on the ground by their bench, twisted into a knot.

# # #

Roger was moody all through dinner that night. He picked at his food and didn't say much. She tried to ask him about the day's routine, about any new crimes, but he had nothing to contribute. Finally, over coffee, he said, "I was driving around downtown this noon. I passed your building."

"Oh? You should have stopped to see me. We could have had lunch together."

"I did see you, in that little park where they have the jazz concerts. You were with another man."

She had to laugh at this evidence of his jealousy. "That was just Carl, one of our artists. I don't take him too seriously — you shouldn't either."

"When I saw you from the car you looked like you were enjoying each other."

She could see he wasn't joking and this annoyed her. "If he bothers you, take heart. He's leaving in two weeks. He's found a better job in the art department at a printer."

"I was just *asking*, for God's sake!"

"What's happening to you? What's happening to *us*? You used to talk about your job, about the cases you worked on. You made it sound like fun, like a game!"

"It isn't a game any more. After so many bodies it stops being a game."

Jenny tried to soothe him. "I just remember how you used to describe a case and give me the clues and let me try to solve it. You called me Watson."

"Yeah, I guess I did." He smiled at the memory.

A few nights later Roger surprised her with his suddenly buoyant spirits. He suggested they go out to dinner and took her to a neighbourhood restaurant they'd frequented when they were first married. "I cracked a case today," he told her over drinks. "An interesting one I've been working on all week."

She knew he was going to tell her about it, and she felt a glow of anticipation. It was almost like the old days. "Do you have pictures?" she asked, remembering the large manila envelope he'd brought home earlier.

"Not before dinner. I'll show you back at the house."

"Tell me about it, at least."

"A man reported that his wife had committed suicide, hanged herself from a rafter in the garage."

"Did she leave a note?"

"No, which is one of the reasons we started investigating."

"What was the other reason?"

"Well, her car was outside in the driveway. Death by carbon monoxide is a lot tidier than hanging."

Their food arrived and the conversation shifted to pleasanter topics. She talked about the office, and some of the ad campaigns they were working on. It was the most pleasant dinner they'd enjoyed in months. Home was within walking distance, and the few blocks' stroll on a late summer evening was invigorating. The cool air against Jenny's face reminded her of the coming of autumn.

Back at the house he showed her the eight-by-ten glossies he'd brought from the office file. Crime scene photographs were usually in colour now, and she was thankful at least that there'd been no blood. The woman's stockinged feet dangled about two feet from the floor, next to an overturned crate of rough wood. "She climbed up on that and put the rope around her neck?"

"Apparently," Roger said with a slight smile. "Come on — you know my methods, Watson."

"First of all, the crate is too flimsy. I can see she's a good-sized woman. More important, in this shot of her from the rear, showing the bottoms of her feet, there are no snags in her stockings. She couldn't have climbed up on that flimsy crate in her stocking feet, adjusted the rope, and then kicked it away, all without getting a run or at least a snag from those wood splinters."

"Go to the head of the class! That's basically what I told her husband, and we had a confession within an hour."

"I'm glad," she whispered into his ear. She was glad he'd caught a murderer and glad he was back to the same old Roger she loved so much.

That night the serial killer struck again.

# # #

The following evening he was worse than ever. "I told you the games were over and I meant it! My job's on the line now. Four killings of bartenders since February is too much for the city fathers to sit still for. If we don't make quick progress they're taking me off the case, and that means I can say good-bye to any chance of promotion. I'll be lucky if I'm not back giving traffic tickets."

"I didn't see the papers. Tell me about it. Was it like the others, in a restaurant?"

"This one was different. He was shot on his way home from work, around three in the morning. The killer apparently was waiting in an alley next to his apartment house."

"But he was a bartender?"

Roger nodded. "He was helping out at the Platt Street Bowling Lanes. Before that he worked at Max's Party House, the same place as victim number two."

"That might be a lead. Maybe they owed gambling debts to one of the customers. Or maybe someone owed them money. Maybe they were dealing drugs on the side."

"We checked all that out on the others. We'll try again but it doesn't look promising. The latest victim was a fill-in bartender. Even when he worked at Max's it was only when they needed extra people for a big party. Victims two and four probably met, but they hardly knew each other, as near as we can tell."

"How about the other victims?"

"No connection."

"And it wasn't robbery?"

"His wallet wasn't touched."

"Could it be just a coincidence?"

Roger shook his head. "Ballistics says it was the same gun all four times — a nine millimetre automatic pistol."

He was glum for the rest of the night, and she could do nothing to shake him out of it. Finally she asked, "Did they give you any sort of deadline?"

"A week or two. They want some action."

"Maybe I can help."

He only sighed and walked away. As he'd told her earlier, the games were over.

# # #

Roger didn't attend the office farewell party for Carl. She hadn't really expected that he would, and when she mentioned it he didn't even bother to reply. Most nights she ate alone, knowing it would be nine or ten before she saw him. She'd never thought it would be like this, being married to a detective.

The party, at one of downtown's fancier hotels, was a welcome relief. Carl himself hadn't had a drink in two years, since his wife was killed in an auto accident, but that didn't stop the rest of the staff from having a good time. Jenny's boss, the production manager, was a beefy man named Herb who imagined every young woman in the office to be fair game, married or not. At one point he had her pressed into a corner, but he was already too far gone to be a real threat. It was the president of the agency who suggested a bit later that perhaps Jenny could drive Herb home.

"He can't drive himself and I don't want another accident, Jenny. If I help you get him into the car could you take him home? It's less than a mile away."

"Certainly, Mr. Miller." She dreaded the idea, but she could hardly suggest that he call a cab for Herb. Miller didn't like anyone to know about drunken employees.

It wasn't till they were on the way that she remembered she hadn't even said good-bye to Carl.

Herb mumbled and snored all the way home, but he came awake as she brought the car to a stop in front of his apartment building and tried to make a pass without fully realizing who she was. She brushed his hand from her breast and he reached into his pocket for a handkerchief, pulling matches, gum and keys with it.

Jenny ran around to the passenger door and helped him out, retrieving his keys and whatever else she could find. The doorman at the building took charge then, betraying no surprise. Perhaps he'd seen Herb in this condition before.

When she got back to her own house, Roger was in the kitchen preparing a sandwich for himself. "I forgot you were going to be out tonight. How was the party?"

She shrugged, dropped her keys on the table, "The usual. My boss got drunk and I had to drive him home. How's the case coming?"

"It's not. Four murders now and we're no closer to an arrest than we were after the first one. My time is running out. The commissioner wants action before the November election."

"Won't you let me work on it with you?" she asked. "Bring home some of the pictures for me to look at. Remember, I spotted the clue in that hanging case right away."

"There's nothing in the pictures," he insisted. "I've been over them a dozen times."

The following morning she found an excuse to leave the office and do some library research. While there she checked the microfilmed copies of the daily papers and read about each of the earlier killings. There was nothing new, nothing to connect the four men except for their occupation. The second victim had worked exclusively at Max's Party House but the others had moved around, mostly filling in part-time at neighbourhood places. The first victim had been the youngest, at twenty-six. The other three were all in their thirties or forties. They lived in different parts of the city and seemed to have been nothing more than passing acquaintances, if that much. Only one had been married at the time of his death. Two of the others were divorced. The youngest victim had never been married.

Was it a random thing, she wondered, just killing bartenders? Or had these four been chosen for a reason?

That night Roger seemed more depressed than ever. He'd brought home some of the crime scene photographs but he never took them out of the envelope. He'd spent the entire day interviewing the girlfriends and ex-wives of the victims, and had nothing to show for it. "No girls in common, no jealous lovers."

Finally, just before bedtime, she asked, "Can I look at these pictures."

"Go ahead. I have to take them back in the morning."

Jenny opened the clasp on the envelope and pulled out a dozen pictures of the various crime scenes. Bodies, four bodies. All shot at fairly close range. The first three were in the barrooms where the men had worked, as they prepared to close up for the night. The fourth was at the mouth of an alley where the killer had waited. One photo showed the cartridge case ejected from the killer's automatic pistol, lying amidst the dirt and trash of the alley.

An empty pack of cigarettes, a torn stub from a nearby movie, the spilled remains of a half-finished container of popcorn, the knotted wrapper off a candy bar, a broken piece of brick —

She went on to the next photo, then quickly turned back to the picture of the alley pavement. Where had she seen a candy wrapper tied in a knot like that? Was it something that people often did, or was it unique?

Then she remembered. Carl had dropped his candy wrapper on the ground that day they'd been listening to the jazz concert on the lunch hour. It was the same brand, Mr. Smiley Nut Cluster, and the wrapper had been twisted and knotted in the same manner.

Of course it proved nothing.

When she slid into bed next to Roger she said. "Those pictures gave me an idea. I want to check on something tomorrow."

"I need all the help I can get. I also need your car in the morning."

"How come?"

"The brakes aren't working on mine. I'll take it in over the weekend."

"You'll have to drop me off at work."

"Can you get home on your own?"

"Sue will give me a ride."

"Fine." He rolled over and was snoring within minutes.

# # #

Jenny searched through the newspaper files for an account of the accident that had killed Carl's wife two years earlier. She'd never heard the details of it, and it had happened before she came to the agency, but something Mr. Miller said — "I don't want another accident" — made her wonder if it might have happened after an office party. It took her a long time to find it, but there it was. Carl's wife had been hit by a truck as she pulled out of the parking lot at Max's Party House shortly after midnight. They'd come to the party in separate cars and he was still inside when it happened. Her blood alcohol level was extremely high at the time, and no charges were placed against the truck driver.

A later article talked about the liability of a place like Max's that continued serving someone who was obviously drunk. There was talk of a lawsuit and the owner stated he was unable to determine which of the four bartenders on duty had been responsible.

Four bartenders.

Why hadn't they seen it? Why hadn't anyone seen it?

The answer to that was simple enough. They had approached the problem from the opposite direction, through the four victims. Jenny was approaching through Carl, and his dead wife, and the accident, and Max's Party House.

That had to be her next stop. Max's.

What a day for Roger to borrow her car!

Back at the office she arranged to take Sue's little Volvo. "I won't be more than an hour," she promised.

She struck it lucky at Max's Party House. Max himself was there. Preparing for a big retirement dinner that evening. "Is this more about that lawsuit?" he asked when she told him what she wanted. "That whole thing was settled last January."

"The newspaper quoted you as saying there were four bartenders working the night of the accident. I want their names."

"Look, the case was settled out of court for a few thousand dollars. The husband's attorney convinced him he couldn't get any more than that. The only reason I paid anything was that she was hit driving out of our parking lot. As for the bartenders, I couldn't tell you if I wanted to. A couple of them were working off the books that night, to avoid paying taxes. It's not unusual in this business."

Jenny opened her purse and took out the list of names. "Just tell me one thing. Are these the four men?"

He glanced at it and then at her. "All right, those are the ones. A couple of them are dead now."

"You don't keep up with the papers. All four of them are dead now."

# # #

Jenny felt a rising excitement all the way home in the car with Sue. She barely heard her friend's chatter as she ran over the facts in her mind. Carl had settled the lawsuit in January, against his wishes, for a figure far less than he thought was justified. A month later, in February, the killings had begun, spaced two months apart in hopes no one would notice the connection right away. They had, of course, by the time of the third one, but then he only had to risk one more.

Four dead — one or more of them the ones who'd been directly responsible for his wife's tragic death. And he'd have gotten away with it if it hadn't been for that knotted candy wrapper dropped to the ground while he waited for the final victim to appear. How had he found out the identity of the four? Probably by getting friendly with the first victim and asking him in some innocent way. That helped explain how he came to be in the bar long after closing. He'd made friends with the first victim, and then killed him when he'd learned the names of the other three.

"Here we are," Sue said, pulling into her driveway. "Home at last. I don't see your car. Roger must be still working."

"He's been working every night lately. Thanks, Sue."

"See you in the morning."

Jenny hurried into the house and got out of her sweaty clothes, silently rehearsing how she'd tell Roger. She slipped into her robe and switched on the television, settling down opposite it without really seeing it.

Roger was very late that night and when he came in she could see that his mood was bad. He unbuckled his holster and tossed the gun onto a chair before he even spoke to her. "What does this mean, Jenny?" he said at last.

"What?" She tried to see what he was holding in his outstretched hand. "What is it?"

"A sealed packet containing an unused condom. I found it under the passenger seat of your car."

"I — "

"Do you have an explanation?"

Her mind was whirling. She could barely recognize this man standing before her. "Roger, let me think — !"

"Make it good — for whatever it's worth."

"My God, Roger! You can't think I was making love to someone in my car!" Then suddenly it came to her. "Herb, my boss! I told you I drove him home from the party because he was drunk. When we got to his apartment he pulled out his handkerchief and a lot of things came with it. I picked them up but I must have missed this."

"Herb, your boss. Am I supposed to believe that?"

All at once the unfairness of his constant jealousy and suspicion moved her to a fury. "I don't give a damn what you believe!" She ripped open the top of her robe. "Here! Do you want to dust my breasts for fingerprints?"

That was when he slapped her. Hard.

# # #

Jenny slept that night curled up on the sofa, somehow protecting herself from further blows. When she awoke, just after dawn, it was raining. Roger came downstairs a little while later, and walked over to her. "I'm sorry about last night. This case has just got me down. I have to see the commissioner this morning and I've got nothing for him."

She got up, wrapping the robe around her, and started making breakfast. Later, while she was drinking her coffee, he remembered to ask, "Did you think of anything yesterday, about the killings?"

"No," she answered softly, staring straight ahead at the rain streaked window. "Nothing at all."

The Altdorf Syndrome

James Powell

Since 1967, when his first story "The Friends of Hector Jouvet" appeared in *Ellery Queen's Mystery Magazine*, James Powell has published more than one hundred short stories of what he describes as "a mysterious and humorous sort." His tales have been reprinted frequently in such anthologies as *The Years Best Mystery and Suspense Stories* and *The Year's Best Fantasy and Horror*. In 1989, Jim's "A Dirge for Clowntown" was voted the favourite story of the year by the readers of *Ellery Queen's*. The following year, a collection of his stories, called *A Murder Coming*, was published in Canada to wide critical acclaim. And in 1992 Jim was co-winner of the Crime Writers of Canada's Derrick Murdoch Award for his exceptional body of work. Born in Toronto, Jim has travelled widely and lived in Europe and New York City. He now lives in Marietta, Pennsylvania, with his American wife. "The Altdorf Syndrome" is an example of Jim at his best, combining both gentle humour and a brilliant plot.

James Powell

The girl at the helicopter counter asked my name. "Philip McGrath," I said and almost added, "the recently appointed vice president in charge of international sales for E. P. McGrath Distilleries." Instead I took a seat on a bench lined with travelers in coats and scarfs to await the next departure.

I had decided to make the trip between Chicago's two airports by helicopter for the simple reason that I'd never flown in one before. It was part of a private little celebration I was having in honour of the fact that I would now spend a good part of my time away from our Toronto home office, away from E.P. McGrath himself. Perhaps other bosses' sons have encountered other problems. But as for me, in the last few years I've found it harder and harder to keep a straight face in my father's presence.

To see him today you'd never believe that during Prohibition he'd been the first man to lay copper tubing under the Niagara River and pump whiskey from the Canadian side to the American. Or that once off Cape Hatteras he had had a rumrunning schooner sunk out from under him by the Coast Guard. In those days he was "Frenchy" McGrath; he talked out of the corner of his mouth and wore loud suits and a fedora. By the end of Prohibition he had made such a success of smuggling that he bought out his major supplier and became a respectable distillery owner. Canadians look to the United States for their image of a successful man, but their notion of respectability is decidedly English. So my father gave up his imitation of Al Capone and started acting like Colonel Blimp.

Spats Larkin, our chauffeur, who raised me on a diet of my father's Prohibition exploits, records the beginning of the transformation about the time my father started courting my mother. It was then he exchanged the Packard for the Rolls-Royce, stopped sitting up front and started calling Spats "Joseph."

I don't blame my mother. At the breakfast table when E. P. starts sputtering from behind his newspaper about the decline of the homely virtues in our times my mother always murmurs in agreement; but sometimes a tired look crosses her face as if she wants to say, "Let's drop the act, dear. You're Frenchy McGrath, the rumrunner, remember?"

My mother could get away with it. But one slight reference to my father's past by me and he would turn a strangled purple and shout, "You are an impertinent puppy, sir! An impertinent young puppy!" And I'm afraid I would laugh out loud.

"Mr. McGrath?"

I looked up. A man in flight boots and parka had read my name from a clipboard. When I stood up, he motioned me through a door opening onto a runway. The others on the bench were waiting for something else. I was to be the only passenger.

Mr. Flight Boots took my suitcase and without a word trotted off across the floodlit runway. I trotted along behind. The helicopter sat on the edge of the concrete just beyond the floodlights. It was small, obviously quite old, and painted a dull black. Behind the pilot's cockpit were two compartments each with its own door, much like compartments in a British railway carriage.

Mr. Flight Boots closed the forward compartment door after me and then went ahead to dispose of my suitcase under the cockpit. The walls of my dimly lit compartment were trimmed with dark varnished wood and the two facing seats were upholstered in a furry material that I hadn't seen since I was a boy and had traveled to out-of-the-way summer camps on half-forgotten railway lines. I was about to take a ride in an antique helicopter.

Flight Boots pounded with his palm on the cockpit window. The propeller began to turn and a few moments later the helicopter lifted off the ground, tilting slightly forward. That, plus the jogging motion of the flight, transformed the compartment into a stagecoach. At any moment I expected either an Indian attack or a brace of pistols to come through the window, followed by a highway man's "Stand and deliver!"

"Are you traveling far?"

I jerked back from the window, surprised by this fellow traveler I hadn't noticed before. In the opposite corner I could make out a face partially concealed by what might have been a collar and a hat, though in the darkness I couldn't be sure. "Omaha," I said.

"Ah," came the reply

"And yourself?"

"Blitzen," he said. "From Altdorf to Blitzen."

"Ah," I said, having no idea where either place was. "That's quite a trip."

"Ten leagues," he said. "Or about thirty miles, if you wish. I have been traveling since 1763."

I laughed. "Sounds like you've made some pretty bad connections."

He didn't laugh back. "Allow me to introduce myself. I am Baron Grindelwald, aide-de-camp to the Duke of Altdorf."

"Philip McGrath, recently appointed vice president in charge of international sales for E.P. McGrath Distilleries."

"Whiskey," he said thoughtfully. "A pity. I'm afraid that isn't going to do you much good. But let us get down to cases. If what I am about to tell you sounds a bit mechanical, that is because I have told it many times before. You may, of course, interrupt at any time with questions. But I strongly advise you to keep them on the essential point. For example, I usually begin with the statement that I was born in 1725, which means I am either almost two hundred and fifty years old or a raving lunatic. I beg you not to waste what time you have left speculating about this. It is completely irrelevant to your situation."

"And what exactly is my situation?" I asked.

"That will become quite clear in a moment," he said. "But let us begin. Of all the petty states in eighteenth-century Germany, the Duchy of Altdorf was by far the pettiest. It comprised less than fifty square miles and contained only one town worthy of the name — Altdorf itself. The principal source of wealth for Karl Ludwig, the Duke, was his small army of five hundred men which he hired out to whomever could pay his price. In addition to the rental fee, if I may use that expression, the Duke was also compensated at an established rate for each wound his soldiers suffered and received a handsome bounty for any soldier who happened to get killed.

"My father, who had the foresight to lose an arm, a leg, and an eye leading his men in three separate battles before being fatally wounded in the fourth, was Duke Karl Ludwig's ideal of what a soldier should be. In my father's memory I was appointed the Duke's aide-de-camp.

"If Altdorf Castle was stark and medieval, the court itself could best be described as frugal and aging. The Duke's idea of hospitality was far from lavish. The entertainments he offered his guests were those that cost him nothing — a row on the moat, for example. The Duke attributed his longevity to regular exercise — more specifically to the fact that Oskar, his trusty manservant, rowed him around the castle several times each morning with the Duke's guests following along behind.

"The fact that the castle was defended by a veterans' guard, old grenadiers in black and yellow uniforms, increased the aura of old age about the court. It was always impressive to see these old soldiers, all over six feet tall and straight as ramrods, stamp their feet and come to attention as the Duke tottered down a hallway. Each soldier would shout in his wheezy voice, 'Here comes the Duke!' Then the next soldier would snap to attention. 'Here comes the Duke!' Being as old as they were, they frequently passed away on the job. I would always warn visitors to watch out for falling guards.

"But to make a long story short, there was a theft one evening at the castle. The Golden Star of Altdorf, the fourth largest diamond in Europe and the pride of the Duke's collection, was stolen. I was ordered to recover the diamond and discover the thief in twenty-four hours or face the gibbet. I failed and rather than take the consequences, as my oath of obedience to the Duke required, I slipped away and caught the diligence for Blitzen. I had the fondest memories of this little town just across the border. I had grown up there and except on feast days when the bell in the church tower would ring gaily, it was the most peaceful place I had ever known

"For over two hundred years now, I have traveled without reaching my destination. I soon realized that my oath to the Duke and my own curiosity would prevent me from arriving at Blitzen until I discovered the name of the thief and how the diamond eluded my most scrupulous searching.

"So far in my journey I believe I have used every means of transportation devised by man. I fall asleep on the Orient Express and when I awake I am in a dugout canoe up the Orinoco, or on a merry-go-round in an amusement park, or in a dog sled crossing an ice field. And always with a traveling companion to whom I can put my story: a polite Japanese naval officer in a midget submarine, perhaps, or a maharaja in a howdah on an elephant during a tiger hunt. Just before I awoke to find myself here, for example, I was in an aerial car on a cable between two Alpine peaks with a Herr Knapp, a Swiss chocolate merchant.

"Depending on your tastes, I imagine you find all this either quite insane or quite Gothic: a man cursed to travel across the years until he can unravel a two-hundred-year-old mystery, and so on. Personally, I find it rather tedious. I never enjoyed traveling very much. One is neither here nor there and time passes very slowly, telling the same story, hearing the same feeble explanations. Believe me, my dear sir, I do want to reach Blitzen so very badly."

"It sounds like you've got yourself a real problem," I said.

"*We* have a problem, Mr. McGrath," he insisted. "You see, if you don't solve my mystery I will kill you." A small pistol appeared in the darkness, perhaps from inside his coat. "I'm sorry," he said. "This is a comparatively recent addition, but I'm afraid it is necessary. Back in the days when travel took longer, there was nothing like a mystery to make the time pass. But since the turn of the century my traveling companions seem to lose interest once they realize that an actual mental effort is expected of them. What should one attribute this to, Mr. McGrath — the rise of the popular press, movies, radio, television? Whatever the reason I have been forced to add an incentive, and this" — he motioned with the pistol — "is it.

"At first I thought the threat alone would be enough. I remember very well the first and only time I tried that. I dozed and when I awoke I was up to my waist in water in a lifeboat off the *Titanic* with an elderly man in evening dress. I recall the moonlight on the ruby in his shirt front. I introduced myself, explained my situation, and said I would shoot him if he could not solve my mystery. I recall his hysterical laughter when I made my threat. I doubt if he heard a word of my story. All he could do was watch the waves wash over the gunwales and croon half-remembered hymns of his childhood in a cracked little voice.

"I realized then that my threat would lack conviction unless I was prepared to carry it out. So you see, whether I am two hundred and fifty years old or a raving lunatic is irrelevant. In either case this gun is quite real and I assure you I will use it."

He spoke calmly and I had no reason to doubt his word. "Herr Knapp, the Swiss chocolate merchant?" I asked.

"Poor Herr Knapp," he said. "He kept insisting the diamond had been swallowed. I explained that this was impossible. But as his time grew to an end in desperation he began swallowing coins and keys to prove that it could be done. He was trying to choke down his wrist watch when I shot him." Baron Grindelwald paused. "Well, shall I proceed with the story?"

"I don't have much of a choice," I answered.

"I'm glad you understand," he said. "Now on the evening of the theft the Duke and his guests had dinner in the small dining room on the third floor of the castle. When the dishes had been removed, the Duke announced that we were going to play 'Find the Pin,' a very popular game in my day.

"One person is sent out of the room. A pin or some other small object is hidden. Then the person is called back and has to find the object while the rest drum with their hands on the table — harder and harder as he gets closer to the object, lighter and lighter as he moves away. The Duke liked to doze at the table after dinner and was greatly addicted to this game because the heavy drumming always woke him up for the final, more exciting moments.

"Oskar, the Duke's servant, came into the room carrying a strongbox. I knew what that meant. Unpredictably, once or twice a year, it tickled the Duke's fancy to play 'Find the Pin' with the Golden Star of Altdorf. It was his idea of entertaining his guests extravagantly at no cost to himself. Perhaps on this particular occasion he wished to impress his unexpected guest, Count Stockhorn, who had arrived that morning.

"The Duke unlocked the strongbox and with a loving cackle withdrew the priceless diamond. I should add that from this moment on until the theft was discovered no one entered or left the room.

"The Duke began by passing the diamond around the table to be admired. And as we follow the clockwise progress of the jewel, let me introduce you to the guests. I was seated on the Duke's left, and having examined the diamond many times before, I quickly passed it on to Count Stockhorn. The Count was a wealthy patron of letters and, more recently, of science. When he had admired the diamond he gave it to Leonia von Hasleburg, a beautiful girl of eighteen. Leonia and her mother were constant guests at the castle. I can say with some authority then that the girl was a complete ninny.

"After gushing over the jewel she passed it on to a certain Marquis of Carabas — or so he called himself. The week before, the Duke had been driving through the countryside when an insolent servant in boots threw himself across the road and stopped the coach. Stroking his mustaches, the servant told the Duke a preposterous story about how his master, the Marquis of Carabas, had gone swimming and someone had stolen his clothes. The Marquis of Carabas — a scoundrel if ever I saw one — had been staying at the castle in borrowed clothes ever since, awaiting, so he said, certain letters of credit that would permit him to resume his travels.

"The Marquis passed the diamond across the table to Wolfgang Brunig, a pale threadbare young man from a respected but impoverished family. Brunig was a poet of some reputation but I understand that his doctors had advised him that without a prolonged stay in Italy he would never live to complete his major opus, a long poem about a young man who falls in love and goes mad. Brunig stared at the Golden Star as though it were the sun of Italy and then passed it to the Baroness von Hasleburg.

"I can only describe the Baroness as an avaricious old hag — in many ways the female counterpart of the Duke of Altdorf. Her supreme ambition was to trade Leonia's beauty for a wealthy husband who would add to the von Hasleburg fortune.

"The Baroness passed the jewel to the final guest, Captain McTavish, a Scottish officer in the Duke's army. Captain McTavish's father had forfeited his title and estates for supporting the Young Pretender in 1745. The Captain's burning ambition was to buy back the acres of heather which would otherwise have been his patrimony. I regret to say that he hoped to accomplish this by marrying the Baroness von Hasleburg. To use an expression I learned from a young man in a Stutz Bearcat, who I later shot right through his raccoon coat, Captain McTavish had been making goo-goo eyes at the Baroness all through dinner. Reluctantly Captain McTavish returned the priceless diamond to the Duke.

"The Duke now slid the diamond down the table to Count Stockhorn. This meant the Count would be the first one to hide the jewel and would choose the person to find it. That person, I might add, would be sent into a curtained alcove while the diamond was being hidden, an alcove that opened only into the dining room. The Count admired the diamond once more and then looked around the table to decide whom he was going to send into the alcove. As he did so, he began throwing the diamond up in the air and catching it in an absent-minded way. Perhaps he was enjoying the expressions on the guests' faces, for there wasn't one of them who didn't covet the priceless jewel, whether for base or worthy motives.

"Finally the Baroness von Hasleburg said, 'If you please, sir. You are making me nervous.'

"'Of course, madam,' said the Count. Ceasing to throw the diamond up in the air, he turned to the Duke and remarked that he had recently become quite interested in precious stones. The Duke cackled and offered to sell him the Golden Star for an astronomical sum. The Count declined politely and returned to the game, choosing the Baroness to leave the room.

"When she had stumped into the alcove with her cane, he hid the jewel in a drawer in a cabinet between two windows. I was disappointed at first in his lack of imagination. But obviously, as a gentleman, he didn't want to make it too difficult for the Baroness, who was quite myopic. Drumming on the table led the Baroness to the cabinet and when she opened the drawer we all applauded politely. But even then, because of her poor eyesight, it took her a moment to see the diamond. When she did she returned it to the Duke.

"Well, there you see how the game was played. I must say it was a bit more interesting with an object smaller than the Golden Star.

"The Duke next slid the diamond down to Brunig, the poet, who, with a blush, chose the beautiful Leonia to go into the alcove. He hid the diamond in the heart of a rose in a vase of flowers on the sideboard. Leonia had some trouble finding it, featherbrained creature that she was. However, I noted this: when she found the jewel she slipped something into the bodice of her gown.

"Let me add here that it was obvious to all of us that Brunig was smitten by Leonia and equally obvious that she had eyes only for the Marquis of Carabas whose resentment at Brunig's attentions to her may have provoked the incident that followed. As Leonia was returning the diamond to the Duke, Brunig drew his snuffbox out of his pocket, as he had done several times that evening. It was a cheap wooden snuffbox, battered and leaking snuff at every seam.

"Carabas sniffed and said with a sneer, 'What an elegant snuffbox, sir.' This from a scoundrel who didn't even own the clothes on his back. Brunig blushed with mortification.

"But Count Stockhorn turned to him at once and said, 'Sir, as an admirer of your poetry, I would be deeply honored to possess a snuffbox which I could say had once belonged to Wolfgang Brunig. But since I would not presume to ask for it as a gift, let us exchange snuffboxes.' Count Stockhorn laid a silver snuffbox of most exquisite workmanship on the table.

"It was a magnificent gesture and the Count spoke with such sincerity that Brunig accepted. Then the Count added to his generous act without alluding to Brunig's poverty. 'Sir,' said the Count, 'you may perhaps find your new snuffbox too elaborate for your taste, as I must admit I have sometimes felt it was for mine. Yet for me it had a certain value, having been in my family for many years. Should you ever wish to dispose of it, I would be pleased to redeem it from you for its weight in gold.'

"You see, Mr. McGrath, Count Stockhorn was a gentleman, while Carabas was an impostor. Breeding always tells.

"But on with the game. The Duke next gave the diamond to me. As I sat there pondering a clever hiding place, I quite absently made several small scratches on the base of my wine glass with the diamond. Later I think you will find this fact important. In any case, I chose Captain McTavish to go into the alcove. I hid the diamond in Oskar's powdered wig, instructing him to go to the sideboard once or twice to confuse the Captain.

"I should explain that we were all drinking wine during the game, but only the Duke was served. The wine was kept on the sideboard in stone pitchers along with a plate of dried herring to be eaten with salt, pepper, and black bread. Oskar served the Duke from the sideboard. The rest of us left the table to help ourselves, the men serving the ladies. Carabas, by the way, claimed that the Duke's vile yellow wine was a fine vintage and drank it in quantity.

"Well, my ingenious little ruse quite confounded Captain McTavish for a time and added to the merriment. Finally the Captain realized why our drumming was not consistent and with a Scottish oath of some kind or another he discovered the jewel.

"Next the diamond went to the Baroness who sent me into the alcove. I quickly found the jewel where she had hidden it in the case of an ormolu clock. Carabas received the Golden Star of Altdorf next and chose Count Stockhorn to find it. With many remarks about his own cleverness, Carabas stood on a chair and hid the diamond among the crystals of the chandelier. But the Count was not taken in and found it in a matter of minutes.

"Next Leonia, with simple-minded symbolism, hid the diamond among some forget-me-nots in another vase of flowers where it was quickly discovered and returned to the Duke by Carabas. Next Captain McTavish slipped the diamond into the padding of an upholstered chair where Brunig finally found it. Then the Duke gave the diamond to me. I chose Count Stockhorn to go into the alcove.

"Here, unfortunately, I had a bit of an accident. My intention to hide the jewel in the heavy, silver salt shaker on the sideboard was frustrated when I found there wasn't enough salt inside to cover it. When I dropped the diamond inside the pepper shaker instead a cloud of pepper rose up in my face and I was caught in a fit of sneezing. The Count, of course, heard me and found the diamond at once. But he commended me on the cleverness of the hiding place and swore he would never have found the diamond if my nose hadn't betrayed me. The Count was a gentleman. Breeding always tells.

"But now to the discovery of the theft. The Duke slid the diamond down the table to the Baroness von Hasleburg. But the Baroness was slow in reaching out for it. The diamond slid off the table — and shattered to bits on the marble floor.

"Confusion swept the table. A diamond, of course, would not have shattered like that. Someone had substituted a paste imitation for the Golden Star of Altdorf. The Duke shouted, 'Grindelwald, take charge!' I immediately announced that everyone in the room would have to be searched. At this the Duke declared that since he was obliged to submit his guests to this indignity, he would allow his own person to be searched as well.

"I called in two guards from the hall, ordering them to see that the guests remained in their places. Then I took the Duke and Oskar into another room, where I searched the Duke from head to toe. 'Grindelwald,' said the Duke, 're-cover my diamond and discover the thief. You have twenty-four hours. If you fail it means the gibbet.' The Duke was stark naked when he said that, but I knew he would carry out his threat.

"Next I searched Oskar, and then, in the Duke's presence, had Oskar search me. Then, while my wife, who had been summoned on my orders and whom I informed of the sentence I was under, searched the women in another room, I searched the male guests in turn.

"What did we find? Several things, but not the diamond. For example, I found hidden about Captain McTavish's person four of the Duke's silver spoons. Brunig, the poet, had stuffed one of his pockets with dried herring and the other with black bread. Petty thefts which under the circumstances I did not call to the Duke's attention. But on the ankles of the so-called Marquis of Carabas I found the scars of galley shackles and that was a more serious matter. Among the men, only Count Stockhorn passed the search successfully. His pockets contained nothing but a handkerchief, a few coins, and some keys. This made me suspicious and I searched him again, but found nothing more.

"Meanwhile, my wife had discovered a secret compartment large enough to conceal the diamond in the head of Baroness von Hasleburg's cane. But the compartment was empty. On the person of Leonia she found two folded pieces of paper. One was a poem entitled 'To Leonia' in which Brunig compared her to the moon, a rose, and the first robin of spring. I understand that several years later this poem was set to music by Franz Schubert. The other paper was a message from Carabas referring to a previously made plan of elopement for that evening which urged her to bring whatever valuables she could lay her hands on so that they could lead a life devoted to love, unencumbered by the petty, material concerns of ordinary mortals. I need not tell you that it gave me the greatest satisfaction to see Carabas escorted to the dungeon where under the mildest of duress he quickly confessed to being a fraud, an itinerant tinker who had escaped from the galleys where he had been condemned for theft.

"As they were searched, the guests were sent to their rooms, accommodations in the castle being provided for Brunig and McTavish, who had only been invited to dinner. When I had searched the last of them I knew the diamond had to be in the dining room or the alcove. There was only one other possibility — the window in the curtained alcove. I assure you the dining room windows had not been opened in the course of the evening. But suppose the thief had thrown the diamond into the moat from the alcove window? Suppose the Golden Star was lying on the bottom under fifteen feet of water or floating on the surface attached to or inside some light object waiting for the thief to recover it the next day during the Duke's rowing excursion?

"I dispatched a rider to Frankfurt-am-Main to hire a team of skilled divers and return as quickly as possible. Then I ordered the Captain of the Guard to send out men in rowboats with torches and bring me everything floating on the moat."

"Suppose the thief had an accomplice who had been waiting in a boat under the window and escaped before your men made their search?" I said.

"Perhaps you are thinking of Carabas' servant, the one in boots," said Baron Grindelwald. "He had spent the evening in the guard room fleecing some old soldiers with a marked deck of cards and quickly joined his master in the dungeon. No, there wasn't any possibility of an accomplice. There were sentry boxes at close intervals all around the perimeter of the moat. Nothing pleased the Duke more than to condemn some sixty-year-old grenadier to run the gauntlet for some minor dereliction of duty. So let me assure you that the veterans' guard, if old, was vigilant.

"In any event, having disposed of the guests and given my instructions about the moat, I returned to the dining room and searched it and the alcove thoroughly, square inch by square inch. And I found nothing. Nothing. I can assure you that the diamond was not there. But then where was it? Ah, you have a question, Mr. McGrath."

"I think you said the Duke only used the Golden Star diamond for playing 'Find the Pin' once or twice a year on a whim," I said.

"Correct," said the Baron.

"Yet the theft must have been premeditated because someone had a paste imitation ready to be substituted."

"Correct again," said the Baron.

"Now if the compartment in the head of the Baroness von Haselburg's cane was large enough to contain the Golden Star of Altdorf, it was also large enough to contain the imitation."

"Correct once more," he said. "And since the Baroness was a constant visitor at the castle, perhaps she had been carrying the imitation with her for some time, patiently waiting the opportunity to make the substitution. But surely the whole point of the substitution was to make the theft pass unnoticed, enabling the Baroness to leave at the end of the evening with the real diamond in her cane."

"Maybe she got rid of it some other way," I said. "Just in case the substitution was discovered by accident."

"That is not impossible," said Grindelwald. "But it leaves us to discover how she disposed of it and to account for one other interesting fact: I am positive that when the imitation was slid down to her that last time, the Baroness deliberately allowed it to fall and shatter on the floor. I am afraid that the secret compartment in her cane was probably for snuff, to which many women of her age were secretly addicted."

"All right, then," I said. "What about Count Stockhorn's silver snuffbox? The one he gave to Brunig."

"Yes," said the Baron. "The Count might well have hidden the diamond in the snuffbox and then proposed the exchange with Brunig along with the generous offer of redeeming it at a later date, an offer the poet could not but accept. If, however, the theft was discovered, then Brunig would run the risk of being caught as the thief. There are three things that contradict this: one, how could the Count know the Golden Star was going to be used that night and thus come provided with a paste imitation? Two, I examined the silver snuffbox very carefully and there were no secret compartments. And three, at the time the snuffbox was given to Brunig the genuine Golden Star of Altdorf was still being used in the game. As I pointed out to you, I accidentally verified this by the scratches I made on the base of my wine glass."

I was starting to get desperate. "The wine then," I said. "To judge from its name, the Golden Star was yellow and so was the wine. You remarked that Carabas said he liked the wine. Suppose — "

But Grindelwald burst out laughing. "I knew you would say that sooner or later," he said. "Eventually everyone conceives of the solution to my mystery in terms of his own field of endeavour. I have encountered this so often I have come to call it the Altdorf Syndrome. Remember Herr Knapp, the Swiss chocolate merchant, who was sure the diamond had been swallowed like candy? Well, I have met cabinet makers who swore by secret compartments in the furniture, cobblers who were certain the diamond had slipped by me in a hollow shoe heel, and fishermen who insisted Brunig carried the diamond out in a dried herring.

"You are in the whiskey business, therefore you think of alcohol. The Altdorf Syndrome. But the wine really isn't a bad guess. The diamond, because of its colouring, would have been almost invisible in the wine. But the fact is, in searching the room I emptied every wine glass and pitcher through my fingers onto the floor. So I'm afraid, as I said in the beginning, the whiskey business isn't going to be of much help to you, unless the thief drank the diamond."

I started to speak but Grindelwald interrupted me. "Listen," he said. "Let me tell you what I did after I had searched the dining room and alcove and found nothing. I called the castle carpenter and had him bore a hole slightly less than the diameter of the Golden Star in an oak plank. Then I called in three trusted servants who, under my supervision, destroyed everything in the dining room and alcove — the table, the chairs, the sideboard, the chandeliers, the silver, the tapestries. Everything was hacked, cut, smashed, and beaten until the pieces would pass through that hole in the oak plank. When the Captain of the Guard arrived with the results of his search of the moat — four dead rats and a week's garbage — that too was forced through the hole.

"When dawn came I found myself alone in a completely bare room. There was not an object left and I had not found the diamond." He paused. "Haven't you any questions to ask me, Mr. McGrath?" he said. "I hope for your own sake you haven't lost interest."

"I'm listening," I said. "I'm just trying to think something out."

"I sincerely hope you think of an answer," said Grindelwald, "for we seem to be losing altitude, which means your time is almost up. But to continue, only one hope stood between me and the gibbet — that the diamond was lying on the bottom of the moat. It was mid-morning before the team of divers arrived. I sent them into the water with specific instructions to bring me anything on the bottom large enough to be or to contain the Golden Star.

"By now I was quite desperate. The Duke and his guests were out in rowboats circling around the castle and each time the Duke passed me he shouted grimly, 'Twenty-four hours, Grindelwald!' The guests, not realizing the sentence I was under, were preoccupied with their own affairs. Since the scoundrel Carabas had been thrown in irons, Brunig was rowing Leonia, whose beauty so hypnotized him that he ran into the side of the moat several times. Poor Captain

McTavish was rowing the Baroness and making goo-goo eyes to win her withered hand. Count Stockhorn, in a boat by himself, invited me to join him but I refused.

"After five hours of searching, the divers had found nothing. I paid them gold out of my own pocket to try again. At sundown, cold and exhausted, they dragged themselves out of the moat empty-handed. In the courtyard of the castle I could hear the hammering as they set up the gibbet. Sending a message to my wife to follow when she could, I caught the diligence from Altdorf to Blitzen. I have never reached my destination. But apparently you have reached yours. Unless you have solved my mystery."

Buildings and lights were rushing up at us. The helicopter settled down onto the edge of a runway, its motor stopped and the propeller began slowly to come to rest.

"What do you want to know first: who the thief was or how the diamond escaped you?" I asked.

Grindelwald laughed incredulously. "Let us save the best to last," he said. "First tell me the name of the thief."

"Count Stockhorn," I said.

"But then," said the Baron warily, "you must expect me to believe that by some wild coincidence the Count just happened to bring a paste imitation of the Golden Star that evening."

"The paste stone wasn't his," I said. "The Baroness von Hasleburg brought it."

"Then why did she deliberately allow it to shatter on the floor?"

"Because she wanted the theft to be discovered," I said. The Baron grunted with disbelief and raised the pistol. "Listen," I said, "before the game started the diamond was passed around the table. The Duke gave it to you. You gave it to Count Stockhorn who saw that it was the real diamond and passed it to Leonia. And so on all around the table and back to the Duke. The Duke then slid the diamond down the table to Count Stockhorn to begin the game.

"To his surprise Count Stockhorn discovered that the stone was now false. Obviously someone had made a substitution as the diamond was being passed around the table. Seeing a chance to obtain the Golden Star for himself, he said nothing. Instead, he began throwing the fake stone up in the air and catching it, studying the faces at the table at the same time. Only one other person knew that the stone was fake and was likely to shatter if it were dropped.

"When the Baroness asked him to stop, Count Stockhorn knew he had found the thief. His little speech about his recent interest in jewels was to convince her that he had spotted the substitution. It did. When Count Stockhorn chose her to go into the alcove, the Baroness knew she had been discovered. She probably thought the Count was giving her an opportunity to return the Golden Star.

"Under the circumstances she had no choice. In the alcove she removed the real diamond from the compartment in her cane and brought it back into the dining room, prepared to make the exchange again. Your drumming led her to the drawer where you had all seen the Count hide the fake stone. Actually, he had palmed it. When the Baroness opened the drawer it was empty. It was then the Baroness realized that Count Stockhorn intended to steal the Golden Star himself. But since you were all applauding, she had no alternative but to produce the real diamond as if she had found it in the drawer and return it to the Duke. The game then resumed with the real diamond, as you proved yourself by scratching the base of your wine glass.

"Now let's consider the Count's situation. He had the fake stone but he couldn't make the substitution again until he had found a way of disposing of the Golden Star whose absence would result in a very intensive search such as the one you made of the guests, the dining room, alcove, and moat."

"I don't follow you," said the Baron. "He had no way of knowing the fake would be smashed and the theft discovered."

"Ah," I said, "he knew that for a certainty. He knew that as soon as the Baroness suspected the substitution had been made and the fake stone was back in the game she would shatter it the first opportunity she got, exposing the Count as the thief and revenging herself.

"Well, Count Stockhorn came up with a way of getting rid of the Golden Star, though it required a gamble on his part. It was only then he made the actual substitution. Remember when Carabas hid the diamond in the chandelier and the Count found it there? That was when the Count made the substitution and returned the fake stone to the Duke. From that moment he had to gamble on one thing — that he would be picked again to go into the alcove before the Baroness got her hands on the fake stone. With your help he won the gamble. You chose him to find the stone that time you hid it in the pepper shaker. While he was in the alcove he disposed of the Golden Star."

"How?" said Grindelwald. His voice was oddly strained. "How did he dispose of it so that I couldn't find it?"

"You always looked in the right place at the wrong time," I said. "Tell me again: what were the contents of Count Stockhorn's pockets when you searched him?"

"A handkerchief, a few gold coins, and some keys," said the Baron.

"But shouldn't there have been something else? Shouldn't there have been a cheap wooden snuffbox?"

"Yes," Grindelwald said thoughtfully. "Brunig's wooden snuffbox that the Count had exchanged for his own." The Baron gave an uneasy laugh. "But you can't be suggesting the Count put the diamond into the snuffbox and threw it in the moat. I examined everything on the surface of the water."

"When you were examining the surface the snuffbox was on the bottom, and when the divers were searching the bottom the snuffbox was back on the surface," I said. "Count Stockhorn — "

"Stop!" shouted Grindelwald. "One more word and I will kill you. I don't think I've been this close to Blitzen before. At this moment I can hear the church bell tolling there. A slow bell. A funeral. Whose funeral, Mr. McGrath?"

"Yours, Baron," I said.

"Yes, mine," he said quickly. "These last two hundred years have been a rather ragged kind of existence. Bits and pieces here and there. Not much of a life. But at least I was alive. Now suddenly I have decided that I don't want to reach Blitzen. I do not want my journey to end. That is why I say, one more word and I will kill you."

"You mustn't threaten me, Baron," I said. "My one word could kill you as quickly as a bullet."

I saw the pistol disappear. "I rather think it could," he said. "The church bell in Blitzen tells me it probably could. So I won't threaten you. Now you will go your way and I will go mine as I have for more than two hundred years, presenting my little mystery to my traveling companions. Without the pistol from now on. The fewer incentives they have to solve it, the better."

A man in flight boots opened the compartment door, gave me a quick glance, and went up front to the cockpit. A moment later he reappeared with my suitcase and started off across the runway toward a well-lit door.

"Goodbye, Mr. McGrath," said the Baron. "Thank you for your company. I hope my little story has made the time pass quickly."

There seemed nothing more to say. I stood up. "Goodbye, Baron," I said, and stepped out through the door and onto the runway.

"Mr. McGrath."

His voice made me turn. I looked back in through the door. He was completely invisible now, sitting in his dark corner. For a moment he didn't speak. Then he said, "It would be quite pointless and absurd, don't you agree, to spend the next two hundred years asking for the answer to a mystery I don't want solved? Blitzen, as I remember it from my childhood, was a peaceful place. Since every journey must come to an end, I think I'll end mine here. Please finish your explanation." I hesitated. "Please continue," he said.

"Do you remember why you hid the stone in the pepper shaker?" I asked. "It was because there wasn't enough salt in the salt shaker to cover it. On one of his visits to the sideboard the Count partially filled the wooden snuffbox with salt. When you sent him into the alcove that last time, he put the Golden Star in the snuffbox and threw it into the moat. Weighed down by the salt, it sank to the bottom.

"But the snuffbox was far from watertight and as the salt slowly began to dissolve, the snuffbox became lighter. Count Stockhorn anticipated your searching the bottom of the moat as well as the surface. But he knew that divers would need daylight, while the surface could be searched at night by men with torches. As a patron of science it was easy enough for Count Stockhorn to calculate how much salt to put in the snuffbox so that it would bob back up to the surface about dawn. Even if they had arrived earlier than they did, your divers would probably have ignored something floating on the surface. As it was, I expect that the Count had already retrieved the snuffbox as he rowed around the moat with the Duke's party even before your divers got into the water."

The Baron sighed in the darkness. "So it was as simple as that." He paused and added, "One last question, Mr. McGrath. And I hope this will not offend you. But in my travels I have met men whom I judge to be more analytical of mind than you and, quite frankly, more intelligent. But in the end my story always baffled them. How were you able to hit upon the answer?"

"Once I figured out how the diamond had been disposed of it wasn't too difficult to work back to who the thief was and how he must have operated," I said. "As for the salt, the moat, the snuffbox — you yourself gave me the idea for that."

"I gave you the idea?"

"Remember when you laughed at my bad guess about the wine? You said that because I was in the whiskey business I thought the thief had drunk the diamond. The Altdorf Syndrome, you called it. But there are more things you can do with whiskey than drink it. You can also smuggle it. During Prohibition the smuggling schooners often weighted down their whiskey cases with rock salt. If they thought they were going to be stopped and searched, they'd dump the cargo overboard, mark the spot, and come back a day later just as the cases were bobbing back to the surface. It was a good trick. My father invented it."

"Ah," said Grindelwald. "As I've said so many times, breeding always tells."

At that moment the headlights of a tractor bringing baggage from another part of the field lit up the inside of the helicopter and gave me my first good look at Baron Grindelwald. He wore a shabby black greatcoat with a high collar and a three-cornered hat with a wilted black and yellow cockade. He looked neither like a lunatic nor a man who was two hundred and fifty years old. But his face was haggard, like the face of someone who had traveled a long distance.

He bowed slightly. "Thank you, Mr. McGrath," he said. Then he closed his eyes. But before I could tell whether his expression was one of peace or simple resignation, the baggage tractor changed direction and the inside of the helicopter went black.

I waited for a moment, wondering if I should call his name. Then I turned and headed across the runway toward the well-lit door that would take me to the next leg of my trip to Omaha.

Double Bogey

John North

For years, John was the regular crime and mystery book reviewer for *The Toronto Star*. His first published crime short story appeared in 1989's *Cold Blood II*. His second story, in the third volume of *Cold Blood*, gained John an Arthur Ellis Award nomination in 1991. Since then he has published a small number of highly accomplished stories. He also worked as co-editor of both *Cold Blood V* and *The Best of Cold Blood* and is now the online mystery reviewer for Indigo.ca. An avid golfer, John has successfully combined that pastime with murder in his best work, as is readily demonstrated here.

John Friesen didn't look worried as he repeatedly bounced the golf ball on the face of his driver — but he was — very worried. While he appeared absorbed with keeping the club and ball moving in unison, his mind was miles away from the golf course and his participation in the Hospital Appeal pro-am. He had triggered a train of events that was now irreversible, and no amount of belated second thoughts could prevent it.

While many of his fellow professionals resented the hours spent humouring amateur partners, he relished this type of charity event where three amateurs and a professional competed as a team. It released him from the day-to-day routines of the workshop, provided an opportunity to promote the customized golf clubs he made as well as the repair side of the business. It also enabled him catch up on the local golf happenings and gossip and even, sometimes, win some money in the simultaneous pro-only competition.

Suddenly he flipped the Titleist high into the air and caught it behind his back. The small audience clapped politely and then moved back to allow the three amateurs from the group playing behind through to the elevated fourteenth tee. John looked to see what had happened to their pro, and saw him talking to a young woman on the edge of the thirteenth green. There always seemed to be a delay on this hole and a glance at the green 180 yards away told him that there would be least five more minutes to wait before his group could resume play. Each member of the group ahead had marked his ball on the putting surface and the foursome was now engaged in confusing itself with conflicting advice on the likely lines of the various putts.

# # #

Thirty minutes earlier the climate control monitoring program running in the microcomputer had changed the setting of the thermostat and the heating system had responded. The temperature in the room was approaching thirty degrees Celsius — the maximum setting of the thermostat over the workshop bench. Under the same bench a small crack in the seam of the metal kerosene drum had already leaked enough of the fluid to create a small pool.

# # #

John walked over to his teenage caddy who was leaning dispiritedly on the golf bag and spitting towards a soft-drink cup near the litter basket. "Practicing for a career in professional baseball or hockey, are you?" John asked. "Make sure you develop as much skill at stick-handling or pitching as you have in the expectorative aspects of the game." He unzipped the side pocket of the golf bag, removed the portable phone and walked off the tee. The caddy gazed blankly after him.

He made two calls, and on each of them hung up before the fifth ring and the intervention of the answering machine. Karen was probably out shopping and the lack of response to the second call reassured him that Don hadn't changed his plan and made one of his infrequent visits to the office. As he folded up the phone he noticed that a mini-cam from the local television station was aimed in his direction. He smiled automatically at the camera and turned to Sharon Villa, the sports reporter, who stood beside it.

"How come you're working?" he said. "I thought you'd be on this side of the camera today." John had made a set of golf clubs for Villa and knew her as an avid and knowledgeable golfer who played whenever she had the chance.

Sharon smiled at him. "That's great, Frank," she said to the cameraman. "Just a few shots of groups coming into the last green and then we're through. Take a break. I'll meet you back at the clubhouse in half an hour."

Sharon turned back to John. "I wish you were the station's News Director," she said. "I was all set to play until Bob got instructions from on high. Seems that the wife of one of the station owners is a mainstay of the Hospital Appeal and she felt that some in-depth coverage might generate additional revenue for the charity. As the station's designated golf expert I was assigned. Anyway, how's the game going?"

"Much the same as any pro-am," John replied. "Three keen, but nervous, occasional golfers who are trying too hard to play shots they'd never attempt at their own courses. As a team we're eight under par, with another couple of birdies on the way in we should finish in the money."

"Lots of luck," said Sharon. "You'll need to be closer to twelve under, Bob Albion and his team of sandbaggers were ten under after the fifteenth."

John laughed with her. Albion was a well-known local golf fanatic who belonged to two local clubs. He could be relied upon to enter each and every available golf tournament within a three-hour drive of the city. He was notorious for his desire to win, and for some of the stunts he had pulled to do so. He was also John's landlord, and if the rent he charged for the renovated barn that housed the golf business was any indicator, he could well afford his hobby.

"What was the point of taping me on the phone? I thought you were here to cover the golf."

"I had a long shot of you doing the traditional ball bouncing act on the face of your driver and I thought the mobile phone would make a great contrasting shot. The modern and traditional aspects of the venerable game." Her voice assumed a serious voice-over tone.

"Well if you use the clip on air, be sure to mention that John Friesen is a respected local club maker and repairer whose craftsmanship and expertise can only improve your game and lower your handicap. I can always use some new business."

A shout from the tee indicated that John's group was waiting for him to hit. He glanced at his watch as he walked back.

# # #

In the workshop liquid continued to drip from the kerosene drum and potentially incendiary fumes were spreading through the workshop. In the office area the phone bell had been switched off and the incoming call was terminated before the answering machine could kick in. The microcomputer hummed gently on its stand and the program now running was due to execute its next command when the internal clock registered three o'clock. The "Housekeeper" program had been changed earlier in the day when the clock had been checked and reset.

# # #

The other members of his group had already hit by the time John joined them on the tee. One of them had hit his ball to the back of the green — about as far from the pin as it was possible to be without leaving the putting surface. The two other golf balls were in the deep bunker at the front left of the green.

With the wind briskly quartering the fairway from behind his right shoulder John asked the caddy for his six iron. He teed up the ball, looked at the pin on the front left of the green long enough to establish the line of flight, and took a couple of slow practice strokes. He settled over the ball, took an easy swing and started the ball towards the right-hand edge of the green. As he had intended the ball rode the wind as it swung gently towards the pin. It landed just short of the green, bounced twice and rolled towards the flagstick. It stopped three feet short of the cup, one of his best shots of the day.

John bowed mockingly to the other golfers on the tee, winked at Sharon and then followed his group towards the green. His excited amateur partners congratulated him on the shot and themselves on drawing him as their pro, while he wondered, for the millionth time, why he couldn't consistently hit shots that good. He knew that the margin of excellence between himself and tour players was extremely small and that on any given day he could turn in rounds as good as any of the well-known tour professionals. What he knew he lacked was the tenacity to do it day in and day out, and enough desire to make the sacrifices necessary to push him over the competitive edge.

Four years ago he had come to terms with his future. He resigned from the staff of the golf club to establish his own golf club business. He didn't want to spend the rest of his life selling shirts, slacks and sweaters; giving lessons doomed to be forgotten within hours rather than days; and playing against the members while trying hard to make it look like a fair contest. He realized he wasn't of tour calibre and that he was better at making clubs than hitting them. In his future competitive golf would be a remunerative hobby rather than a way of earning his living.

# # #

In the workshop the kerosene drum had reacted to the increased heat by expanding very slightly. The tiny increase in the size of the crack that John had made earlier in the day allowed more liquid to dribble down to the floor. The ensuing pool eventually overflowed the slight depression in which the drum sat and a small stream of fluid trickled towards the interior partition separating the workshop from the office. There it disappeared through a crack in the floor.

# # #

John's present dilemma was caused by money or rather the lack of it. His initial dream of his own small independent business had been rudely shattered as soon as he and Karen started to plan the project in detail. Even with their joint savings and a loan from her parents they were barely able to get together enough cash for stock and raw materials, let alone rent and equip a workspace. They soon realized that the choice was between abandoning the idea of striking out on their own or looking for a partner with capital. After asking around some of their friends and members at the golf club they had been introduced to Don Partick, a young accountant who had inherited a sizable legacy when his parents died in a car crash. Partick was a social golfer who played only a few times a year and who made it clear that he had absolutely no desire to become involved in the technical side of the business. He had checked John's plans and reputation carefully and was convinced of his competence, diligence and honesty. Partick admitted that the golf side of the business was not the reason for his participation. He simply preferred the role of instant independent entrepreneur to the grind of junior associate in a multinational accounting conglomerate. With no misgivings on either side the partnership documents were signed and the business was born. John's current problem was an inadequate income. Although the business generated more income than he had originally anticipated, splitting it with a partner kept him perpetually poor.

# # #

Below the floor the kerosene flowed along the metal edge of the partition wall to form a larger pool in a depression in the concrete foundation of the building. As luck would have it, the pool formed just underneath the area where the solvents were stored and close to the point at which the natural gas line entered the premises.

# # #

In the first year the partnership had worked well. John had immersed himself in the technical aspects of the business and had spent countless hours developing suitable working space, selecting stock, testing and lining up operating supplies for the repair work, and establishing and cementing links in all areas of the local golfing community. Don's training and business contacts had been invaluable in getting the venture off the ground, and his infusion of capital had enabled them to present a prosperous and progressive business image. His initial insistence on quality had gone unquestioned by the busy John, and the result had been such items as the smart premises, quality stationery, and essential business trappings — such as the oversize desks, the black leather chairs and sofa, the fax machine, an office computer that even regulated the environment of the building, and the portable phone John now carried in his golf bag. Despite his misgivings about the scale of the expenditures, John had gone along with the Don's wishes, since he was the source of the money.

# # #

In the office, the internal clock in the computer triggered another sequence of commands. The first command activated the power to the workshop exhaust fan and the second one erased the program the machine had just run. The computer had barely executed the erase sequence before the effects of the first command were felt.

# # #

After a slow but satisfactory first year, business had picked up, and both partners were pleased with what they had accomplished. However, as year two progressed problems began to emerge. John was kept increasingly occupied with the golf end of the business and his new daughter Tracey, while Karen became less tolerant about the time he spent on the business and a lower living standard than she had anticipated. Meanwhile, Don's initial enthusiasm waned and his visits to the shop grew further apart. He came in only when he had to and clearly saw his role as a passive investor rather than a working partner. Once the initial euphoria had worn off, it became apparent that Don's main interest was in what the business provided for him rather than what he contributed towards its success. He saw his share of the operation as a framework for a lifestyle, and as a way to provide the tax-free peripherals essential to support it. Don's detachment and lack of participation made it easy for John to resent his partner's share of the growing profits. Don had moved from saviour to albatross.

While John walked onto the green, marked his ball and went to assist the player on the back of the green line up his putt, he sneaked another glance at his watch. It must have happened by now — if all had gone well his problems should be almost over. He and Karen would be able to start over and nobody would have lost out.

#

The exhaust fan never switched on. The electrical wire to its motor had been unclipped from the wall and rerouted to floor level where it passed through a plastic bottle sitting on a floor heating vent. There was an inch of liquid in the bottom of the bottle which bulged slightly from the pressure of the fumes within. The points at which the wire entered and left the bottle had been sealed with a caulking compound, and inside the bottle the wire had been stripped of its insulating plastic, scraped to a narrower diameter and had several thin strips of paper wound loosely around it.

#

John looked over the long putt of his amateur partner. The ball was two inches off the edge of the green, sixty downhill feet from the flagstick over a slick green with at least two changes of direction. John knew the man would be pleased to get down in three from there, but gave the optimistic support he was supposed to provide. "Leave the stick in," he said. "Give it a good rap, though. What do you think — aim about a foot from the right-hand edge?" His partner nodded nervously and then jabbed at the ball. From its initial path and velocity the ball looked as if it would pass at least two feet to the right of the cup and run right off the green. However as it sped across the green it tracked inexorably towards the left and began to look as if it would pass close to the hole after all. As if drawn by a magnet the ball closed in on the flagstick and as John prepared encouraging remarks about the line being good even if the speed was wrong, the ball slammed into the flagstick, popped up several inches in the air and dropped into the cup. There was a moment of complete silence and then the whole team exploded into a round of congratulations and back-slapping. Once the excitement had died down John quietly sank his own short birdie putt to count in the separate competition among the professionals.

# # #

When current flowed into the wire leading to the fan, events happened so fast that they seemed virtually simultaneous. The wire heated up and began to glow red at its narrowest point inside the bottle. The paper started to burn igniting the gasoline fumes in the plastic bottle. As the bottle exploded the liquid gasoline in the bottom caught fire and the fumes from the pool of kerosene burst into flames. While a fireball enveloped the area of the workbench a tongue of flame ran along the kerosene trail to the crack in the wall, along the metal base of the wall and ignited the pool of fluid trapped on the foundation. The ensuing explosion set light to the contents of the storage cupboard and broke the gas main resulting in two further explosions that leveled all the internal walls and severely damaged two of the outer ones. Large sections of the roof fell in and the flames, fed by the gas line, leaped dozens of feet into the air.

# # #

The improbable putt seemed to galvanize the team and they managed to gain another two strokes on par over the next three holes. As the game progressed John tried to shake off his preoccupation with what should be taking place at the workshop. He had given it his best shot and it was too late to do anything about it now. His basically honest nature had caused him severe qualms about setting the fire, but as the scheme had evolved it seemed to provide a win-win situation. He and the family would be better off, Don would suffer no financial loss, and the landlord of the building would be compensated by his insurance. Defrauding the insurance company was wrong, but it was a victimless crime and the relatively small amount of his subsequent claim wouldn't even be noticed on their corporate balance sheet. The fire would provide the excuse to sever the unsatisfactory partnership with Don, and furnish enough cash to indulge Karen and Tracey in some long overdue luxuries before he re-established the business with himself as the sole proprietor.

# # #

The last drum of solvent had exploded in the ruins of the workshop. The oily black smoke from the boxes of rubber golf club grips was sucked skyward along with the cleaner fumes generated by the burning wood of the furniture and fittings. Occasional tongues of flame still flared from the rubble as pockets of combustible material caught fire. The burnt timbers from the fallen roof and walls collapsed even lower as the material underneath burned away. Two cars and a truck stopped on the nearby road, and the occupants leaned on the vehicles as they watched the fire. The siren from an approaching fire truck could be heard in the distance.

# # #

At ten minutes to four they arrived at the eighteenth tee to learn from one of the spectators that the Albion group had finished at twelve under par — one stroke better than their score. The last hole was a downhill par five with a long dogleg to the left through stands of mature trees. The golfer had to avoid the trees and the stream which meandered along the right edge of the fairway, before attempting to clear the pond created by the dammed stream. A green that sloped away from the fairway and a large trap at the rear made this a difficult and memorable finishing hole. When his three partners had hit their tee shots towards the corner of the fairway John took the driver that the caddy offered him. He decided to go for broke. If he could carry the corner of the trees he would be able to reach the green with his second shot. He decided he might as well give his amateur partners their money's worth and he took a long slow backswing and started the club forward as hard as he could. The ball almost looked like a flat line drive as it went straight for the corner of the trees, about a hundred yards from the tee it started to climb higher until it disappeared from sight. If it made it over the trees it should be in excellent shape for a shot to the green.

#

The firefighters continued to pump water onto the soggy black remains of the structure. Parts of the uneven rubble held small pools of water that reflected the afternoon sun while other areas steamed intensely as the heat underneath vapourized the water. The roadside spectators had now grown to the point where a policeman was having trouble keeping the traffic moving.

#

The four golfers reached the corner of the fairway having discussed every possible way they could beat, tie or fall short of the score posted by Albion's team. While the three amateurs continued to hope for a miracle finish John, seasoned by years of the golfing applications of Murphy's Law, kept his reservations to himself. Two of the balls were in the fairway and had almost reached the corner of the dogleg. The third had rolled into the ditch on the right edge and its owner retrieved it and put it in his pocket. John's caddy came back to report that his ball had cleared the trees and was in the centre of the fairway. The two amateurs in the fairway played different shots. The better of the two played a high wedge shot over the corner of the trees and left himself a long iron shot to the green. The other, the possessor of an awesome hook that had got him into trouble all day, decided to hook a three iron around the trees. The rest of the group, who knew from bitter experience that deliberate attempts to hook or slice shots invariably deliver miraculously straight results, watched and anticipated the worst. The ball started well to the right of the trees and turned slowly to the left as it climbed past them. When it disappeared from their view they looked at the caddy who had stationed himself at the corner. He looked down the fairway for some time before he turned to the group and shook his clasped hands over his head. The ball had finished on the left edge of the fairway, short of the pond and about ninety yards from the green. It was one of those rare shots that convince amateur golfers that on a good day they are only a few strokes away from breaking par.

# # #

A black waterlogged mess was all that remained of a thriving business. The fire was completely extinguished, and the firefighters were putting their equipment back into their trucks. The gas company had turned off the gas lines and the police had managed to persuade the last of the bystanders to leave.

# # #

When the group arrived at John's ball they were all excited. Not only had it cleared the trees but had taken a favourable bounce on the firm fairway. He was left with a shot of one hundred and forty-five yards with an excellent angle to the flagstick. Behind the green the flagpole on the clubhouse lawn drooped languidly and indicated no wind. He shook off the eight iron the caddy held out and reached for the nine iron. As he took a last glance at the green to align his shot he noticed a police car pull up the clubhouse and park under the portico. He took several deep breaths to try to settle down, but he rushed the backswing and hit into the ground well behind the ball. The last they saw of the ball was the splash of water as it finished in a watery grave in the exact centre of the pond.

John was furious at his lapse of concentration and the poor execution of such a routine shot. Probably the arrival of the police car had nothing to do with him and all he had managed to do was deprive himself of some prize money. He immediately apologized to his partners and handed the club back to the caddy who was trying unsuccessfully to stifle a smirk of misplaced satisfaction which John pretended not to notice.

The amateur who had played the safe shot over the corner of the trees managed to reach the green, but his ball rolled down the slope and into the trap beyond. Unless the other player could pull off the impossible and hit two more good shots, it looked as if the best the team could hope for would be to get a par and finish one stroke behind Albion's team. Realizing the fate of the team was in his hands the nervous golfer seemed to be having trouble selecting a club. John put the pitching wedge in his hands and placed a reassuring hand on his shoulder. "Hit it hard and aim for the centre of the green. Anywhere on the putting surface gives us a chance for a birdie and a tie."

"Close only counts in horseshoes and grenades," said the golfer. "I might as well hole it out for a clean win."

"Go for it. You can do it," encouraged John. One of the other golfers, with a more pragmatic outlook, mumbled something about John's mouth and God's ear.

A short fast swing started the ball climbing towards the right corner of the green. At its highest point over the pond it began to curve gracefully towards the left hand side of the green and the flag. The entire group held their breaths as the ball plummeted towards the green, bounced once and disappeared into the hole. The stunned amateur had scored the first eagle of his life and had managed the difficult task of hooking a pitching wedge. The whole group, including the phlegmatic caddy, rushed over to congratulate the unexpected hero. Once the excitement had died down John dropped a ball close to the pond and pitched onto the green about fifteen feet from the pin. As the group walked on the cart-path around the pond, the small group of spectators around the green gave them a round of applause. Up at the clubhouse John could see the manager of the club pointing his group out to a man in a grey suit. John's par putt stopped on the edge of the hole. He tapped in for the bogey and joined his waiting partners. While the group signed their scorecard on the edge of the green, the man in the suit went over to the police car and spoke briefly into the radio. John shook hands with his partners and agreed to meet them in the bar a few minutes.

He gave the caddy his car keys and told him to clean the clubs, put them in the trunk and then meet him in the locker room. The policeman who had pulled a small black book from his jacket pocket waited and approached John as the caddy shambled out of earshot.

"Mr. Friesen?"

"Yes?"

"Inspector Bristol, Township Police. I'm afraid there's been a bad fire at your workshop. We tried to contact your partner, Mr. er . . . " He glanced at his notebook. " . . . Partick, and when we couldn't reach him we called you. Eventually we sent a car to your house and your neighbour told us where you were."

"What happened? Is the damage bad?"

"Pretty bad I'm afraid, sir. The whole place was completely destroyed. It looks as if there was an explosion and then a fierce fire. The firefighters said there was almost nothing left when they arrived. Right now though I'd like to know if anyone was likely to have been in the building."

"No, everyone was away today, thank God. Our receptionist is away on vacation, my partner is down in the city meeting with our lawyers and I have been here all day. I'd better get cleaned up and then go out there. Is there anything you want me to do?"

"In view of the explosion and the possibility of arson, we've asked the fire investigator to check the site over. However, he won't be able to get there for a couple of hours. I'd appreciate it if you could keep clear until he's finished. There's nothing you can do at the moment, sir. I expect you'll be wanting to get in touch with your partner, landlord and people like that. I assume you were insured."

"I hope so," said John nervously. "Don takes care of the business side of things, but I expect he put it through Russ Thompson's agency — I know he handles the insurance for our company cars."

"Well that's all we can do for now, sir. If you could drop in at the police station sometime tomorrow, we can tie up any loose ends and I'll give you a copy of the investigator's report. The insurance company will probably want it later."

"Thanks very much for letting me know," said John. "I'd like to take a look at the damage on the way home, if that's OK? I'll certainly call in at the police station tomorrow morning."

"No problem, Mr. Friesen, so long as you just look. I'll warn our man at the site to keep an eye open for you, and I'll expect you tomorrow."

They had walked up to the clubhouse as they talked. Bristol climbed into the police car and drove away and John went to the locker room in search of his caddy. Forty minutes later he was ready to leave. He had turned in the scorecards, showered and changed, paid his caddy, informed the organizers he could not stay on for the dinner, congratulated his jubilant team-mates on their unexpected victory and made his excuses to leave what promised to be a prolonged celebration. He swung his van out of the golf club parking lot and headed towards the workshop.

Even though the excitement was long over and the fire trucks had departed, traffic still slowed on the highway to look at the police car and the area of charred devastation. When he pulled into the muddy ruts and puddles of the small parking lot, a policeman climbed out of the cruiser parked near the entrance. John wound down his window and stared aghast at the ruins. The devastation was unbelievable. The building had been completely flattened to the point where no part of the debris was more than waist high.

"Mr. Friesen? Inspector Bristol warned me to expect you."

"Yes, that's right."

"I'm afraid you'll have to stay away from actual ruins until the inspection team has had a look at the site. Not that there seems much left for them to look at."

John could not believe the extent of the destruction. When he had planned the fire he had expected a charred building with the contents destroyed. He certainly had not anticipated anything on this scale.

Accompanied by the policeman he skirted the ruins in silence. When they'd finished he shook his head in disbelief, thanked the constable and climbed into the van. If he'd known the result would have been like this he would never have had the courage to do it. He hoped Albion had enough insurance to replace the building — it needed rebuilding not restoration. He drove slowly off the site and the policeman returned to the police cruiser to await the inspection team.

When he arrived home he saw Tracey playing in the sandbox in the front yard of the house next door. Mrs. Poole was watching her from the rocker on the porch. Tracey ran across the lawn towards her father and threw herself into his arms when he climbed from the van.

"Hi, Daddy. I had hot dogs and chocolate ice cream. Can I watch TV before bed?"

"Sure, honey," John replied. "Let me just have a few words with Mrs. Poole first." Tracey ran back over to the sandbox as he walked over to the porch.

He had known Mrs. Poole a long time. She had lived there when he was a child and in the intervening years she had become a trusted friend. His parents had died several years earlier and she slipped naturally into the role of Tracey's surrogate grandmother. Since her husband's death the previous year Tracey had given her a new interest in life and she had almost become one of the family. She put down her book as John approached.

"How was the golf? You don't look very happy."

"Oh the golf went well enough, but that was the only thing that did. The police came to tell me that the workshop had burned down."

"Yes. They came here and I told them where to find you. Tracey enjoyed the excitement. They came about an hour after Karen dropped her off here. Apparently the Cancer Society needed a last-minute replacement for one of their volunteer drivers. She asked me to look after Tracey for a couple of hours while she drove a patient to the clinic in the city. She should have been back by now though."

"You know what those out-patient clinics are like. Sometimes you're in and out of there before the engine cools down, and other times it seems to take forever. This must be one of their slow days."

John took Tracey home and let her put one of the *Sesame Street* tapes into the VCR. While she lost herself in the activities of Bert, Ernie and Big Bird, John thought about the fire and worried if there were any traces of arson. By the time he had bathed Tracey, read her a story and put her to bed darkness had fallen and Karen had still not returned. He called Don's number again, but only got the answering machine.

John wasn't much of a drinker, but he made himself a large scotch and water and sat by the empty fireplace drinking it. His mind kept replaying the picture of the burnt-out workshop. He shook his head in irritation and wondered where Karen was. The clinic closed at five o'clock. She should have been home hours ago. He walked into the kitchen and looked on the list of phone numbers taped to the wall. He tapped out the number against Cancer Soc. (Mrs. Stoner) and the woman who answered was very surprised to hear from him. Mrs. Stoner had scheduled no runs to the clinic that day, and she assured him that she had not phoned Karen. He took a deep pull of his drink and phoned several of her friends. None of them had seen her, or heard from her, that day. He made one more call to Don's answering machine, hung up in disgust and returned to the den to replenish his glass.

Several drinks later he had still not been able to reach Don, and his worry about Karen's whereabouts had swung from concern to anger and back to concern again. He made a sandwich and ate it while he watched the coverage of the fire and the pro-am on the local news program. He was surprised at how he looked on TV. While the medium made some people look deranged, it seemed to flatter him. He even liked the sequence of him using the cellular phone despite Sharon Villa's somewhat breathless remarks about him being a high-tech golfer on the move. At least she had mentioned his name and that of the now-defunct business. He switched off the set and glumly stared at the screen. When he found himself thinking in clichés such as "what's done is done" and "it would probably work out best for all concerned," he drained his glass, cleared up the kitchen and went to bed.

While John tossed and turned in an uneasy sleep, Inspector Bristol was hard at work. He too had watched the TV program of the pro-am but his reaction was very different. Several minutes after the golf finished Bristol was still sitting in his armchair. The TV now showed a supposedly adult comedy show but Bristol was thinking about what he had just seen from the golf course. The phone interrupted his musing and he turned off the TV before answering it. The report from the fire site inspection team caused him to get his jacket and return immediately to the police station.

By midnight, when he returned home for the second time, Bristol had interviewed the chief investigator from the inspection team, brought his Superintendent up to date and issued several series of orders to members of his team. He decided against contacting John Friesen until the morning when both would be more refreshed and one of them would be far better informed. Rather than stick around the station and needlessly supervise his capable staff, Bristol opted for the rest he would need to get him through tomorrow. He also had a whisky before turning in, but in his case it was only one and his sleep was immediate and restful.

Bristol was in the office at six thirty the next morning reading the results of the inquiries he had instigated the night before. By seven o'clock he had scanned each of the reports and finished one mug of coffee. He was just settling down to a second mug and the careful rereading of the reports when the desk sergeant appeared in the doorway.

"Excuse me, Inspector. Mr. Friesen is here and would like to see you urgently."

"Sure. Show him in would you and bring him some coffee. He's going to need it." Bristol stacked the reports he had been reading and placed them face-down on the desk.

"Good morning, Mr. Friesen. Have a seat, please."

He got no further since John started speaking immediately he entered the room. "It's Karen, she didn't come home last night. My wife, I mean. She's disappeared. I had to leave my daughter with the neighbour. I've brought in a picture of her. She's never done this before. You must help me find her." He sat down abruptly in the chair facing the desk and stared at Bristol.

"Take it easy, sir. The Sergeant's getting you some coffee. Then we'll get it all sorted out. When I asked you to call round this morning, I hadn't exactly expected you this early in the day."

There was a brief knock on the office door and the Sergeant returned with a round plastic tray bearing a mug of coffee, a jar of creamer, sugar, a spoon and a small plate of digestive biscuits. Without saying a word he placed it on the corner of Bristol's desk and left the room.

Bristol gestured towards the tray and waited silently while John fixed his coffee. By the time his visitor had taken his first sip, Bristol was ready.

"I'm afraid I have some more bad news for you, Mr. Friesen. We now believe that your wife and partner perished in the explosion at your workshop yesterday. Last night the team of investigators found two badly burned bodies in the rubble. Later examination of a wedding ring and an identity bracelet found at the site indicate that the bodies were those of your wife and your partner." He forbore to mention that the two bodies had been discovered unclothed and joined permanently together in death among the burnt remains of the office sofa.

John was stunned. "What? Karen and Don? I don't believe it. There's no way!" He slumped back in his chair and most of the coffee spilled in his lap.

Bristol pulled a box of tissues from a drawer and pushed it across the desk. "I'm afraid there's no mistake, Mr. Friesen. I'm very sorry."

"It must be a mistake," John insisted. "Don was at a meeting. Karen didn't even have a key. How could they have been there? Whatever were they doing there? The place was closed yesterday . . . " He stopped abruptly. Don's meeting in the city, Karen's phoney phone call from the Cancer Society, his all-day commitment at the pro-am and the times involved coalesced into the most likely explanation. When the realization of what must have occurred struck him John went white and seemed to shrink in the chair.

Bristol was surprised at the reaction to his news. There was another knock at the door and a constable came in and handed Bristol a folded piece of paper. He opened it and glanced at the contents, then nodded to the constable who left the room.

"There's no doubt about the identities, I'm afraid. We've been trying to check with both local dentists. Both your wife and partner were patients of Dr. Crystal and his office has just confirmed that their dental charts match the teeth of the two bodies." He waved the piece of paper he had just received.

"I'm sorry to have given you such a shock, Mr. Friesen. Look, let me get you another mug of coffee while you dry yourself off and collect your thoughts." He took the mug from John's unresisting hand and swiftly left the room.

He delayed his return to the office by checking his phone messages, returning a call to the Superintendent, and visiting the washroom. When he returned to his office with the refilled coffee mug five minutes had elapsed. John had used several of the tissues to soak up coffee from his trousers and was leaning on the desk smoking a cigarette.

"I helped myself to one of your cigarettes, I hope you don't mind. I quit six years ago, but just now what I needed more than anything else in the world was a cigarette."

"No problem," Bristol replied. "I've tried give up several times, but I just can't break the habit. It seems to be my answer to stress, and if anyone deserves a cigarette it must be you."

John drew heavily on the cigarette and sipped his coffee. "I just don't know where to start. It's all too much," he said. "Yesterday my only problem was my golf swing, but now I've got to cope with child-care, funeral arrangements, wills, settling the business, the landlord, and God knows what else."

He looked as if he was about to burst into tears and Bristol tried to divert his attention. "Is there anyone I can contact to help you with all this?" he asked.

"My brother Jim is a lawyer. He'll know what to do."

"Do you know his number, Mr. Friesen? I'll call him."

John searched through his wallet until he found Jim's business card. "He'll probably be at the office by now, he always was an early riser."

Bristol took the card and dialled. John stared out of the window as he tried to think what to do. He was vaguely aware of Bristol's telephone conversation.

"He'll be here in about thirty minutes, Mr. Friesen. As you heard I just gave him a brief outline of what had happened."

Friesen was relieved that his brother was coming to collect him. Jim would know what to do, he probably dealt with this sort of thing all the time. He would keep John on track and make sure he did all the bits and pieces necessary. It didn't seem that Bristol had any suspicion that the fire was deliberately set. Surely it would be silly and dangerous to ask. He decided he needed time alone to think.

"I wonder if I could use the washroom?"

"Of course. Let me show you where it is."

Fifteen minutes later they were back in Bristol's office. John had combed his hair and washed his hands and face. The left leg of his trousers was damp from his further efforts to remove the coffee stain. He looked, and felt, much better. Bristol leaned over the desk to offer John another cigarette.

He accepted reluctantly. "You realize, of course, that you've just rekindled my addiction. I think I'm a smoker again."

Bristol laughed. "That's not my only recent bad deed, I'm afraid. I have a confession and an apology to make. When I went to bed last night I had you figured for one of the most cold-blooded and calculating killers I had ever encountered." John suddenly sat very still in his chair. He tried to breathe normally.

Bristol gave another self-conscious laugh. "I have an unfortunate tendency to look for complicated solutions to crimes I'm investigating. I know from experience that the most direct solution is usually correct, but it doesn't stop me. It's probably the result of reading too many detective stories. Last night I saw the TV coverage of the pro-am and the segment about you carrying the phone in your golf bag. This was only minutes before I heard about two bodies found at the fire and the tentative identification. I wondered if you'd taken out massive insurance on your wife and then murdered her with a bomb triggered by a telephone call."

John stared at him. He was beyond speech. How could Bristol suspect him of deliberately killing anybody?

"Even if anyone thought of a bomb set off by phone, you would have a perfect alibi. On a golf course — miles way from a phone. Who would think of a cellular phone in a golf bag unless, like me, they saw you on TV in that exact situation? Simple, eh? Just get her to the office on some excuse, make the call and set off the bomb."

John didn't trust himself to try and speak. He seemed to have gone into shock and he just stared at Bristol.

"The investigators looked for evidence of arson as a matter of routine, but didn't spot any of the obvious giveaways. There appears to be no sign of foul play, and they said the fire and explosion started in the workshop, nowhere near a phone. That, by the way, is another thing that went against my theory — the total devastation at the scene. That fire and explosion could only have been the work of a demolitions expert or one of those freak occurrences that you read about only in textbooks."

John still said nothing. He continued to stare blankly at the Inspector. How could Karen and Don deceive him like that?

"Anyway, just to be sure, I checked with the phone company about calls from your portable phone. They showed that calls were initiated to your home and office during the times you were on the course yesterday, but neither was completed."

"I was trying to save money by hanging up before the answering machines cut in," John said. "I didn't realize they could trace calls like that. It's just as well I have nothing to hide."

Bristol smiled. "Anyway, before I abandoned my master criminal scenario I made one more call to Russ Thompson about your insurance coverage. He said that your partner had arranged the usual business types of coverage, but that you had terminated the insurance coverage on your wife several years ago. That's where my theory finally collapsed, and that's why I owe you the apology."

Bristol stood, came around the desk and stretched out his hand. "Unless there are any unexpected developments, it looks as if we shan't have to bother you again. There will be an inquest, of course, but it looks as if you are a victim rather than a culprit. Oh, by the way, here's a copy of the preliminary report from the fire investigation team."

John shoved the report into his jacket pocket before he reached out to shake the policeman's hand. He thanked him for his concern and walked slowly out of the office. As he walked towards the main door to wait for Jim he thought about Karen and Don and the irony of their illicit meeting crossing with his plan designed to benefit them both. He wondered if Bristol would be so sympathetic if he knew about the terms of the partnership insurance Don had insisted on when they started out. The cost of maintaining it had been a bone of contention, but the unanticipated windfall of the $250,000 survivor's benefit would go a long way to making some of his unexpected problems easier to handle.

Generation Y

Nancy Kilpatrick

A winner of the Arthur Ellis Award for her short story "Mantrap," and a three-time finalist for the Horror Writers Association's Bram Stoker Award, Nancy is one of the world's most respected writers of dark fantasy. In addition to more than a hundred short stories, she has published numerous novels including the acclaimed *Power of the Blood* trilogy (*Near Death*, *Child of the Night* and *Reborn*). Nancy has also been nominated for the Aurora Award, Canada's top prize in science fiction and fantasy writing. Nancy's gifts as a writer are balanced by equal skill as an editor. Her numerous anthologies of horror, dark fantasy and erotic writing include *In the Shadow of the Gargoyle*, *Graven Images*, and five anthologies under her pseudonym, Amarantha Knight, among them *Seductive Spectres* and *Sex Macabre*. In much of her best short fiction, such as "Generation Y," Nancy blends elements of the crime and horror genres into a seamless nightmare.

"I'm *not* 'menacing'!"

"Rand, I'm sure he didn't mean to upset you. I think he just meant that, well, under the circumstances . . . " The Psychiatrist turns her palms up, and scans the prison's interview room. "Your statement about being a sensitive male *is* odd." The Psychiatrist crosses her short legs and leans forward, resting both forearms on her thigh, clasping her hands together as if she is pleading.

Rand likes the shape of her thigh, the way the pastel silk skirt clings to the taut skin and just lies there, passive, resting, waiting for fingers to reach out and separate fabric from flesh.

"Can you elaborate?" The Psychiatrist asks. "How do you see yourself as a sensitive young man?"

"There's lots of guys like me. Regular guys. Sensitive. Decent," Rand says.

"Yeah. A regular, sensitive, decent serial killer!" The Reporter's remarks are aggressive. Hostile. Violent.

Rand focuses on The Reporter. "A lot of guys are serial killers. More and more every day. You see it on TV. In the news. Guys like you write about guys like me. Guys who are trying to help."

"Help? Right!" The Reporter stabs symbols into his notebook, barely glancing down. The carved lines of his face deepen under the glare of brilliant TV lights.

"You created me."

The Reporter looks disgusted. His skin is tight, but with no appealing insulation beneath his cheeks. Just bone, nothing but bone. Hard, not subtle. Holding up a face with limited flexibility. He starts to say, "Look, you little sh — "

"Rand, I think what you're trying to get at," The Psychiatrist interrupts, "is that the media portrays violence and that in turn encourages violence in young people like yourself, with a predisposition."

"Fuck!" The Reporter mutters under his breath, low enough that the microphone will not pick it up. Rand watches him glance at The Guard by the door, whose eyes are non-committal, but whose mouth — the one that spits saliva when he talks, that opens and closes like the jaws of a vice, that utters sound bytes that Rand breaks into chunks and swallows whole — whose mouth twitches at the left corner. Nice touch, Rand thinks. But too far in the background to be effective.

"Well, Rand?" The Psychiatrist says. "Do you see yourself as a victim of media violence?"

"Oh, come on!" The Reporter says. "Tell us why you mutilated all those — "

"Let him answer the question," The Psychiatrist interrupts again.

The Reporter crashes back against the chair. Rand knows The Reporter would love to jump to his feet and punch The Prisoner in the face. The Reporter is violent by nature, that's clear. His turn to ask the questions is coming. They are supposed to take turns. Politely. That's the way it's supposed to go.

"I love television," Rand says. His voice is not as sincere as he wants it to sound, so he concentrates on lowering his eyes, dropping his head down a fraction. He looks up through his long lashes at The Psychiatrist. The dark eyelid hairs cut her body into strips. "And newspapers. It's important to know what's going on in the world around you."

Her face softens. She reminds him of The Teacher, and The Minister's Wife. The Others in the room wouldn't notice that her face has changed, but Rand does. She understands. "Tell us about your childhood," The Psychiatrist says gently.

This script is familiar. He has repeated these lines many times and knows them by heart. He wants to sigh, but that would not be the right thing to do. In a moment of inspiration, he tilts his head and looks away. If only his hands were free, but the chain keeps them six inches apart, which means he cannot rely on his hands to speak for him, and they speak eloquently.

"I had a very normal life," he says matter-of-factly, repeating by rote what he has said so often. Why won't they believe him? "My parents were divorced, but that wasn't a problem. Mom was great. She took real good care of me."

"How so?" asks The Psychiatrist.

"From when I was a baby. She had a monitor in the nursery and everything. So nothing bad would happen."

He remembers the monitor, even when he got old enough to go to school. His mother hovered just in the next room, always listening, waiting, as if for a sign.

"And there were home movies, then videos," he adds. Many. Endless tapes. She recorded them from before he could walk: Rand strapped into his cradle, the television set on — he still remembers his favourite show, the cartoon with the blood-red lion that chomped off the heads of its enemies; moving images of Rand eating meatloaf with his hands in front of the TV in a highchair; wandering the mall in his toddler harness, so he wouldn't get lost, or be stolen or be violated by some sick man. "She liked to shoot me. She said I was a natural on tape."

The Psychiatrist smiles.

The Reporter scribbles more notes.

The Guard shifts his weight to his other leg.

This room is small, like the set at a television station Rand saw once on a school tour. They had been broadcasting the news. The set, the size of a bathroom, consisted mainly of a plywood desk, the front veneered so it looked like real wood on tape. Two cameras. A control room with a bank of monitors before The Reporters. The Class visited the control room. The Technicians sat at the panels of switches and buttons and levers, wearing headsets, sending and receiving instructions as directed, zeroing in on The Female Reporter, then The Male Reporter. Back and forth, back and forth. Then The Weatherperson. The Technical Director controlled how everyone looked, what they said and how they said it. It was just like a movie.

"I'm sorry," he says when he realizes The Psychiatrist has asked a question.

"I asked if you would try to explain your motivation. Why you did what you did, to all those people . . . You must have felt very angry — "

"I never feel angry."

The Reporter leans forward.

The Psychiatrist sits back.

"Who's the first person you killed?" The Reporter demands.

"I never killed a person."

"Your DNA matches the DNA found at the scene of six murders. Six mutilations. And the jury found you guilty of — "

"They were wrong. I'm innocent. DNA can be wrong, you know. I saw a show on *60 Minutes* — "

"Yeah, kid, I know the stats. If you're not an identical twin, it's one in a million — "

"Two million. One in two million, depending on the tests used. But two million and one could be a match — "

"How did it feel to just tear off — "

"Please!" The Psychiatrist grips The Reporter's arm, tempering him. Reluctantly, he moves back in his chair. His face tightens. The Psychiatrist moves forward. This is her territory.

"Rand, I read the reports and evaluations. What you told the court. What you told the other doctors. You said you never felt the slightest bit of anger toward anyone."

"That's right," Rand agrees. "I don't believe in getting angry. That's how Mom raised me."

"But you must have been angry at your mother now and again. And your father — "

"Nope." He knows he's answered too quickly. It sounds like he is trying to hide something, but he isn't. Not at all. There's nothing to hide.

"My father wasn't around, so why would I get angry at him?"

"He was around until you were ten."

"I didn't notice. He was always at work."

"Rand, there's a history of domestic violence, your father assaulting your mother, and — "

"Yeah, well, she divorced him. Besides, she protected me. I didn't know about it until later. I was busy."

"You played a lot of video games," The Reporter says, struggling to get with the program at last.

"Sure. Some D&D stuff, then Nintendo when I got older. Doesn't everybody?"

"Yeah, but everybody doesn't — "

"I mean, doesn't everybody like video games? All the kids at my school did."

"Rand . . . " The Psychiatrist searches for another avenue, as though if she keeps probing he'll split apart, spill what's inside him. Bleed for the camera. But there is nothing to say that he hasn't said before. "Some of those games get pretty violent, don't they?"

"I guess."

"After you played them, you went out and played them in real life, didn't you?" The Reporter interjects, blurring the picture again.

"No."

"Sure you did!"

"Why should I? I had the games."

"And the urges — "

"Nope."

Rand looks up, presenting the face of The Innocent to The Videographer, a slim-bodied young woman with the head of a camera. How many hundreds of thousands, maybe millions of people will watch this drama unfold? he wonders. Most, he is certain, will understand. Most are against violence.

The Lawyer sits beside him, prepared to nip any compromising questions or answers in the bud. So far she has said nothing. Now she does.

"My client's answers to these questions are a matter of record. It's all in the trial transcripts."

"What's the basis of your final appeal?" The Reporter asks.

The Videographer shifts the camera to the left, to capture The Reporter's profile.

"Evidence that should never have been admissible," The Lawyer says.

"The video tapes?"

"Yes, the tapes."

A flash-fire races through Rand — The Reporter isn't supposed to steal the limelight! Rand is The Prisoner. The-Juvenile-Sentenced-To-Death. The one who has agreed to this three-way exclusive. The *only* one the camera should be focused on!

Rand knows he should say nothing but he needs to regain control.

"The only urges I have are to get rid of The Evil."

The Lawyer jumps in.

"Don't say another word — "

"What is The Evil?" the Psychiatrist asks, leaning far forward, until Rand can smell her perfume.

"You mean evil, like you?" The Reporter says sharply.

Rand smiles slightly and gazes seductively into the impassive camera eye. For effect, he fingers the white ribbon he always wears on his prison shirt, over his name. "I just mean, the world is full of violence. I wish it wasn't, but it is."

"That's enough, Rand! My client is — "

"Men are the violent ones. Everybody says so. The TV, the newspapers. So men have got to stop the violence. 'A man's gotta do what a man's gotta do.' John Wayne said that, you know. My mother used to quote him."

"Rand, have you heard of the psychiatric term 'projection'? It's — "

"If men don't do it, who will? The good guys have to stop the bad guys, or there's gonna be violence."

"Listen, kid, I've been a reporter for twenty years, and I know BS when I smell it — "

"My mother didn't raise me to be violent. She didn't want me to be like my father."

"As your counsel, Rand, I must advise you — "

"Most men are violent, don't you think so doctor? You're a woman."

"Rand, people can project feelings they have onto someone else — the way a camera projects an image. Angry feelings, or feelings of wanting to harm someone we fear will harm us — "

But Rand tunes her out. He directs his remarks exclusively toward The Videographer, to her cold, precise eye, studying him, controlling him, never letting him slide out of her objective sight.

"If there were no men in the world, there wouldn't be any violence. Isn't that right?"

Silence cuts the air for barely a second.

"I'm sorry, people, but as Rand's attorney, I must protect my client's interests. This interview is — "

"Deny it! Go ahead and deny it!" Rand shouts at the retreating camera, using emotional charge to lure it back. "You say it all the time, all of you. How can you say something different now? You're phonies!"

"Rand, do you feel attacked? No one here is attacking you — "

"All of you! You want all males dead!"

"Turn off the camera, or I'll file a civil action — "

"So do I! Then there won't be any more violence."

"Listen, you little shithead, *you're* the violent male!"

Rand lunges. He is aware of the camera zooming in on his hands. The chain from the wrist cuffs is hooked to a waist chain and his reach stops inches from his grasp.

Silence clutches the air. The Videographer has captured all. The shocked looks. The gasp from The Lawyer. The cry of "No!" from The Psychiatrist. The Guard drawing his gun. The Reporter, struggling to protect his genitals, what would have been seconds too late, but for The Prisoner's restraints.

Rand stares down at his hands. They are bony and thin, 'sensitive' his mother always said. The fingers stretch like talons, ready to claw The Evil from its roots. Ready to deposit it into his hungry mouth, where powerful jaws can pulverize and razor teeth rend. Where what should not exist, by being devoured, can be eliminated forever.

That would have made a great shot. His mom would have loved it. Rand sits back and smiles into the camera's eye. He just hopes that The Videographer had the lens in sharp focus when she captured him.

Trophy Hunter

Peter Sellers

Regarded as Canada's leading anthologist of short crime fiction, Peter was the founder and editor of the critically acclaimed *Cold Blood* series of Canadian short crime fiction anthologies. He has also edited two single-author collections: *Fear is a Killer* featuring stories by William Bankier and *A Murder Coming*, stories by James Powell. In addition to working as an editor, Peter has written numerous short stories that have been published in such places as *Ellery Queen's* and *Alfred Hitchcock's Mystery Magazines*, as well as various crime and dark-fantasy anthologies. A collection of his stories, *Whistling Past the Graveyard*, was published in 1999 by Mosaic Press. He has twice served as President of the Crime Writers of Canada, and received that organization's Derrick Murdoch Award in 1992.

"I want you to find my new wife, Mr. Daniher."

The little cash registers in Milo's head started ringing as soon as the rich man spoke.

"I want you to find my new wife."

Milo didn't have to be a detective to know the guy was rich. He knew it the minute he got the address over the phone. He had it reconfirmed as soon as he saw the house. And when the door opened and he saw Cross standing there he had unassailable proof. Milo recognized the face from countless newspaper and magazine photo ops. And he knew all the stories about the various businesses Cross owned or was reputed to own.

"Find my new wife."

Milo had worked for rich people before and he knew immediately how this job was going to go. If there was one thing Milo prided himself on, it was knowing how other people's clocks were wound. And he knew that this would be the kind of job he had come to treasure. Not hard. Not dangerous. Pushing yourself definitely not required. And at the end, a major payday. It meant he could write his own ticket. It meant clearing enough to cover the cost of life for a few months and then taking Cara to Jamaica for a week, or to Vegas or the Bahamas. And he knew how appreciative she could be on the rare occasions when he took her away somewhere.

"My new wife."

A lot can happen to a wife. She could have been kidnapped and the rich man was scared to go to the cops. He liked press, but not that kind. She could have wandered off from the old folks' home in nothing but a bathrobe and furry slippers. She could have split for Niagara Falls with the delivery guy from the drug store. He called her his new wife so maybe she got disappointed that he couldn't hold up his end in bed or maybe she didn't like the fact that it was up all the time. Milo didn't know whether it was one of those or something else entirely, but he didn't much care. Because he did know one thing for sure. He knew how to work this.

How it worked was like this. Milo sets it up about how tough it is to track somebody all by yourself in a city of three and a half million people. He'll do his best but it'll take time. And if somebody doesn't want to be found at all, well, it's a big wide world out there. Then, having set the stage, Milo hits the rich man for a big day rate, takes a couple of weeks up front as retainer, then fucks the dog. Looks a bit, calls in every couple of days to update on nothing. Every so often he picks up a couple of receipts and floats them past the rich guy's nose as expenses. After a month or so he calls it a day, packs a suitcase, and takes Cara somewhere she can get an all-over tan.

"Do you have a picture of her?" Milo asked.

"No." Cross sounded surprised. "I'm afraid I don't."

Now that was odd. Not many people don't have a picture of the person they're married to. At least, not many people who care enough to hire a private detective to track down a wife who's gone missing. Oh well, Milo thought, maybe she's got some weird phobia. Maybe she's just ugly as homemade sin. Maybe she's from some tribe somewhere that thinks cameras steal your soul. Doesn't matter. Fact is it made things better. Without a picture to show around he could make the case that the job'd be that much tougher, take him that much longer. Make him that much richer.

"Can you describe her to me, then?" Milo reached in his pocket for a chewed up pen and a half used note pad.

"Well." Cross sat back, looking up at the ceiling as if fixing an image in his mind. "I can definitely do that, Mr. Daniher. She is between twenty-four and twenty-six years old. She weighs between one hundred fifteen and one hundred twenty-five pounds. She has shoulder length hair, wavy but not curly, some shade of brown, but definitely not blonde. She has long legs and neither tattoos nor pierced body parts except her ear lobes. She stands between five feet six and five feet eight inches tall."

Milo stopped writing. He knew that a lot of women kept their age secret, and some outright lied about it, so there had to be husbands who didn't know exactly how old their wives were. He knew that everyone's weight fluctuated. And with the way a lot of women dieted and binged they could roller coaster up and down ten pounds from one week to the next. And hair could change length and colour in the bathroom between halves of a football game. But a person's height tended to be pretty consistent. That's what really threw Milo. It didn't sound like

Cross was describing someone he knew. It sounded like he was telling the guy at the dealership what options he wanted on his new 4x4.

"Hold on," Milo said. "Can't you be a little more precise? You don't know how tall your wife is?"

"Not yet." The smile again.

Milo scratched his jaw. "I'm sorry, but you lost me back there."

"What do you mean?"

"I mean, it sounds like you're describing types of people, not one in particular. What's going on here?"

"Did I not make myself clear, Mr. Daniher? I said I want you to find my new wife. The woman I intend to marry. If I'd already met her, I wouldn't need the services of a detective."

Milo blinked hard several times then dug his little finger into his right ear and shook it. He'd done a lot of things for money in his time. He'd chased away raccoons and stolen garbage bags off ritzy front lawns at two in the morning. He'd videotaped every kind of couple imaginable. He'd dragged runaways back to the families they probably had good reason for leaving in the first place. He'd pissed into empty pickle jars sitting up nights in his car waiting for guys who'd skipped on their bondsmen to come up for air. He'd repoed cars and intercepted mail and made harassing phone calls. But he'd never played matchmaker. "Let me get this straight. You want to hire me to find you a co-ed you can marry. You don't need me, pal. You need a dating service."

"Oh no, Milo. May I call you Milo?"

Milo figured it didn't matter whether he minded or not. So he just shrugged.

"Well then, Milo, you're quite wrong. I need you very much."

"How so?"

"I want this done discreetly. I don't want my name and personal data keyed into some computer system that spits out desiccated spinsters and blubbery widows with condos in Pompano Beach. I want women who fit my specifications exactly. I want it done with no fuss whatsoever. And I have been told, Milo, that you are nothing if not discreet."

In the end, Milo took the job. He quoted a day rate that was twice what he usually got and Cross slipped him three grand up front. Cash.

"Anything else I should know about your sweetheart?" Milo asked.

"A couple of small things, Milo. Intelligence is not an issue. I want a woman who looks very attractive. I'm not interested in intellectual discussions. There are plenty of people with whom I can have those. Indeed, since her opinion will neither be sought nor appreciated, it would be much better if she didn't have one. Also it would be better — in fact it is a prerequisite — that she not have a family."

Milo's eyebrows went up.

"It's simple, Milo. I'm a very rich man. I make no secret of it. And my friends tend also to be very rich men. Many of them, like me, have taken younger wives. In at least two cases of which I am aware, these wives had families. And members of those families had" — he paused as if searching for the right word — "avaricious tendencies. The situations became very unpleasant. Such unpleasantness is something I am determined to avoid."

"Understood," Milo said. "You're not looking for love then. Good. Because I can find you a chick for the rate we discussed. But love costs extra. Anything else?"

"I think that's everything. I expect to hear from you within a week with a progress report. Within two weeks, I expect to begin meeting candidates. Please be aware that I do not want a cattle call. I haven't the time to waste." He stood up and ushered Milo out of the room. They walked along the panelled hallway toward the front door.

Milo marveled again at the suit of armour standing guard at the foot of the stairs. A suit of armour with a big double-headed axe in one hand.

"Lovely piece, isn't it?" Cross said. He reached out and touched the blade of the axe with his thumb. "Feel it," he said.

Milo pressed the ball of his thumb against the blade and felt it slice the skin. "Sharp."

"Yes. Some day I must outline for you the provenance of the piece, but I'm sure you're too busy for that now." Then he crossed to a set of double doors and opened them wide. "Before you go, I thought you might be interested in this. My trophy room." It was dark with wood panelling, stone fireplace, leather chairs and severed heads sticking out from the wall. There was a moose, a twelve point buck, a bear and several animals that Milo was sure were on endangered lists somewhere. There were fish too. Trout and muskie and a big billfish on the far wall. The only area of wall with nothing on it was above the fireplace.

Milo pointed at the open space. "What's going up there? You want something pretty big. What's that mantel? About six feet? That marlin'ld look good."

"Yes, it actually was there for a time. It took me seven hours to land off Zihouatanejo. It was a wonderful challenge. But beautiful as it is, it felt too common. I want a more exotic trophy." Then he smiled and showed Milo the door.

# # #

"I have an idea," Cara said.

"Yeah, what's that?" Lying on his back with his eyes closed, Milo felt like a lizard on a hot rock.

"I'll do it."

"You'll do what?" Cara was not one for doing things for other people unless money changed hands, so Milo got nervous right away.

"I'll marry the rich guy."

"What?" He opened his eyes and turned his head to look at her.

"You heard me. I'll marry him. Then I'll ditch him. And we'll get half of everything. That's how community property works, isn't it?"

Milo had explained the job to her over dinner and she listened with an unusual amount of interest. When he was finished she got quiet for a time, then laid this at his door. "I'll do it." Like she was saying yeah, she'd pick the milk up on the way home from the hair salon. She was unpredictable. That was one of the things Milo liked best about her.

He didn't concern himself much with most of her inconsistencies. It flashed through his mind that she had told him more than once that she really didn't like men. This didn't exactly jibe with suggesting that she marry someone she'd never met, but then Milo knew that people were seldom simple or consistent.

She got out of bed to dress and Milo studied her. This time with more purpose than just enjoyment. She was exactly what Cross had in mind. The right age. The right colouring. The right height and weight and shape. She was smarter than the person Cross was looking for, but that only meant she was smart enough to play dumb. Milo was just thankful that he'd been able to talk her out of getting her navel pierced on her last birthday. "You have an amazing body," he said.

"Thanks," she said. "I like yours too."

"I'm serious. I think you look great. I think Cross'll think you look great. But I think you should give this thing some deeper thought," Milo said. Something about the idea didn't sit comfortably in the back of his head.

"I will." She slipped into a pair of jeans and did up her belt. "It's only about the money, Milo. I'm tired of feeling stressed over not having enough money."

"So move in with me." It was the umpteenth time of asking. She was renting a house down in the Beaches and it was eating up too big a chunk of her pay.

She pulled on a shirt that didn't reach her waist and then she stretched, showing him her smooth and flat belly. "I don't think that's a good idea, Milo. Not yet, anyway."

He thought, but you're ready to move in with some rich guy you've never even talked to. But he kept his mouth shut. Instead, he said, "I just don't want to make this look too easy or too much like a set up. Leave it with me. I'll make it so it can't fuck up."

"I like a man who takes charge," she said.

# # #

For the next week, Milo pretended to work. He placed ads in the classified sections of several newspapers, giving an anonymous post office box. *"Successful, established businessman seeks . . . early- to mid-twenties . . . no children . . . send letter and photo . . . "* He knew the ads would most likely turn up nothing. Any candidates who did have potential he could just shitcan.

He took out ads in foreign papers too. In England and Ireland and Australia, for women looking to emigrate to Canada. Women for whom marrying a Canadian was the easiest route. This wasn't what Cross wanted, but Milo had to show some effort and, as he'd explain it, you never knew. You don't ask, you don't get. Bearing in mind Cross's desire for brown hair, Milo also advertised in France and Spain, specifying absolute fluency in English. Although, since Cross didn't seem to care if they never opened their mouths for anything but a blow job, that might not matter.

Milo saw women on the street occasionally who were close to the type but, he suspected, not perfect. Sometimes he would follow them and take pictures with a telephoto lens. More useless evidence of his keen efforts.

All this information, including clippings of the various ads, copies of the bills, and some early and unacceptable local responses, were presented to Cross during Milo's first update.

# # #

"Surely there's something more personal you can do." Cross sounded irritated.

"I am," Milo said. "I'm asking people all the time. 'Do you know somebody?' Things like that. But you have to be careful. You're not going to make much progress using that approach on someone in a bar. And is that who you'd want anyway?"

"I suppose not."

"No, I figured."

Milo left with a week's extension and another grand in his pocket.

Slowly, the responses from overseas started to trickle in. Most of them were useless, but a couple had potential merit. Those Milo ripped up and threw away. He was amazed by the photos some of them sent him. Several were topless. Some totally naked. A few actually sent pictures of themselves, or women they were palming off as themselves, having sex. Milo put those photos in a special file. After two weeks, it was time to up the stakes a notch.

He went to see Cross again, bringing the next batch of mailed-in replies, plus some of his telephoto shots. Included in the pictures he'd taken himself were three women who he was going to have Cross meet. Before he got to meet the woman of his dreams.

Going through the options with Cross, Milo pushed the three ringers hard. They had the look, he pointed out. They didn't have families. At least, none that he'd been able to dig up so far. And he was sure he could interest them in the proposition. Cross bit. Bring them in. Tuesday night. One at eight. One at eight fifteen. One at eight thirty. Cross didn't say it in a way that gave Milo the feeling he could negotiate.

One of the three was an acquaintance of Milo's. A friend who did amateur theatricals and was close to Cross's description. The others were friends of hers. They all were active in little theatre and wanted to try out their skills in a real life drama. Milo hired them all, for a modest sum. Then he sketched the details. Just enough so they'd know what to do. Not enough that they'd screw the deal.

Tuesday at quarter to eight, he met the first potential Mrs. Cross at the front door. She was perky, with an athletic build and auburn hair. Milo escorted her to the trophy room. "Everything'll go fine," he said. "Piece of cake." There was a fire burning in the hearth that accentuated the wall above the mantel. "This is Janet," Milo said.

Cross was sitting in a wing chair, angled slightly away from the fireplace. He looked at the woman carefully, then motioned for her to turn around. "Tell me something about yourself, Janet."

"Like what?"

"Anything at all. About your childhood."

She thought for a moment and then started talking enthusiastically about the pets she'd had, the cottage she'd loved to visit with her family each summer, the friends she'd shared secrets with. Cross shut his eyes while she spoke and gave Milo the impression that he wasn't so much listening to what she said as to the quality of her voice. She was in the middle of a story about a rabbit she'd been particularly fond of when Cross opened his eyes again and interrupted her, "That's enough."

She looked startled, but stopped talking.

"Now," Cross said, "take off your clothes."

Leaning back against the wall by the door, Milo's pulse quickened. He hadn't anticipated this, although it made sense, given what Cross was looking for. He hadn't prepared any of the women for it. This was going to be more interesting than he'd figured.

"Pardon me?" Janet said.

"You heard me," Cross said softly. "Remove your clothes. How you look nude is a significant part of my decision." He looked at her evenly, but Janet didn't reach for button or zipper. Instead she turned, picked up her purse and overcoat from the love seat, gave Milo a hurt and angry look, and left.

"Clearly," Cross said, "she won't do."

"Probably won't do much of anything," Milo joked, but Cross didn't even smile.

The next one worked better. Her name was Mary and when the request was made she didn't hesitate. She simply dropped her clothes in a pile on the floor and turned slowly so that Cross could see her fully. As she faced Milo she winked and stuck out her tongue. "Want me to bend over?" she asked Cross over her shoulder.

Mary's undoing was a small rose tattooed on her behind. As soon as Cross saw it, he said, "Get dressed. You won't do."

"Your loss, my friend," she said as she went through the door.

At Milo's suggestion, the third candidate had become a brunette two days before. She had no tattoos and taking off her clothes was not a problem. But Cross felt her thighs were too heavy and she, too, was sent home.

"So far, Milo, I'm less than impressed."

It became clear to Milo that Cross had been spun along as far as possible. It was time the rich guy got to know Cara.

"Mr. Cross," Milo said over the phone the next day, "I think we have a strong contender."

"Tell me," Cross said.

# # #

The meeting with Cross went just the way Milo figured it would. He got there a couple of minutes before eight. Cross was never on time, but Milo knew that he got mad as hell if you weren't there when you were supposed to be.

He waited in the library. It was packed with books, floor to ceiling, on dark wooden shelves that covered almost every inch of wall. Once, Milo had made the mistake of taking a book off the shelf. It was selected works of Milton, beautifully bound and quite old. Milo was reading *Samson Agonistes* aloud when Cross came into the room. "Don't ever touch my books," Cross said, taking the volume from Milo's hand.

"It's Milton," Milo said, but Cross was not impressed by Milo's taste in literature.

"Don't ever touch anything that belongs to me," Cross said. Then he smiled and offered Milo a coffee.

That's how Milo learned. He never touched anything, never sat down or opened a door, unless the rich man told him to. The last thing he wanted to do was fuck up the deal.

Cross motioned for Milo to come into the trophy room. The space above the fireplace was still vacant, Milo noticed. Cross was taking his time deciding what to put there. Maybe he had a trip to Africa coming up or Borneo, and he was waiting to see what he bagged while on safari. Milo sensed that Cross was impatient. He didn't sit down himself. He didn't motion for Milo to sit either. He just held out his hand for the photographs. Milo handed them over.

Cross flipped through them once quickly, then a second time, studying each one at length. They were a mixed bag of images. Some candid shots of Cara walking along the street or sitting at outdoor cafes. Some were studio shots. They were all pretty wholesome, a couple just bordering on cheesy. But he knew by now what the rich guy went for. He didn't like aggressive women. He didn't want one who would look him in the eye and ask him, "Do you want to fuck?" Cara could play it both ways.

Milo figured Cross liked what he saw. "Bring her here. Tomorrow night. This same time." And then Milo was outside heading for his car.

# # #

It was all turning real. Milo took a long route home, doubling back on himself and circling like a hawk. His mind was cranking all the way. Here it was. If he shut his eyes he could almost smell the money, almost feel how different life would be to the touch. It would feel like silk and chenille and twenty-year-old malts. But that wasn't all he thought about. He worried too. This was not unusual and it wasn't necessarily bad either. Milo worried about a lot of things. He sweated the details. That's why things worked out so well for him all the time. That's why this thing was going so smooth. Had been ever since Cara suggested it and Milo cooked up the scheme. But whenever he thought about Cara being involved in it right up to her tender neck, he had mixed feelings.

Of course, he had mixed feelings about Cara most of the time. He wasn't in a position to say, forget it. Forget the money. Let's walk away while we can. No, much as he thought about it he couldn't bring himself to make that big a sacrifice. On the other hand, he couldn't tell her that he'd stick around after she'd taken half the rich guy's dough. He couldn't make that promise. He'd be just as likely to take his cut and head for greener pastures.

He loved her, or thought he did. He certainly liked the way her body looked and the way she moved it. But he hated the fact that she was secretive. He was good at laying secrets bare most of the time. But he couldn't dig far into her.

He knew the facts that she'd given him. But he also knew that it was far from everything. It was like her life was a panoramic photograph that she had carefully cropped down to wallet size and given to him. This is what he knew.

She never talked about her childhood. The story she told Milo started when she was fourteen and doing a lot of drugs. She smoked a plantation's worth of grass and hash and dropped acid. Nothing heavy, she said. Nothing in the vein. She left home when she was seventeen. She got an apartment with a friend and began a series of nothing jobs she didn't like. Often, she dropped them at a moment's notice, going out for lunch and simply not going back. At nineteen she married a guy she claimed she didn't want to marry and went west with him. They lived for a time in Vancouver, which she loved, then Edmonton, which she hated. She hated the cold and the tedium and the marriage and she fell into a clinical depression. At some point along the road she told Milo she'd thought about suicide. But he got the sense maybe she'd done more than think.

At another point, she picked up a major case of panic and didn't go outside for months. It lingered still. She wouldn't ride the subway or get on a plane or step into an elevator. She left her husband. Left him, more or less. She still spent one night a week with the guy even after she started going out with someone new. Then she moved in with the new guy. Another thing she claimed she didn't want to do. Eventually, she stopped spending nights with the ex-husband and stayed home most evenings. Until she met Milo. And that was it. Everything else was secret. She even refused to tell him how old she was. But he guessed she was in Cross's range.

He had problems with turning her over to Cross. On the other hand, there was probably more money than he could count. He started for home.

# # #

"You ready?"

They were sitting in the car out front of Cross's place. Cara hadn't given away anything when she saw it. "Big," was all she said.

"Wait'll you see the inside."

She said nothing at all to that.

It was about ten to eight. "We still have a few minutes," Milo said. Cara was staring out through the windshield. It wasn't bright in the car, but the security floodlights shining on the property let Milo see enough of her face. She had this look on her that Milo never knew if he was decoding right.

"We don't have to go through with it," he said. He put his hand on top of hers. She didn't pull away, but neither did she respond. "We can just leave." He felt better saying it. Like a responsibility was lifted off him. "We can drive home and I'll tell Cross to forget it. There's lots of money to be had out there. We can pick ours up somewhere else."

Cara shook her head. "No. I can't get out of this now."

"You mean you don't want to."

"I mean I can't." She opened her door. "Let's go," she said. "Get me to the church on time."

Milo followed her to the house.

# # #

Inside, Cara stopped for a moment in the foyer and looked around. She took in the vaulted ceiling and the circular staircase and the gilt framed oil paintings. But all she commented on was the suit of armour. "Look at that," she said and went up to it, reaching out to the blade of the axe.

"Careful," Milo said. "It's sharp."

"I guess you'd want it to be," she said.

Cross didn't say it when he opened the door to let them in, but Milo could tell that he was pleased. Cross was checking Cara out while she checked out the suit of armour. The armour didn't pay any attention. Then Cross led them into the trophy room. He told Cara to undress. She did it right away, but mechanically. The mask was still in place. When she was naked, she stood waiting with her arms at her sides.

As Cara waited, Cross lifted a pair of surgical gloves from his desk and put them on. He didn't say anything. Milo didn't say anything. Neither did Cara. The sucking sound of rubber seemed very loud. When the gloves were on, Cross wiggled his fingers. Then he motioned for Cara to turn around.

She did and Cross walked across the carpet and stood very close to her. In the middle of her back was a large mole. Cross reached out with his right hand and pressed it, then bent his index finger back and flicked it hard, like a child shooting a marble. Cara winced and Cross said, "This can be fixed."

Then he grabbed her hair and lifted it up, peering at the skin of her neck. He placed his free hand on the top of her head and twisted it sharply to the left and then to the right. Still holding her hair, he bent her ears forward with his thumb, one then the other. Milo figured he was looking for face lift scars.

Cross seemed satisfied because, without letting go of her hair he stepped around in front of her. "Bend forward," he said, pulling downward. "Not that far." He jerked her head backward and she whimpered.

Milo was starting to feel uncomfortable. "Mr. Cross . . ."

"It's okay, Milo," Cara said.

"You can leave if you like," Cross said, but Milo didn't move.

When Cara was bent forward at the angle Cross wanted, the rich man started pawing at the top of her head. Pushing her hair around with rough, sharp motions. Looking for dark roots, Milo supposed.

Satisfied with her head, Cross put a hand under Cara's chin and jerked up. "This won't take much longer," he said. But to Milo it seemed to take quite some time.

# # #

"Tomorrow at eleven, have her at this address." He handed Milo a card with the name of a well known cosmetic surgeon. "Get him to look at that thing on her back. If he says it can be fixed with no sign, call me right away. If he says there'll be a problem with scarring or something, call me in two days with other possibilities." Cara was standing near the front door with her coat bunched around her. Her chin was tucked down into the collar and she looked cold. Cross never looked at her.

"Good work, Milo. We're very close with this one." He gave Milo one of his rare smiles. "I hope to hear from you tomorrow," he said.

# # #

"Are you all right?"

"Sure." She said it without conviction. Just the way she said it when Milo suggested doing something together other than going to the two or three restaurants she liked.

Milo's feelings of discomfort weren't going away in a hurry. "We don't have to go see that doctor tomorrow," he said. "I don't have to call him."

"I can't get out now," she said. "Take me home. I want a bath."

# # #

The plastic surgeon was expecting them. They saw him right on the dot of eleven o'clock. Milo was impressed. Cross must have really had some sway to get a doctor to see someone on time. Of course, you paid cash for this type of treatment. It wasn't a medicare thing, necessary because of an accident or something. Cash made a difference. Milo knew it. So did Cara.

The doctor seemed very gentle. He told Milo to wait in the reception area, then he asked Cara to go into an examining room and remove her shirt. She would find a gown to wear hanging on the back of the door. He gave her a few minutes while he checked some charts and made a phone call, then he went to the examining room and tapped lightly on the door. "May I come in?"

Milo did not hear Cara's response, but the doctor opened the door and went inside. He was not gone long. He came out, making notes. Cara followed a minute or two later.

"I have to tell you," the doctor said, "that based on a preliminary examination there's no medical reason to remove that mole. Cara, you tell me that it's always been there. It hasn't changed in size or colour or texture — hasn't changed in any way at all. We can do a biopsy, but my feeling is it won't show anything abnormal. Sometimes, to be quite frank, removing a benign growth such as this can trigger cancerous growth."

"Thank you, doctor, but there are other issues here. If you do remove it, will there be any scarring or anything?"

The doctor shook his head. "No, it's a very straightforward procedure. Any mark left behind will be so insignificant as to be unnoticeable. But again I have to tell you that there's no medical reason to do this."

Cara put on her jacket. "It's not being done for medical reasons," she said.

# # #

Cross was happy with the news, as far as Milo could tell. The rich man's voice didn't change very much. "This is good. Tell her to be ready tomorrow evening at seven. Have her dressed for a wedding. Not a white gown. I'm not a traditionalist. But something demure and simple. I'll have a car pick her up. She needn't pack anything. Clothes will be arranged."

"You're getting married tomorrow night?"

"Yes. I'm sorry, but it will be a private affair. But we do have business to conclude. Come and see me now."

As he listened to the phone humming in his ear, Milo's head started to swim. This was moving faster than he'd planned. He wished everything would slow down for a second so he could think.

Until that happened, he had to keep moving at the pace that was set. That or get left behind. He went to see Cross. They met in the trophy room as usual. Milo took a good long look around because he sensed he might never see it again.

Cross handed him a fat envelope. "What's this?" Milo asked. Cross had more than paid up already.

"A bonus. You've outdone yourself. Once that small disfigurement is corrected, she'll be perfect. I assure you that, should any of my friends need the services of a private detective, I'll be sure to recommend you highly." He placed a hand on Milo's back and guided him to the door. "I also trust that I can count on your continued discretion."

"You bet," Milo said. He looked at the space over the mantel again and for the first time an uncomfortable thought crossed his mind. "Good luck finding something for up there."

"Yes," Cross said. Then he laughed. Milo had never heard him do that before.

# # #

Almost three weeks and not a word from Cara. Milo knew that most honeymoons were over in a week or two. But he had no idea how long rich guy honeymoons lasted. Did they go to Europe for the season? Were they on a round-the-world cruise? Were they backpacking in the Andes or spending a month in an ashram getting cleansed? He didn't have a clue.

The evening of the wedding he'd waited with Cara until Cross's car pulled up out front. She was wearing a short red sleeveless dress and a gold chain with her name on it around her right ankle. Her legs looked great and Milo wished she wasn't leaving. Milo wasn't sure the outfit qualified as demure, but that was not his problem.

The driver honked from the street. Cara gave Milo a brief smile and a quick kiss on the cheek. "So long, Milo." He went to hug her, but she'd already turned away, picked up her small purse and taken hold of the door handle.

"Be careful," he said. "Call me and let me know what's happening. We still have details to work out. And if you want out, any time, all you have to do is phone. Or come see me. I'll haul you out of there in a second."

She smiled at him again and then she left. Through the living room window he saw her walk across the porch, down the steps and out to the car. The driver stood by the door which he shut as soon as she was inside. The windows were tinted so Milo couldn't tell if she looked back at him or not.

Not a word since. No post cards from the South of France or letters carried by llama down from some Andean retreat.

There were still things they needed to go over. Parts of the plan that had to be worked out now that she was inside. He'd tried to do it before she ever met Cross, but she kept putting him off. Always had a reason. Always told him not to worry, though. They'd work everything out soon.

While he waited for soon to arrive, Milo just kept telling himself that he trusted her. He had to. Otherwise, he was fucked.

He took a couple of other cases in the meantime. Some guy wanted to scare a couple of his wetback employees for some undisclosed reason. Milo didn't ask why. He just showed up at the factory pretending to be from Immigration. They got scared enough. He had a couple of beers afterwards and thought about how much he wanted to stop doing this kind of work.

He got passed an insurance claim that the company was sure was bogus. Sometime in the middle of the night he set fire to the guy's shed. It was located at the back of his yard, a good sixty feet from the house. As he watched the man hobble desperately across his yard, hauling a garden hose in his one good arm, Milo figured the claim was legit. But he took pictures. Telephoto. Infrared.

That kind of gig was okay. It paid well enough, though not like Cross. But his heart wasn't in much of anything for those weeks. He missed Cara. And he wondered where the hell she was.

# # #

Patience was never Milo's long suit and finally he couldn't wait any more. He had phoned her number at home a couple of times, never expecting her to pick up but just to hear her voice on the answering machine. "You have reached . . . No one is available to take your call at this time . . . " He was always amused by the careful enunciation of each word. No endings dropped. Nothing slurred over. He'd hear the message through and then hang up before the beep sounded. Then one day he phoned and, instead of her voice, he got the phone company's. "I'm sorry, the number you have dialled is not in service."

He dialled the number again. Maybe, despite the fact that he'd called it a thousand times, he'd made a mistake. But no. The number was gone. He knew he shouldn't have been shocked. But he felt numb.

He knew there was only one cure. It was time to take charge again.

Milo phoned Cross from a pay phone several blocks from his office. Just in case the rich guy had call display. This time, though, he didn't call Cross's private line — the one that rang only in the trophy room or very softly in the library. He called the general house number. Unlisted, but Milo was a fair to middling detective.

If Cross answered, or the housekeeper, Milo would just hang up. If Cara answered, he'd feel a lot better.

The phone rang three times and then Milo heard a click and "Hello?" Milo caught himself smiling at the sound of her voice.

"Hi, it's me." He realized he was whispering.

"Milo? Why are you calling me?"

That was not the reaction he had anticipated. "Because I miss you every day. And I want to know what's going on. We still have details to work out."

"Details?"

"Yeah." He didn't want to say too much just in case the rich guy was insecure enough to have the phone bugged. "You know, details. About the deal."

"Oh, right."

She didn't sound good. Milo knew something was wrong. "Look, can you get out? Can we meet for dinner or something?"

"Sure," she said. Flat and unenthusiastic.

Milo felt her hesitation and pushed harder. "When? Tonight? Tomorrow?"

"I'll have to call you back."

"We have to get together. We have to work out the details. I have to know what's going on."

"I'll tell you," she said. "Just let me do it in my own way."

"You'll call me?"

"Yes, I'll call you."

"When? Tonight?"

"I'll try."

He felt like telling her there was no such thing. She'd either do it because she wanted to or not do it because she didn't. Instead, he softened his voice and tried a gentler tack. "Will you try really hard?"

She made a noise that might have been the least part of a laugh. "Bye," she said and hung up.

She did call him that night, but late. He'd given up. He was lying in bed reading Yeats out loud when the phone rang. He knew it had to be her. He seldom got calls at home. Never at that hour. But even when he picked up the phone and heard her voice it surprised him.

"I can't talk long," she said. "He's in the shower so I've only got a minute. We can have dinner tomorrow night."

"Where?"

She named a restaurant that she liked, where it was quiet and they didn't rush you to get out. "I'll tell you as much as I can then."

"What time?"

"Seven thirty."

"Great," he said. "I love you." But she was already gone.

#

From seven thirty till eight, Milo figured she was tied up. From eight till eight thirty, he figured she'd just forgotten. By quarter to nine he was ready to leave. He was standing with his coat on when she breezed in.

"Sorry," she said but offered no explanation. She wore jeans and a brown leather jacket he'd never seen before.

"That's nice," he said.

"It was a gift." She sat and looked at him, but didn't say anything more.

"So what's the story?" he asked.

"Story?"

Jesus Christ. "Yeah. What's going on? What's your sense of how we play this? How long does he hang on until we can take him? Or does he have some heart condition and maybe he'll kick sometime in the next few months?"

"No," she said, "he definitely doesn't have a heart condition." She laughed, but it was awkward and nervous. "Look, there are some strange things happening, Milo."

No shit. "Strange like what?" he said.

"There's no prenuptial agreement."

Milo had never even considered that. It had never entered his head that Cross would want Cara to sign something before the wedding. He never even considered that his plan might be killed like that, with the stroke of a pen, before it even began. He kicked himself for overlooking something so basic. But, odd that it was that Cross hadn't asked for an agreement, it was a good thing. It meant Milo had dodged the bullet. "Well, that's good," he said. "Something like that could've really fucked us up."

"It's not good, Milo. It's weird. This guy's got so much money he wipes himself with twenties. And what he's got he hangs on to. Why would he marry a trophy wife and not take every precaution to protect his dough? You read about it all the time, old rich guys getting taken. You told me, he mentioned that kind of thing to you himself. Why wouldn't he protect himself, Milo? Why?"

Milo thought about it but couldn't come up with a reason that made sense. "Maybe he trusts you," he said doubtfully.

"Yeah, right." She looked back over her shoulder, then leaned in halfway across the table. "I don't think he trusts gravity to hold him down. No, I think it's something else. The only thing I can figure is it's like he knows I'm never going to leave him." She looked back again, as if she were expecting Cross to loom in the doorway any second. "Look, I gotta go. He likes me to stay close to home. That's what he said to me the first day. 'I want to keep you close to hearth and home.' There's something really weird going on."

Milo grabbed her hand across the table. They used to touch fingertips during dinner, but this was different. He grabbed her hand and gripped it tight. "If it's that weird, maybe it's time we got you out of there," he said. "Let's take what we can get now and get you out of there."

She pulled her hand away. "Soon, Milo," she said. "But not yet."

# # #

The stress was getting to Milo. He went to the gym. He figured he could sweat some of it out. But no matter how hard he pushed himself it didn't help much. He kept thinking hard. Something had to be done. He felt like he was losing Cara. She was being sucked away from him by the vacuum of Cross. That was bugging him plenty. But it wasn't the only thing. There was something Cara had said that was jangling in his brain — way off in the distance like an alarm clock the instant before you wake up.

Milo finally woke up in the shower. He was standing there with the hot water pelting down on the back of his head and his neck. The water ran around the sides of his head and poured off his face. His eyes were shut and he played images of Cross and Cara over and over in his head, trying to work it out.

And, for no reason he ever understood, all of a sudden it was clear to him. He opened his eyes and the water streamed over them. "God help me, what have I done?" he said

As he frantically half dried himself and dressed, Milo's mind conjured up pictures. He couldn't stop himself. Cross standing in his trophy room. The empty patch of wall above the mantel. Cross asking for a woman with no family. Cross describing the look he wanted. Cara saying he wanted her close to hearth and home. God, that was a sick joke. He wanted something exotic to hang over the fireplace. He wanted a trophy wife. Jesus H. Christ. Milo clenched his teeth to hold down the panic. What have I done? What have I done? Oh God, what have I done?

Outside the gym he found a phone booth. He dropped in a quarter and pounded the keys so hard his finger hurt after. As soon as she answered he wanted to scream at her down the phone line, Get out! Get out now! But he didn't want to look out of control. Didn't want to make her panic. He stopped himself and breathed in deeply. Well, buddy, he said to himself, you asked for rescue time. Here it is. Don't fuck it up.

The phone rang and Milo thought about what he'd say when she answered. He'd keep his voice calm and tell her that despite what she said, it was time to go. That he was coming for her now. That he'd be there in twenty minutes. The phone rang and rang and Milo would tell her that she didn't need to pack because as soon as he picked her up they were heading for Pearson and next stop was the nude beach at Negril. The phone rang and rang and rang and Milo slammed the receiver down. Why didn't she answer? He didn't want to consider the possibilities.

Milo left the phone booth and ran to his car. Oh, man, he thought. I'm getting old and stupid. Why didn't I see it?

Just past eight thirty. Milo pulled to the curb a fair distance from Cross's place. He got there early on purpose. To do a recee. To make sure there wasn't something going on he hadn't planned for.

The street was empty. Rich people didn't walk much at night, Milo had noticed. The streetlights were set far apart and the maple trees cast the street and the big houses in shadow. Milo got out of the car and eased the door shut. He was wearing the clothes he usually wore when he worked nights. Black jeans, black canvas high tops, black jacket zippered to the neck. He kept them in a chewed up Adidas bag in the trunk in case of emergencies.

He looked around one more time, but nobody was watching that he could see. He started walking to Cross's place. It took him five minutes and when he got there he could see lights burning on all three floors. Good. Cross was home. That meant maybe nothing had happened to Cara yet. If something had happened, at least Milo wouldn't have to wait to mete out justice.

He went up the flagstone walk and up the stone steps to the big front porch. He'd been in the house enough to know what was alarmed and what wasn't. He knew if Cross was inside there'd be no alarm on the front door and the motion detectors would be off. He had no idea how he'd get in. If worse came to worse he could just knock, force his way in, and confront Cross right then and there.

He moved quickly to the door, put his ear to it and listened. He couldn't hear anything inside. He listened longer. Then, before he pushed the bell, he grabbed the doorknob. He'd known some burglars and they always told him, you'd be amazed at how often that works. The knob turned and Milo opened the door. There was nobody in sight. Just the suit of armour standing by the stairs, axe raised.

Milo looked to his right. The double doors to the trophy room were closed. He took a deep breath, prayed that Cross wasn't in the room. Prayed that there was no one in there he knew. Then he went in the house, shut the door behind him and went to the trophy room.

He turned one door handle and pushed. The door didn't budge. He tried the other handle. That door didn't open either. Milo thought back. In all the times he'd been here Cross had never locked this room. The doors were always either wide open, one of them at least, or they were shut but unlocked and Cross just opened them and walked in. Why would they be locked now? Milo tried each handle again. He tried them one at a time and then together. He shook them and pounded his shoulder against them. Why were they locked? Why? He rattled and banged and threw himself against them again and again. His desperation made the noise not matter. The doors, however, would not open.

Milo backed up several steps. He'd run at the door. Launch himself and burst it open. He'd never done that before. He figured it was something for TV, but he didn't know what else to do. Then out of the corner of his eye he saw the armour and the glint of the axe.

He ran across the foyer and grabbed at the handle held in the metal gloves. He tried to pull it free but the gloves held on tightly. He pulled again but that was no more effective than cranking the door handles.

That's when Milo tried lifting the axe up. It moved. He tugged upward again and the axe rose a little further. Milo pulled harder and, hand over hand, he lifted the axe higher and higher. Then it was free of the armoured gloves and in Milo's hands. It was heavier than he'd expected and it fell to the floor with a clang.

He picked it up and held the blade at shoulder height and turned to the double doors. He was trying to figure out which door to hit and exactly where when he saw the handle turn, the door opened just enough to show that it was very dark inside and Cross stepped out. He shut the door again and turned to lock it. Then he turned back to Milo.

"What are you going to do with that?" he asked. "It's easier if you use the key." He held it out between his thumb and forefinger and shook it in Milo's face.

"Let me in there," Milo said.

"I don't think so. I didn't even let you in my house. Get out of here now."

"I don't think so," Milo said, then he took a swing with the axe. It felt really good. Whoever made it back in the Dark Ages surely knew his stuff, Milo thought. The weapon was beautifully balanced and it swung like a perfect pendulum. Milo did it again. It made a swish as the blade cut through the air. He took a step forward and swung the axe a third time. "It's really sharp, you know. I could cut off your arm just like that." He lunged forward slightly and swung the axe again, aiming it vaguely at Cross's free left arm.

Cross jerked back. "Are you mad?"

"Oooh," Milo said. "There's a thought. Maybe I am." He swung the axe again.

"Put that down and get out of my house." Cross sounded shrill but he still had the voice of a man who was used to having his orders obeyed.

Milo didn't pay any attention. "You never told me the provenance of this thing," Milo said. "But lemme guess. They used to use it to cut the dicks off guys who fucked other men's women." The axe was swinging back and forth now like a metronome. Cross's gaze kept drifting back to it like it was a mesmerist's watch — shifting from Milo's face to the blade. Milo pressed forward and Cross backed up the same distance.

"I want in that room," Milo said. Then he pulled the axe back and swung it hard at Cross's belly.

Cross lurched backwards, startled when he hit the wall. The blade sliced by within inches of him. He dropped to the ground and the backswing whistled above his head. Cross pressed himself flat to the shiny floor, his hands grasping the back of his head. He whimpered as Milo lifted the axe high in the air.

"Is Cara in that room?" Milo asked. He thought his voice sounded very soft and calm.

"Yes," Cross said. It sounded like he was sobbing. "Yes. Yes. Cara's in that room."

Milo remembered the most effective technique for chopping wood from summers when he was young. He'd worked on a farm and splintered cord after cord. He knew he was still in good enough shape that he could drive an axe this sharp and this heavy clean through anything if he swung it properly and if his mind was just as sharply focused.

He held his right hand at the base of the axe handle and his left hand up near the blade. As he brought the axe back over his head he'd slide his left hand down the handle to touch his right, giving him maximum momentum and impact when the axe came up over his head and then down fast and very hard. Milo knew that, if he did it just right, someone would have to come repair the gouge he left in the hardwood floor. And, of course, a painter would have to be called in too.

Milo fixed his eyes on the target and began his swing. The handle slipped through his left hand smoothly and he had the axe poised, held high, just ready to drive downward. He felt good. He was perfectly balanced. The target had stopped moving. The axe was steady and his mind was made up. Then he heard a sound behind him that made him change his mind. It was a sound that had made him freeze the first time he heard it. It was instinctive. In the same way that a kitten knows to be afraid of a dog the first time it sees one. And every time since it had the same effect on him.

Someone behind his back had cocked a gun. Milo lowered the axe slowly and turned to look.

"Don't, Milo," Cara said. She was standing in the door of the trophy room, open again.

Milo started to set the axe on the floor, but Cross had risen to his knees and made a tut-tutting noise. "Put your toys back where they belong when you're finished playing with them," he said. Milo walked over to the stairs and slipped the handle of the axe back into the clutches of the armour.

Milo breathed deeply. He was glad Cara had stopped him from killing Cross. That would have been a tough one to get out of. And he was glad that he'd gotten there in time. Glad that she was alive.

He started to go over to her. To take the gun from her. So he could cover Cross while she packed and they got the hell out. But she poked the barrel at him, motioning for him to back off. He was startled but he did it. You didn't want to mess with a woman with a gun.

He decided to pretend the weapon wasn't there. "Run upstairs," he said, "and grab a few things. Some jewels or some cash or something. We can catch a flight at the airport. The first thing going anywhere."

But she didn't run upstairs. She didn't grab anything. Instead, she walked over to Cross and handed him the pistol. Cross lowered the gun, pointing it at the floor. "Would you care for a cognac?" he asked. Milo didn't want to hang around. He wanted to get the hell out of there and he wanted to take Cara with him. But Cross had a gun in his hand and he was holding it like he really knew what he was doing, and that made Milo cautious.

Then again, after nearly just killing a guy, a cognac would taste pretty good. And maybe in the act of pouring it the rich man would put the gun down. "Yeah. If it's old and expensive, make it a big one."

Cross went to the small bar beside his desk and took up a decanter. Milo had drunk from it before and knew that it was good. But as the rich man took the stopper out of the decanter and raised it and poured into two matching glasses, the gun never left his other hand. Milo settled for Plan B.

He took the cognac. His hand was shaking and he felt all of a sudden weary as the adrenalin left him. He swallowed quickly. The cognac burned all the way down. "Thanks," he said. "I have to go now." He put the glass down, looked at Cara. Then he started to turn for the door. But Cross raised the gun and pointed it at him. Milo froze.

Cross stood by his desk, sipping his drink and holding the outstretched pistol at Milo's stomach. He made it all look very elegant and sophisticated. Like something from a Noel Coward play. "Don't go just yet," he said.

"I got to," Milo said. "I'm parked illegally."

"They don't ticket much in this neighbourhood." Cross began to pour himself more cognac. He held the decanter out to Milo and raised an eyebrow. Milo nodded and Cross poured more for him, too. He motioned with the gun for Milo to pick up his drink.

As Milo did so, he asked, "What calibre is that?"

"It's big enough to hurt you quite badly," Cross said. "Now tell me why you're here?"

Milo shrugged. "I thought Cara was in trouble. I thought she needed me."

"Is that it? You came because you thought Cara was in trouble?"

"Yes," Milo said.

Cross moved away from the desk and walked across the room, past Cara, and stood by the fireplace. He set his drink down on the mantel. "What kind of trouble, Milo?"

Milo stared at him and didn't answer.

"It doesn't matter. I know what you thought. Truth to tell, you were in the ballpark. I also know that you wanted my money, very likely that you wanted to live in my house. Well, Milo, part of your wish is about to come true."

"What are you talking about?"

Cross never took his eyes off Milo. "Show him, Cara."

She lifted something off the desk top and handed it to Milo. It was a small pile of Polaroid pictures. They were of Milo. He was naked and asleep, the covers pulled back. Every part of his body had been photographed. "Where did you get these?" he asked. But he knew and answered his own question. "You took these," he said to Cara.

"Finally, an accurate deduction," Cross said.

Milo looked at him and then beyond him to the wall. He looked at the photographs in his hand again and then at Cara and then at the other heads stuck on the wall and then back at the space above the mantel. "Oh my God. You two knew one another all along."

"Would you care for another cognac?" Cross asked.

Milo shook his head, but it was as much in disbelief as in answer. "Why? Why me?"

"You fit all the criteria. And you're very discreet. I know you've told no one about this. No one will miss you." Cross walked over and took the photographs from Milo's hand. Then he fanned them and gazed down at them. "And you'll look lovely up there," he said softly.

"But why the charade? Why spin it out so long? Why didn't you just kill me and get it over with?"

Cross pointed at a tiger's head on the wall. "I tracked that magnificent creature for four days through the jungles of Sumatra. It was a fascinating experience, seeing what the quarry would do. It was a challenge. I learned much. I know of men who have dug pits in the jungle and covered them over and waited for big cats to fall into them. Then, from the edge of the pit, they shoot. The animal can't run or hide. It's slaughter that does nothing to help those men grow and I have no respect for them." He waved his hand around the room. "Each of these trophies is hard won. And each of them taught me a great deal about myself and about animal behaviour."

Milo digested this. "So was this a growth experience for you?"

Cross shook his head. "Unfortunately, you did nothing that hadn't been predicted."

Milo sometimes wondered how he would feel at the end of his life. But he had never imagined it quite like this. He imagined being surrounded by people who cared about him. He imagined tears and death bed reconciliations and immortal last words. But all he could think to do was turn to Cara and say, "You told me you loved me."

"Did I?" she replied. "Oh." When she looked at Milo, there was nothing in her eyes to suggest that they had ever known one another. No hint that she had whispered to him in the dark.

Milo felt numb with humiliation. He looked at Cross. "You used her as bait."

"Oh, Milo, what a pathetic detective you are. You still don't get it, do you?" Cross gave him a cold smile. "She wasn't the bait," he said. "I was. And it was all her idea."

Milo looked at Cara's blank face and could think of nothing more to say.

Gifts

Rosemary Aubert

For her first published crime short story — "Night Boat to Palermo," which appeared in the anthology *Cold Blood V* — Rosemary won the Arthur Ellis Award in 1995. A published poet and writer of romance novels, Rosemary further secured a place among Canada's leading crime writers with the publication of *Free Reign*, her first novel about disgraced judge turned street person Ellis Portal which captured an Arthur Ellis Best Novel Award nomination. A trained criminologist, Rosemary's articles on the subject have been widely published and, in addition to teaching writing at the college level, she has served as a public-education specialist for clients involved in the criminal justice system.

My uncle Salvatore — Sammy — stuck out his hand as if he expected me to shake it. I didn't do a double take or anything like that. I've been a lawyer now for nearly twenty years, and I'm as good at keeping emotion out of my face as a cop, a poker player or a nun. But all the same, Sammy could tell I couldn't bring myself to touch him. I motioned toward one of the wing-chairs in front of my desk. "Please . . ."

Sammy sat, but he kept his stocky body on the edge of the seat, as if he was afraid to soil it somehow.

"Relax," I said, "take it easy. Have some wine...."

I reached over to the carafe and poured him a small glass of sweet vermouth.

"*Grazie*," he said softly, then sank back into the chair.

He rested his head against the leather. I noticed that his grey hair was thin. In the first memory I have of Sammy, his hair was a black, curly bush. "Your Uncle Sammy looks like Groucho Marx," my mother had commented, "too bad he isn't funny..."

There'd never been a time when he hadn't been in my life. When I was a kid, he'd told me bedtime stories, strange bedtime stories about Mafia hits and complicated scams. I loved them.

In fact, I'd often thought it was Sammy's stories that inspired me to enter law. Good thing, too, as far as he was concerned. I'd pulled Sammy out of a number of scrapes. Only a few months before, I'd had homicide charges against him dropped for lack of convincing evidence. Now, he was in trouble again. Big trouble.

"You want to tell me how it happened?" I asked him. I poured myself a drink, then came around and sat on the corner of my desk. It was late afternoon, and a ray of sunlight bounced off the glass door of one of my bookcases and spread its reflected flush across the rug, making its pattern look blurry and vague. Sammy looked vague, too, staring at the rug instead of looking me in the eye as we talked.

Sammy made his living as a fraud artist. It was a trick of his trade to look a person straight in the eye no matter what. It seemed to be failing him now.

"I did just as you instructed," he said. "I flew to Boston. I called on your mother. I told her and your father that I'd been sent by you to give them a special gift for their fiftieth anniversary. You did a good job with those pardons and all — I sailed through customs like a breeze. When I reached Logan, I had a redcap handle the baggage. I can't — I mean I couldn't — manage to carry much, as you know."

Over the years, Sammy had taught himself to behave and speak like an educated man. He never slipped up. His speech patterns had been honed by years of bending the ears of his victims, dazzling them until they stopped paying attention just long enough for Sammy to slip them over the line and into the red.

"At first," he said, "your mother was a little wary. It's understandable. She's never forgiven me for what happened to your Aunt Mary's pension — "

I nodded, but he didn't see. He still hadn't looked up.

"She took my word for it that I was straight now," he went on. "That I'm getting by on my disability pension plus what I get working for you. She don't — doesn't — know anything about those last charges, about that guy in my rooming house getting killed. About my alibi and that. I haven't told my sister anything about my work in years. But still, she seemed sort of doubtful. Maybe she had some kind of premonition or something." Sammy swallowed, almost as if he were choking something back.

I reached across and touched his shoulder. "Don't worry. It'll be okay — " Without warning, my mind flashed back to the first time I'd ever said that to him. It was while I was still articling — working on bail cases. I'd gone into a police lock-up and stumbled on him sitting there, awaiting a show-cause. I'd never seen him down and out before. My mother had told me he was a businessman. She'd just neglected to mention the business.

Now he reached up and grabbed my fingers in his own. I almost jumped.

"Forget about those charges," I told him. "You are no longer a suspect. Never really were, as far as I'm concerned. No one can accuse you of choking that man. Clearly, it would have taken a man with two strong hands."

Now he looked up. His eyes held something I'd never seen there before: terror.

"It's my whole life," he said in the modulated tones that had calmed many a wealthy widow. "I've wasted my whole life. And now, near the end of it, when I'm finally as respectable as anybody else in this family . . . Now this."

He held up his hand, the long straight fingers, the firm palm, the supple wrist. "And now, this. . . . "

For a moment, we just sat there in silence. The sun, with the slowness of early autumn, shifted to amber, then rust. Then the air in my office seemed to become a soft blue, like the stained glass wings of angels. I turned on a lamp.

"Your mother and father were really thrilled when I told them about your gift," Sammy resumed. "I tried to be a little suspenseful. I played around with my suitcoat pocket, pretending to be looking for something. Then I pretended to find the envelope. 'What's this?' I asked, as if I'd never seen it before. 'Seems to be plane tickets to Paris!' 'Paris?' your father asked. 'Why in heaven's name would my son think that his mother and I would want to go to Paris?'"

Despite everything, I had to smile. Sammy mimicked my father exactly. He could imitate anybody's voice. Of course he could.

"'Because,' I told him, 'that's where you go first when you're on your way from Boston to Lourdes.'

"I watched them carefully," Sammy said, "so I could tell you just how they looked. Well, I thought your mother was going to cry, she was so surprised and happy. Your dad — well, he's always said he's happy if she is, and maybe it's true. Anyway, it was perfect. I wished you could have been there — the two of them staring at those tickets as if they were tickets to heaven itself." He stopped and took another sip of vermouth.

"Yes, your folks looked like a couple of angels," Sammy said. "I should have stopped then. I should have left well enough alone instead of shooting my mouth off." His voice seemed to quaver. In his line of work, a steady voice was as much a necessity as if he'd been a radio announcer.

"I told your parents that you were so excited about all the arrangements that you'd made for them that you'd said a little joke, that you'd said the only thing that you were unable to arrange was for them to actually witness a miracle."

Sammy drained his glass. And he slid his hand beneath the lapel of his jacket, as if to hide it from view. I had known him all my life, and I had *never* seen him try to hide his hand, though anybody would have forgiven him for doing so.

"They didn't laugh at the joke, did they, Sammy?" I knew my mother.

"No. We never mentioned it again. All the way over, your mother was so quiet. Almost like she knew something really big was going to happen. Your father was quiet, too, but then he always is. I figured maybe they were praying.

"We got to Lourdes. There's a lot of tourist business, and I was feeling upset by it. It's noisy. Crowded. And my hand started to ache. It hadn't done that in years, but I figured it was because on the way over, I had to help your mother carry her tote bag, and I'd held it in both hands for a couple of minutes—something I almost never do.

"Anyway, I took them around a little. Your mother sees the wheelchairs, the abandoned crutches — the whole thing. It's impressive. I have to admit. But I'm not a religious man. With my history how could I be?"

"Plenty of people with your background become very religious later in life," I reminded him.

He gave me a look as if to say, "Let's be serious — "

"Finally," he went on, "it's the big event. A Healing Mass at the shrine. Now your mother's more like herself. Excited. And she wants everything perfect. She's got a new dress. Your father's in that suit he wore when he stood up for me in court the last time. Nice.

"And I'm dressed, too. Only I can hardly do up my shirt because my hand is hurting so bad. I had to get your mother to help. And when she did, she accidentally touched my bad hand. I never knew her to touch it before. Nobody ever touched it, really. Anyway, nothing happened. It still hurt.

"We went to Mass. It was scary. I saw an awful lot of really sick people. I didn't know what to think about it all. One was a kid. A bald kid. I was watching this kid while the priest was giving some sort of blessing. She was just kneeling there, looking up. I remember thinking that even bald she was a beautiful kid.

"All of a sudden, she closes her eyes and starts to sway, like she's going to faint. Without thinking, I reach out to catch her. And then I see what's happening. I'm reaching out with my bad hand. It's hurting like hell, but it don't look like hell. Not any more. My fingers are straightened out. I'm not a cripple anymore! Before I can even think about what's going on, I hear your mother shouting, 'It's a miracle! Sammy is cured!' Then everybody is screaming and shoving and touching me...."

Sammy shivered. So did I. I felt sick. I didn't know what to say. There were tears in Sammy's voice, and I think on his face, too, but I couldn't really force myself to look.

"Sammy," I said, "Nobody's come by your place, have they? None of those detectives you talked to before . . . ?"

He shook his head. "No," he said, "but somebody's going to spill the beans on me sooner or later. They'll show up. Cops always do. And what am I going to tell them? That yes, I'm an able-bodied man now but that I was crippled at the time that guy got killed? I'm innocent. You know I am. But I'm also the last person who saw him alive and — aside from the real killer — the only person in the whole world who doesn't have an alibi. And I've got a rap sheet as long as a rope. . . " He took a gulp of vermouth, swallowed hard. Choked out the words, "How are you going to keep me from being hauled in this time?"

"You're a fraud artist, Sammy. Not a killer. It's the wrong M.O. You've never gone down for a violent offense before. That's got to count for something."

But not much. We both knew it. For whatever reason my Uncle Sammy was a cured man. But he was also a man with a dead neighbour and a story nobody could believe.

I poured us both another vermouth. I handed him back his glass. He reached out and took it in his straight fingers. They trembled a little, the way a baby's legs tremble when he's just learning how to walk.

You See But You Do Not Observe

Robert J. Sawyer

Maclean's says, "Robert J. Sawyer is the science fiction genre's northern star—in fact, one of the hottest SF writers anywhere. By any reckoning Sawyer is among the most successful Canadian authors ever." He won the Science Fiction and Fantasy Writers of America's Nebula Award for Best Novel of 1995 (for *The Terminal Experiment*). Rob also won an Arthur Ellis Award for Best Short Story of 1993, and has been nominated twice more, including for his novel *Illegal Alien*, which *The Globe and Mail* called "the best Canadian mystery of 1997." With David Skene-Melvin, he co-edited *Crossing the Line: Canadian Mysteries with a Fantastic Twist* for Pottersfield Press, a 1998 anthology of mystery stories that also happen to be science fiction, fantasy, or horror. Rob lives just north of Toronto with his wife, Carolyn Clink; visit his web site at www.sfwriter.com. "You See But You Do Not Observe" was originally published in the anthology *Sherlock Holmes in Orbit*, and won France's top SF award, *Le Grand Prix de l'Imaginaire*.

I had been pulled into the future first, ahead of my companion. There was no sensation associated with the chronotransference, except for a popping of my ears which I was later told had to do with a change in air pressure. Once in the twenty-first century, my brain was scanned in order to produce from my memories a perfect reconstruction of our rooms at 221B Baker Street. Details that I could not consciously remember or articulate were nonetheless reproduced exactly: the flock-papered walls, the bearskin hearthrug, the basket chair and the armchair, the coal-scuttle, even the view through the window — all were correct to the smallest detail.

I was met in the future by a man who called himself Mycroft Holmes. He claimed, however, to be no relation to my companion, and protested that his name was mere coincidence, although he allowed that the fact of it was likely what had made a study of my partner's methods his chief avocation. I asked him if he had a brother called Sherlock, but his reply made little sense to me: "My parents weren't *that* cruel."

In any event, this Mycroft Holmes — who was a small man with reddish hair, quite unlike the stout and dark ale of a fellow with the same name I had known two hundred years before — wanted all details to be correct before he whisked Holmes here from the past. Genius, he said, was but a step from madness, and although I had taken to the future well, my companion might be quite rocked by the experience.

When Mycroft did bring Holmes forth, he did so with great stealth, transferring him precisely as he stepped through the front exterior door of the real 221 Baker Street and into the simulation that had been created here. I heard my good friend's voice down the stairs, giving his usual glad tidings to a simulation of Mrs. Hudson. His long legs, as they always did, brought him up to our humble quarters at a rapid pace.

I had expected a hearty greeting, consisting perhaps of an ebullient cry of "My Dear Watson," and possibly even a firm clasping of hands or some other display of bonhomie. But there was none of that, of course. This was not like the time Holmes had returned after an absence of three years during which I had believed him to be dead. No, my companion, whose exploits it has been my honour to chronicle over the years, was unaware of just how long we had been separated, and so my reward for my vigil was nothing more than a distracted nodding of his drawn-out face. He took a seat and settled in with the evening paper, but after a few moments, he slapped the newsprint sheets down. "Confound it, Watson! I have already read this edition. Have we not *today's* paper?"

And, at that turn, there was nothing for it but for me to adopt the unfamiliar role that queer fate had dictated I must now take: our traditional positions were now reversed, and I would have to explain the truth to Holmes.

"Holmes, my good fellow, I am afraid they do not publish newspapers anymore."

He pinched his long face into a scowl, and his clear, grey eyes glimmered. "I would have thought that any man who had spent as much time in Afghanistan as you had, Watson, would be immune to the ravages of the sun. I grant that today was unbearably hot, but surely your brain should not have addled so easily."

"Not a bit of it, Holmes, I assure you," said I. "What I say is true, although I confess my reaction was the same as yours when I was first told. There have not been any newspapers for seventy-five years now."

"Seventy-five years? Watson, this copy of the *Times* is dated August the fourteenth, 1899 — yesterday."

"I am afraid that is not true, Holmes. Today is June the fifth, *anno Domini* two thousand and ninety-six."

"Two thou — "

"It sounds preposterous, I know — "

"It *is* preposterous, Watson. I call you 'old man' now and again out of affection, but you are in fact nowhere near two hundred and fifty years of age."

"Perhaps I am not the best man to explain all this," I said.

"No," said a voice from the doorway. "Allow me."

Holmes surged to his feet. "And who are you?"

"My name is Mycroft Holmes."

"Impostor!" declared my companion.

"I assure you that that is not the case," said Mycroft. "I grant I'm not your brother, nor a habitué of the Diogenes Club, but I do share his name. I am a scientist — and I have used certain scientific principles to pluck you from your past and bring you into my present."

For the first time in all the years I had known him, I saw befuddlement on my companion's face. "It is quite true," I said to him.

"But why?" said Holmes, spreading his long arms. "Assuming this mad fantasy is true — and I do not grant for an instant that it is — why would you thus kidnap myself and my good friend, Dr. Watson?"

"Because, Holmes, the game, as you used to be so fond of saying, is afoot."

"Murder, is it?" asked I, grateful at last to get to the reason for which we had been brought forward.

"More than simple murder," said Mycroft. "Much more. Indeed, the biggest puzzle to have ever faced the human race. Not just one body is missing. Trillions are. *Trillions.*"

"Watson," said Holmes, "surely you recognize the signs of madness in the man? Have you nothing in your bag that can help him? The whole population of the Earth is less than two thousand million."

"In your time, yes," said Mycroft. "Today, it's about eight thousand million. But I say again, there are trillions more who are missing."

"Ah, I perceive at last," said Holmes, a twinkle in his eye as he came to believe that reason was once again holding sway. "I have read in *The Illustrated London News* of these *dinosauria*, as Professor Owen called them — great creatures from the past, all now deceased. It is their demise you wish me to unravel."

Mycroft shook his head. "You should have read Professor Moriarty's monograph called *The Dynamics of an Asteroid*," he said.

"I keep my mind clear of useless knowledge," replied Holmes curtly.

Mycroft shrugged. "Well, in that paper Moriarty quite cleverly guessed the cause of the demise of the dinosaurs: an asteroid crashing into earth kicked up enough dust to block the sun for months on end. Close to a century after he had reasoned out this hypothesis, solid evidence for its truth was found in a layer of clay. No, that mystery is long since solved. This one is much greater."

"And what, pray, is it?" said Holmes, irritation in his voice.

Mycroft motioned for Holmes to have a seat, and, after a moment's defiance, my friend did just that. "It is called the Fermi paradox," said Mycroft, "after Enrico Fermi, an Italian physicist who lived in the twentieth century. You see, we know now that this universe of ours should have given rise to countless planets, and that many of those planets should have produced intelligent civilizations. We can demonstrate the likelihood of this mathematically, using something called the Drake equation. For a century and a half now, we have been using radio — wireless, that is — to look for signs of these other intelligences. And we have found nothing — *nothing!* Hence the paradox Fermi posed: if the universe is supposed to be full of life, then where are the aliens?"

"Aliens?" said I. "Surely they are mostly still in their respective foreign countries."

Mycroft smiled. "The word has gathered additional uses since your day, good doctor. By aliens, I mean extraterrestrials — creatures who live on other worlds."

"Like in the stories of Verne and Wells?" asked I, quite sure that my expression was agog.

"And even in worlds beyond the family of our sun," said Mycroft.

Holmes rose to his feet. "I know nothing of universes and other worlds," he said angrily. "Such knowledge could be of no practical use in my profession."

I nodded. "When I first met Holmes, he had no idea that the Earth revolved around the sun." I treated myself to a slight chuckle. "He thought the reverse to be true."

Mycroft smiled. "I know of your current limitations, Sherlock." My friend cringed slightly at the overly familiar address. "But these are mere gaps in knowledge; we can rectify that easily enough."

"I will not crowd my brain with useless irrelevancies," said Holmes. "I carry only information that can be of help in my work. For instance, I can identify one hundred and forty different varieties of tobacco ash — "

"Ah, well, you can let that information go, Holmes," said Mycroft. "No one smokes anymore. It's been proven ruinous to one's health." I shot a look at Holmes, whom I had always warned of being a self-poisoner. "Besides, we've also learned much about the structure of the brain in the intervening years. Your fear that memorizing information related to fields such as literature, astronomy, and philosophy would force out other, more relevant data, is unfounded. The capacity for the human brain to store and retrieve information is almost infinite."

"It is?" said Holmes, clearly shocked.

"It is."

"And so you wish me to immerse myself in physics and astronomy and such all?"

"Yes," said Mycroft.

"To solve this paradox of Fermi?"

"Precisely!"

"But why me?"

"Because it is a *puzzle*, and you, my good fellow, are the greatest solver of puzzles this world has ever seen. It is now two hundred years after your time, and no one with a facility to rival yours has yet appeared."

Mycroft probably could not see it, but the tiny hint of pride on my longtime companion's face was plain to me. But then Holmes frowned. "It would take years to amass the knowledge I would need to address this problem."

"No, it will not." Mycroft waved his hand, and amidst the homely untidiness of Holmes's desk appeared a small sheet of glass standing vertically. Next to it lay a strange metal bowl. "We have made great strides in the technology of learning since your day. We can directly program new information into your brain." Mycroft walked over to the desk. "This glass panel is what we call a *monitor*. It is activated by the sound of your voice. Simply ask it questions, and it will display information on any topic you wish. If you find a topic that you think will be useful in your studies, simply place this helmet on your head" (he indicated the metal bowl), "say the words 'load topic,' and the information will be seamlessly integrated into the neural nets of your very own brain. It will at once seem as if you know, and have always known, all the details of that field of endeavour."

"Incredible!" said Holmes. "And from there?"

"From there, my dear Holmes, I hope that your powers of deduction will lead you to resolve the paradox — and reveal at last what has happened to the aliens!"

# # #

"Watson! Watson!"

I awoke with a start. Holmes had found this new ability to effortlessly absorb information irresistible and he had pressed on long into the night, but I had evidently fallen asleep in a chair. I perceived that Holmes had at last found a substitute for the sleeping fiend of his cocaine mania: with all of creation at his fingertips, he would never again feel that emptiness that so destroyed him between assignments.

"Eh?" I said. My throat was dry. I had evidently been sleeping with my mouth open. "What is it?"

"Watson, this physics is more fascinating than I had ever imagined. Listen to this, and see if you do not find it as compelling as any of the cases we have faced to date."

I rose from my chair and poured myself a little sherry — it was, after all, still night and not yet morning. "I am listening."

"Remember the locked and sealed room that figured so significantly in that terrible case of the Giant Rat of Sumatra?"

"How could I forget?" said I, a shiver traversing my spine. "If not for your keen shooting, my left leg would have ended up as gamy as my right."

"Quite," said Holmes. "Well, consider a different type of locked-room mystery, this one devised by an Austrian physicist named Erwin Schrödinger. Image a cat sealed in a box. The box is of such opaque material, and its walls are so well insulated, and the seal is so profound, that there is no way anyone can observe the cat once the box is closed."

"Hardly seems cricket," I said, "locking a poor cat in a box."

"Watson, your delicate sensibilities are laudable, but please, man, attend to my point. Imagine further that inside this box is a triggering device that has exactly a fifty-fifty chance of being set off, and that this aforementioned trigger is rigged up to a cylinder of poison gas. If the trigger is tripped, the gas is released, and the cat dies."

"Goodness!" said I. "How nefarious."

"Now, Watson, tell me this: without opening the box, can you say whether the cat is alive or dead?"

"Well, if I understand you correctly, it depends on whether the trigger was tripped."

"Precisely!"

"And so the cat is perhaps alive, and, yet again, perhaps it is dead."

"Ah, my friend, I knew you would not fail me: the blindingly obvious interpretation. But it is wrong, dear Watson, totally wrong."

"How do you mean?"

"I mean the cat is neither alive nor is it dead. It is a *potential* cat, an unresolved cat, a cat whose existence is nothing but a question of possibilities. It is neither alive nor dead, Watson — neither! Until some intelligent person opens the box and looks, the cat is unresolved. Only the act of looking forces a resolution of the possibilities. Once you crack the seal and peer within, the potential cat collapses into an actual cat. Its reality is *a result of* having been observed."

"That is worse gibberish than anything this namesake of your brother has spouted."

"No, it is not," said Holmes. "It is the way the world works. They have learned so much since our time, Watson — so very much! But as Alphonse Karr has observed, *Plus ça change, plus c'est la même chose.* Even in this esoteric field of advanced physics, it is the power of the qualified observer that is most important of all!"

# # #

I awoke again hearing Holmes crying out, "Mycroft! Mycroft!"

I had occasionally heard such shouts from him in the past, either when his iron constitution had failed him and he was feverish, or when under the influence of his accursed needle. But after a moment I realized he was not calling for his real brother but rather was shouting into the air to summon the Mycroft Holmes who was the twenty-first-century savant. Moments later, he was rewarded: the door to our rooms opened and in came the red-haired fellow.

"Hello, Sherlock," said Mycroft. "You wanted me?"

"Indeed I do," said Holmes. "I have absorbed much now on not just physics but also the technology by which you have recreated these rooms for me and the good Dr. Watson."

Mycroft nodded. "I've been keeping track of what you've been accessing. Surprising choices, I must say."

"So they might seem," said Holmes, "but my method is based on the pursuit of trifles. Tell me if I understand correctly that you reconstructed these rooms by scanning Watson's memories, then using, if I understand the terms, holography and micro-manipulated force fields to simulate the appearance and form of what he had seen."

"That's right."

"So your ability to reconstruct is not just limited to rebuilding these rooms of ours, but, rather, you could simulate anything either of us had ever seen."

"That's correct. In fact, I could even put you into a simulation of someone else's memories. Indeed, I thought perhaps you might like to see the Very Large Array of radio telescopes, where most of our listening for alien messages — "

"Yes, yes, I'm sure that's fascinating," said Holmes, dismissively. "But can you reconstruct the venue of what Watson so appropriately dubbed 'The Final Problem'?"

"You mean the falls of Reichenbach?" Mycroft looked shocked. "My God, yes, but I should think that's the last thing you'd want to relive."

"Aptly said!" declared Holmes. "Can you do it?"

"Of course."

"Then do so!"

# # #

And so Holmes and my brains were scanned and in short order we found ourselves inside a superlative recreation of the Switzerland of May, 1891, to which we had originally fled to escape Professor Moriarty's assassins. Our re-enactment of events began at the charming Englischer Hof in the village of Meiringen. Just as the original innkeeper had done all those years ago, the reconstruction of him exacted a promise from us that we would not miss the spectacle of the falls of Reichenbach. Holmes and I set out for the falls, him walking with the aid of an alpenstock. Mycroft, I was given to understand, was somehow observing all this from afar.

"I do not like this," I said to my companion. "'Twas bad enough to live through this horrible day once, but I had hoped I would never have to relive it again except in nightmares."

"Watson, recall that I have fonder memories of all this. Vanquishing Moriarty was the high point of my career. I said to you then, and say again now, that putting an end to the very Napoleon of crime would easily be worth the price of my own life."

There was a little dirt path cut out of the vegetation running halfway round the falls so as to afford a complete view of the spectacle. The icy green water, fed by the melting snows, flowed with phenomenal rapidity and violence, then plunged into a great, bottomless chasm of rock black as the darkest night. Spray shot up in vast gouts, and the shriek made by the plunging water was almost like a human cry.

We stood for a moment looking down at the waterfall, Holmes's face in its most contemplative repose. He then pointed further ahead along the dirt path. "Note, dear Watson," he said, shouting to be heard above the torrent, "that the dirt path comes to an end against a rock wall there." I nodded. He turned in the other direction. "And see that backtracking out the way we came is the only way to leave alive: there is but one exit, and it is coincident with the single entrance."

Again I nodded. But, just as had happened the first time we had been at this fateful spot, a Swiss boy came running along the path, carrying in his hand a letter addressed to me which bore the mark of the Englischer Hof. I knew what the note said, of course: that an Englishwoman, staying at that inn, had been overtaken by a hemorrhage. She had but a few hours to live, but doubtless would take great comfort in being ministered to by an English doctor, and would I come at once?

"But the note is a pretext," said I, turning to Holmes. "Granted, I was fooled originally by it, but, as you later admitted in that letter you left for me, you had suspected all along that it was a sham on the part of Moriarty." Throughout this commentary, the Swiss boy stood frozen, immobile, as if somehow Mycroft, overseeing all this, had locked the boy in time so that Holmes and I might consult. "I will not leave you again, Holmes, to plunge to your death."

Holmes raised a hand. "Watson, as always, your sentiments are laudable, but recall that this is a mere simulation. You will be of material assistance to me if you do exactly as you did before. There is no need, though, for you to undertake the entire arduous hike to the Englischer Hof and back. Instead, simply head back to the point at which you pass the figure in black, wait an additional quarter of an hour, then return to here."

"Thank you for simplifying it," said I. "I am eight years older than I was then; a three-hour round trip would take a goodly bit out of me today."

"Indeed," said Holmes. "All of us may have outlived our most useful days. Now, please, do as I ask."

"I will, of course," said I, "but I freely confess that I do not understand what this is all about. You were engaged by this twenty-first-century Mycroft to explore a problem in natural philosophy — the missing aliens. Why are we even here?"

"We are here," said Holmes, "because I have solved that problem! Trust me, Watson. Trust me, and play out the scenario again of that portentous day of May fourth, 1891."

# # #

And so I left my companion, not knowing what he had in mind. As I made my way back to the Englischer Hof, I passed a man going hurriedly the other way. The first time I had lived through these terrible events I did not know him, but this time I recognized him for Professor Moriarty: tall, clad all in black, his forehead bulging out, his lean form outlined sharply against the green backdrop of the vegetation. I let the simulation pass, waited fifteen minutes as Holmes had asked, then returned to the falls.

Upon my arrival, I saw Holmes's alpenstock leaning against a rock. The black soil of the path to the torrent was constantly re-moistened by the spray from the roiling falls. In the soil I could see two sets of footprints leading down the path to the cascade, and none returning. It was precisely the same terrible sight that had greeted me all those years ago.

"Welcome back, Watson!"

I wheeled around. Holmes stood leaning against a tree, grinning widely.

"Holmes!" I exclaimed. "How did you manage to get away from the falls without leaving footprints?"

"Recall, my dear Watson, that except for the flesh-and-blood you and me, all this is but a simulation. I simply asked Mycroft to prevent my feet from leaving tracks." He demonstrated this by walking back and forth. No impression was left by his shoes, and no vegetation was trampled down by his passage. "And, of course, I asked him to freeze Moriarty, as earlier he had frozen the Swiss lad, before he and I could become locked in mortal combat."

"Fascinating," said I.

"Indeed. Now, consider the spectacle before you. What do you see?"

"Just what I saw that horrid day on which I had thought you had died: two sets of tracks leading to the falls, and none returning."

Holmes's crow of "Precisely!" rivaled the roar of the falls. "One set of tracks you knew to be my own, and the others you took to be that of the black-clad Englishman — the very Napoleon of crime!"

"Yes."

"Having seen these two sets approaching the falls, and none returning, you then rushed to the very brink of the falls and found — what?"

"Signs of a struggle at the lip of the precipice leading to the great torrent itself."

"And what did you conclude from this?"

"That you and Moriarty had plunged to your deaths, locked in mortal combat."

"Exactly so, Watson! The very same conclusion I myself would have drawn based on those observations!"

"Thankfully, though, I turned out to be incorrect."

"Did you, now?"

"Why, yes. Your presence here attests to that."

"Perhaps," said Holmes. "But I think otherwise. Consider, Watson! You were on the scene, you saw what happened, and for three years — three years, man! — you believed me to be dead. We had been friends and colleagues for a decade at that point. Would the Holmes you knew have let you mourn him for so long without getting word to you? Surely you must know that I trust you at least as much as I do my brother Mycroft, whom I later told you was the only one I had made had privy to the secret that I still lived."

"Well," I said, "since you bring it up, I *was* slightly hurt by that. But you explained your reasons to me when you returned."

"It is a comfort to me, Watson, that your ill-feelings were assuaged. But I wonder, perchance, if it was more you than I who assuaged them."

"Eh?"

"You had seen clear evidence of my death, and had faithfully if floridly recorded the same in the chronicle you so appropriately dubbed 'The Final Problem.' "

"Yes, indeed. Those were the hardest words I had ever written."

"And what was the reaction of your readers once this account was published in the *Strand*?"

I shook my head, recalling. "It was completely unexpected," said I. "I had anticipated a few polite notes from strangers mourning your passing, since the stories of your exploits had been so warmly received in the past. But what I got instead was mostly anger and outrage — people demanding to hear further adventures of yours."

"Which of course you believed to be impossible, seeing as how I was dead."

"Exactly. The whole thing left a rather bad taste, I must say. Seemed very peculiar behaviour."

"But doubtless it died down quickly," said Holmes.

"You know full well it did not. I have told you before that the onslaught of letters, as well as personal exhortations wherever I would travel, continued unabated for years. In fact, I was virtually at the point of going back and writing up one of your lesser cases I had previously ignored as being of no general interest simply to get the demands to cease, when, much to my surprise and delight — "

"Much to your surprise and delight, after an absence of three years less a month, I turned up in your consulting rooms, disguised, if I recall correctly, as a shabby book collector. And soon you had fresh adventures to chronicle, beginning with that case of the infamous Colonel Sebastian Moran and his victim, the Honorable Ronald Adair."

"Yes," said I. "Wondrous it was."

"But Watson, let us consider the facts surrounding my apparent death at the falls of Reichenbach on May fourth, 1891. You, the observer on the scene, saw the evidence, and, as you wrote in 'The Final Problem,' many experts scoured the lip of the falls and came to precisely the same conclusion you had — that Moriarty and I had plunged to our deaths."

"But that conclusion turned out to be wrong."

Holmes beamed intently. "No, my Good Watson, it turned out to be *unacceptable* — unacceptable to your faithful readers. And that is where all the problems stem from. Remember Schrödinger's cat in the sealed box? Moriarty and I at the falls present a very similar scenario: he and I went down the path into the cul-de-sac, our footprints leaving impressions in the soft earth. There were only two possible outcomes at that point: either I would exit alive, or I would not. There was no way out, except to take that same path back away from the falls. Until someone came and looked to see whether I had re-emerged from the path, the outcome was unresolved. I was both alive and dead — a collection of possibilities. But when you arrived, those possibilities had to collapse into a single reality. You saw that there were no footprints returning from the falls — meaning that Moriarty and I had struggled until at last we had both plunged over the edge into the icy torrent. It was your act of seeing the results that forced the possibilities to be resolved. In a very real sense, my good, dear friend, you killed me."

My heart was pounding in my chest. "I tell you, Holmes, nothing would have made me more happy than to have seen you alive!"

"I do not doubt that, Watson — but you had to see one thing or the other. You could not see both. And, having seen what you saw, you reported your findings: first to the Swiss police, and then to the reporter for the *Journal de Genève*, and lastly in your full account in the pages of the *Strand*."

I nodded.

"But here is the part that was not considered by Schrödinger when he devised the thought experiment of the cat in the box. Suppose you open the box and find the cat dead, and later you tell your neighbor about the dead cat — and your neighbor refuses to believe you when you say that the cat is dead. What happens if you go and look in the box a second time?"

"Well, the cat is surely still dead."

"Perhaps. But what if thousands — nay, millions! — refuse to believe the account of the original observer? What if they deny the evidence? What then, Watson?"

"I — I do not know."

"Through the sheer stubbornness of their will, they reshape reality, Watson! Truth is replaced with fiction! They will the cat back to life. More than that, they attempt to believe that the cat never died in the first place!"

"And so?"

"And so the world, which should have one concrete reality, is rendered unresolved, uncertain, adrift. As the first observer on the scene at Reichenbach, your interpretation should take precedence. But the stubbornness of the human race is legendary, Watson, and through that sheer cussedness, that refusal to believe what they have been plainly told, the world gets plunged back into being a wave front of unresolved possibilities. We exist in flux — to this day, the whole world exists in flux — because of the conflict between the observation you really made at Reichenbach, and the observation the world *wishes* you had made."

"But this is all too fantastic, Holmes!"

"Eliminate the impossible, Watson, and whatever remains, however improbable, must be the truth. Which brings me now to the question we were engaged by this avatar of Mycroft to solve: this paradox of Fermi. Where are the alien beings?"

"And you say you have solved that?"

"Indeed I have. Consider the method by which mankind has been searching for these aliens."

"By wireless, I gather — trying to overhear their chatter on the ether."

"Precisely! And when did I return from the dead, Watson?"

"April of 1894."

"And when did that gifted Italian, Guglielmo Marconi, invent the wireless?"

"I have no idea."

"In eighteen hundred and ninety-*five*, my good Watson. The following year! In all the time that mankind has used radio, our entire world has been an unresolved quandary! An uncollapsed wave front of possibilities!"

"Meaning?"

"Meaning the aliens are there, Watson — it is not they who are missing, it is us! Our world is out of synch with the rest of the universe. Through our failure to accept the unpleasant truth, we have rendered ourselves *potential* rather than *actual*."

I had always thought my companion a man with a generous regard for his own stature, but surely this was too much. "You are suggesting, Holmes, that the current unresolved state of the world hinges on the fate of you yourself?"

"Indeed! Your readers would not allow me to fall to my death, even if it meant attaining the very thing I desired most, namely the elimination of Moriarty. In this mad world, the observer has lost control of his observations! If there is one thing my life stood for — my life prior to that ridiculous resurrection of me you recounted in your chronicle of 'The Empty House' — it was reason! Logic! A devotion to observable fact! But humanity has abjured that. This whole world is out of whack, Watson — so out of whack that we are cut off from the civilizations that exist elsewhere. You tell me you were barraged with demands for my return, but if people had really understood me, understood what my life represented, they would have known that the only real tribute to me possible would have been to accept the facts! The only real answer would have been to leave me dead!"

# # #

Mycroft sent us back in time, but rather than returning us to 1899, whence he had plucked us, at Holmes's request he put us back eight years earlier in May of 1891. Of course, there were younger versions of ourselves already living then, but Mycroft swapped us for them, bringing the young ones to the future, where they could live out the rest of their lives in simulated scenarios taken from Holmes's and my minds. Granted, we were each eight years older than we had been when we had fled Moriarty the first time, but no one in Switzerland knew us and so the aging of our faces went unnoticed.

I found myself for a third time living that fateful day at the falls of Reichenbach, but this time, like the first and unlike the second, it was real.

I saw the page boy coming, and my heart raced. I turned to Holmes, and said, "I can't possibly leave you."

"Yes, you can, Watson. And you will, for you have never failed to play the game. I am sure you will play it to the end." He paused for a moment, then said, perhaps just a wee bit sadly, "I can discover facts, Watson, but I cannot change them." And then, quite solemnly, he extended his hand. I clasped it firmly in both of mine. And then the boy, who was in Moriarty's employ, was upon us. I allowed myself to be duped, leaving Holmes alone at the falls, fighting with all my might to keep from looking back as I hiked onward to treat the nonexistent patient at the Englischer Hof. On my way, I passed Moriarty going in the other direction. It was all I could do to keep from drawing my pistol and putting an end to the blackguard, but I knew Holmes would consider robbing him of his own chance at Moriarty an unforgivable betrayal.

It was an hour's hike down to the Englischer Hof. There I played out the scene in which I inquired about the ailing Englishwoman, and Steiler the Elder, the innkeeper, reacted, as I knew he must, with surprise. My performance was probably half-hearted, having played the role once before, but soon I was on my way back. The uphill hike took over two hours, and I confess plainly to being exhausted upon my arrival, although I could barely hear my own panting over the roar of the torrent.

Once again, I found two sets of footprints leading to the precipice, and none returning. I also found Holmes's alpenstock, and, just as I had the first time, a note from him to me that he had left with it. The note read just as the original had, explaining that he and Moriarty were about to have their final confrontation, but that Moriarty had allowed him to leave a few last words behind. But it ended with a postscript that had not been in the original:

> My dear Watson [it said], you will honour my passing
> most of all if you stick fast to the powers of observation.
> No matter what the world wants, leave me dead.

I returned to London, and was able to briefly counterbalance my loss of Holmes by reliving the joy and sorrow of the last few months of my wife Mary's life, explaining my somewhat older face to her and others as the result of shock at the death of Holmes. The next year, right on schedule, Marconi did indeed invent the wireless. Exhortations for more Holmes adventures continued to pour in, but I ignored them all, although the lack of him in my life was so profound that I was sorely tempted to relent, recanting my observations made at Reichenbach. Nothing would have pleased me more than to hear again the voice of the best and wisest man I had ever known.

In late June of 1907, I read in the *Times* about the detection of intelligent wireless signals coming from the direction of the star Altair. On that day, the rest of the world celebrated, but I do confess I shed a tear and drank a special toast to my good friend, the late Mr. Sherlock Holmes.

Ice Bridge

Edo van Belkom

The author of more than 150 crime, horror, science fiction and erotic stories, Edo won the 1997 Bram Stoker Award from the Horror Writers Association for "Rat Food" (co-authored with David Nickle), and the 1999 Aurora Award — Canada's top honour in SF — for "Hockey's Night in Canada." He has also been nominated twice for the Arthur Ellis Award. Edo's *Northern Dreamers*, a collection of interviews with Canadian science fiction, fantasy and horror writers, is soon to be joined by *Northern Schemers*, a collection of interviews with Canadian mystery writers. His novels include *Wyrm Wolf*, *Lord Soth*, and the forthcoming *Teeth*. Edo's first collection of stories, *Death Drives a Semi*, was published in 1998, and he now serves as the editor of genre fiction titles for Quarry Press. In "Ice Bridge," reprinted here from the 1997 anthology *Northern Frights IV*, Edo uses horror technique to great effect, creating a tale of steadily mounting suspense.

The continuous diesel-driven thrum of the loader was only occasionally drowned out by the crash of logs being dumped into place. The loud noise was followed by the faint groan of metal and the slight rumbling of frozen earth as the truck dutifully bowed to accept its load.

Ice Bridge

Rick Hartwick mixed his coffee with a plastic stir-stick and walked casually toward the far end of the office trailer. At the window, he blew across the top of his steaming cup and watched his breath freeze against the pane. Then he took a sip, wiped away the patch of ice that had formed on the glass, and watched his truck being loaded one last time.

As always, the loader, a Québécois named Pierre Langlois, was making sure Rick's rig was piled heavy with spruce and pine logs, some of them more than three feet in diameter. Langlois liked Rick, and with good reason. Every other week throughout the season, Rick had provided Langlois with a bottle of Canadian Club. He'd been doing it for years now, ever since he'd called a loader an asshole during a card game and wound up driving trucks loaded with soft wood and air the rest of the winter.

He'd been lucky to hang on to his rig.

The next winter he began greasing Langlois' gears with the best eighty proof he could find and since then he'd never had a load under thirty tonnes and only a handful under thirty-five.

He owned his rig now, as well a house in Prince George.

As he continued to watch the loading operation, Jerry Chetwynd, the oldtimer who manned the trailer for the company came up behind Rick and looked out the window. "That's a good load you got going there."

"Not bad," said Rick, taking a sip.

"Are you gonna take it over the road, or take a chance on the bridge?"

Rick took another sip, then turned to look at the old man. They said Chetwynd had been a logger in the B.C. interior when they'd still used ripsaws and axes to clear the land. Rick believed it, although you wouldn't know it to look at him now, all thin and bony, and hunched over like he was still carrying post wood on his back. "Is the ice bridge open?"

Chetwynd smiled, showing Rick all four of the teeth he'd been able to keep from rotting out. "They cleared the road to MacKenzie last night and this morning," he said. "But the company decided to keep the bridge open one more day seeing as how cold it was overnight."

Rick nodded. Although the winter season usually ended the last two weeks of March, a cold snap late in the month had lingered long enough for them to keep the bridge operating a whole week into April. And while they'd been opening and closing the ice bridge across Williston Lake like a saloon door the past couple days, the few extra trips he'd been able to make had made a big difference to Rick's finances — the kind of difference that translated into a two-week stay at an all-inclusive singles resort on Maui.

"Anyone use the bridge today?"

Chetwynd scratched the side of his head with two gnarled fingers. "Not that I know of. Maybe an empty coming back from the mill. Harry Heskith left here about an hour ago . . . But he said he wasn't going to risk the ice. Said the road would get him there just the same . . . "

"Yeah, eventually," Rick muttered under his breath.

The ice bridge across Williston Lake was three kilometres long and took about four minutes to cross. If you took the road around the lake you added an extra fifty kilometres and about an hour's drive to the trip. That might have been all right for Harry Heskith with a wife, mortgage, two-point-three kids, and a dog, but Rick had a plane to catch.

Maui was waiting.

"Up to you," Chetwynd said, shrugging his shoulders as he handed Rick the yellow shipping form.

The loader's throaty roar suddenly died down and the inside of the trailer became very quiet.

Uncomfortably so.

Rick crushed his coffee cup in his hand and tossed it into the garbage. "See you 'round," he said, zipping up his parka and stepping outside.

"If you're smart you will," said Chetwynd to an empty trailer. "Smart or lucky."

# # #

The air outside was cold, but nothing like the –35 Celsius they got through January and February. Between –15 and –35 was best for winter logging — anything colder and the machinery froze up, anything warmer and the ground started getting soft. The weather report had said −15 today, but with the sun out and shining down on the back of his coat, it felt a lot warmer than that.

Rick slipped on his gloves and headed for his rig, the morning's light dusting of snow crunching noisily underfoot.

"You got her loaded pretty tight," he called out to Langlois, who had climbed up onto the trailer to secure the load.

"Filled the hempty spaces wit kindling," Langlois said with obvious pride in his voice.

"Gee, I don't know," chided Rick. "I still see some daylight in there."

"All dat fits in dare, my friend, is match sticks hand toot picks," Langlois said, his French-Canadian accent still lingering after a dozen years in the B.C. interior.

Rick laughed.

"You know, I uh, I haven't seen you in a while and I been getting a little tirsty . . . You know what I mean?"

Rick nodded. Of course he knew what Langlois meant. He was trying to scam him for an extra bottle before he went on holidays, even though he'd given the man a bottle less than a week ago.

"I'll take care of you when I get back next week," Rick said, knowing full well he wouldn't be back for another two.

Langlois smiled. "Going somewhere?"

"Maui, man," said Rick, giving Langlois the Hawaiian 'hang loose' sign with the thumb and little finger of his right hand.

"Lucky man . . . Make sure you get a lei when you land dare."

"When I land," Rick smiled. "And all week long."

The two men laughed heartily as they began walking around the truck doing a circle check on the rig and making sure the chains holding the logs in place were tight and secure.

"You load Heskith this morning?" Rick asked when they were almost done.

"Yeah."

"What do you figure you gave him?"

"Plenty of air," Langlois smiled. He had struggled to pronounce the word *air* so it didn't sound too much like *hair*.

"How much?"

"Twenty tonnes. Maybe twenty-two."

"He complain about it?"

"Not a word. In fact, he ask me to load him light. Said he was taking the road into MacKenzie."

Rick shook his head. "Dumb sonuvabitch is going to be driving a logging truck into his sixties with loads like that."

"Well, he's been doing it twenty years already."

"Yeah, and maybe he's just managed to pay off his truck by now, huh?"

"He seem to do okay," Langlois shrugged. "But it's none of my business anyway, eh?"

"Right," said Rick, shaking his head. The way he saw it, truck logging was a young man's game. Get in, make as much as you can carrying as much as you can, and get out. So he pushed it to the limit every once in a while. So what? If he worked it right he could retire early or finish out his years driving part-time, picking and choosing his loads on a sort of busman's holiday.

They finished checking the rig.

Everything was secure. "How much you figure I got there?" asked Rick, knowing Langlois could usually estimate a load to within a tonne.

"Tirty-six. Tirty-seven."

"You're beautiful, man."

Langlois nodded. "Just get it to the mill."

"Have I failed you yet?"

"No, but dare will always be a first time."

"Funny. Very funny."

There was a moment of silence between them. Finally Langlois said, "So, you taking it over the ice?"

"The bridge is open isn't it."

"Yeah, it's *open*."

Rick looked at him. Something about the way he'd said the word *open* didn't sit right with him. It sounded too much like *hope* for his liking. "Did Heskith say why he wasn't taking the bridge?"

"Uh-huh," Langlois nodded. "He said he had no intention of floating his logs to the mill."

Rick laughed at that. "And I got no intention of missing my flight."

Langlois nodded. "Aloha."

For a moment, Rick didn't understand, then he smiled and said, "Oh, yeah right. Aloha."

# # #

The interior of the Peterbilt had been warmed by the sunlight beaming through the windshield. As Rick settled in he took off his hat and gloves and undid his coat, then he shifted it into neutral and started up the truck. The big engine rattled, the truck shivered, and a belch of black smoke escaped the rig's twin chrome pipes. And then the cab was filled with the strong and steady metallic rumble of 525 diesel-powered horses.

He let the engine warm-up, making himself more comfortable for the long drive to the mill. He slipped in a Charlie Major tape, and waited for the opening chords of "For the Money" to begin playing. When the song started blaring, he shifted it into gear and slowly released the clutch.

His first thought was how slow the rig was to get moving as the cab rocked and the engine roared against dead weight of the heavy load. It usually didn't take so long to get underway, Rick thought. Must be a bit heavier than Langlois had figured.

Inch by inch, the truck rolled forward. At last he was out of first and into second, gaining small amounts of momentum and speed as he worked his way up through the gears.

A light amount of snow had begun to fall, but it wasn't enough to worry about, certainly nothing that would slow him down.

The logging road into MacKenzie was wide and flat, following the southern bank of the Nation River for more than a hundred kilometres before coming upon the southern tip of Williston Lake. There the road split in two, one fork continuing east over the ice bridge to MacKenzie, the other turning south and rounding the southern finger of Williston Lake before turning back north toward the mills.

Rick drove along the logging road at about sixty kilometres an hour, slowing only once when he came upon an empty rig headed in the opposite direction. Out of courtesy, he gave the driver a pull on the gas horn and a friendly wave, then it was back to the unbroken white strip of road cut neatly through the trees.

The snow continued to fall.

When he turned over the Major tape for the second time he knew he was nearing the bridge. He hated to admit it, but a slight tingle coursed through his body at the thought of taking his load over the ice.

When Rick first began driving logging trucks the idea of driving across lakes didn't sit all that well with him. To him, it was sort of like skydivers jumping out of perfectly good airplanes — it just wasn't right. Six-axle semi-trailers loaded with thirty-five tonnes of logs weren't meant to be driven over water — frozen or otherwise.

It was unnatural . . .

Dangerous.

But after his first few rides over the ice, he realized that it was the only way to go. Sure, sometimes you heard a crack or pop under your wheels, but that just made it all the more exciting. The only real danger about driving over the ice was losing your way. Once your were off the bridge there were no guarantees that the ice beneath your rig would be thick enough to support you. And if you did fall through, or simply got stuck, there was a good chance you'd freeze to death while searching for help.

Even so, those instances were rare, and as far as Rick knew, no one had ever fallen through the ice while driving over an open bridge.

And he sure as hell didn't intend to be the first.

Up ahead the roadway opened up slightly as the snow-trimmed trees parted to reveal the lake and the ice bridge across it. In the distance, he could see the smoke rising up from the stacks of the three saw mills and two pulp mills of MacKenzie, a town of about 5,000 hardy souls.

He turned down the music, then shut it off completely as he slowed his rig to a stop at the fork in the road.

He took a deep breath and considered his options one last time.

Across the lake at less than three kilometres away, MacKenzie seemed close enough to touch. But between here and there, there was nothing more than frozen water to hold up over thirty-five tonnes of wood and steel.

He turned to look down the road as it curved to the south and pictured Harry Heskith's rig turning that way about an hour before, his tracks now obscured by the continuing snowfall.

The road.

It was Heskith's route all right . . .

The long way.

The safe way.

But even if Rick decided to go that route, there were no guarantees that the drive would be easy.

First of all he was really too heavy to chance it. With its sharp inclines and steep downgrades there was a real risk of sliding off the snow-covered road while rounding a curve. Also, although it hadn't happened to him yet, he'd heard of truckers coming across tourists out for Sunday drives, rubbernecking along their merry way at ten or fifteen kilometres an hour. When that happened, you had the choice of driving over top of them, or slamming on the brakes. And on these logging roads, hard braking usually meant ending up on your side or in the ditch, or both. And that might mean a month's worth of profits just to get back on the road.

But even if he *wanted* to take the road, it would mean spending another hour behind the wheel and that would make him late for his flight out of Prince George. Then he'd miss his connecting flight out of Vancouver which meant . . .

No Maui.

And he wasn't about to let that happen, especially when he'd been told that the resort he'd be staying at discreetly stocked rooms with complimentary condoms.

Man, he couldn't wait to get there.

He looked out across the lake again. The snow was still falling, but a light crosswind was keeping it from building up on the ice. He could still clearly see the thick black lines painted onto the ice surface on either side of the bridge. With those lines so visible, there was really no way he could lose his way.

He took one last look down the road, thought of Heskith heading down that way an hour ago and wondered if he'd catch up with good ole Harry on the other side.

If he did, maybe he could race him into Mackenzie.

The thought put a dark and devilish grin on Rick's face.

He slid the Charlie Major tape back into the deck, turned up the volume and shifted the truck into gear.

"Here goes nothing," he said.

The rig inched forward.

# # #

It took him a while to get up to speed, but by the time he got onto the bridge he was doing fifty, more than enough to see him safely to the other side.

The trick to driving over the ice was to keep moving. There was incredible amounts of pressure under the wheels of the rig, but as long as you kept moving, that pressure was constantly being relieved. If you slowed, or heaven forbid, stalled out on the ice, then you were really shit-out-of-luck.

He shifted into sixth gear, missed the shift and had to try again. Finally, he got it into gear, but in the meantime he had slowed considerably and the engine had to struggle to recover the lost speed.

Slowly the speedometer's red needle clawed its way back up to sixty, sixty-one, sixty-two . . .

And then he heard something over the music.

It was a loud sound, like the splintering of wood or the cracking of bone. He immediately turned down the music and listened.

All he could hear was the steady thrum of his diesel engine.

For a moment he breathed easier.

But then he heard it again.

The unmistakable sound of cracking ice.

It was a difficult sound to describe. Some said it was like snow crunching underfoot, while others compared it to fresh celery stalks being snapped in two.

Rick, however, had always described it as sounding like an ice cube dropped into a warm glass of Coke — only a hundred times louder.

He looked down at the ice on the bridge in front of him, realized he was straddling one of the black lines painted on the ice and gently eased the wheel to the left, bringing him back squarely between the lines.

That done, he breathed a sigh of relief, and felt the sweat begin to cool on his face and down his back.

"Eyes on the road," he said aloud. "You big dummy — "

Crack!

This one was louder than the others, so loud he could feel the shock waves in his chest.

Again he looked out in front of his truck and for the first time saw the pressure cracks shooting out in front of him, matching the progress of his truck metre for metre.

Finally Rick admitted what he'd known all along.

He was way too heavy.

And the ice was far too thin.

But 20/20 hindsight was useless to him now. All he could do was keep moving, keep relieving the pressure under his wheels and hope that both he and the pressure crack reached the other side.

He stepped hard on the gas pedal and the engine responded with a louder, throatier growl. He considered shifting gears again but decided it might be better not to risk it.

He firmed up his foot on the gas pedal and stood on it with all his weight.

The engine began to strain as the speedometer inched past seventy . . . He remained on the pedal, knowing he'd be across in less than a minute.

The sound grew louder, changing from a crunching, cracking sound to something resembling a gunshot.

He looked down.

The crack in front of the truck had grown bigger, firing out in front of him in all directions like the scraggly branches of a December birch.

"C'mon, c'mon," he said pressing his foot harder on the gas even though it was a wasted effort. The pedal was already down as far as it would go.

Then suddenly the cracking sound grew faint, as if it had been dampened by a splash of water.

A moment later, crunching again.

Cracking.

He looked up. The shoreline was a few hundred metres away. In a few seconds there would be solid ice under his wheels and then nothing but wonderful, glorious, hard-packed frozen ground.

But then the trailer suddenly lurched to the right, pulling the left-front corner of the tractor into the air.

"C'mon, c'mon," Rick screamed, jerking back and forth in his seat in a vain attempt to add some forward momentum to the rig.

Then the front end of the Peterbilt dipped as if it had come across a huge rent in the ice.

"Oh, shit!"

The tractor bounced over the rent, then the trailer followed, each axle dipping down, seemingly hesitant about coming back up the other side, and then reluctantly doing so.

And then, as if by some miracle . . .

He was through it.

Rolling smoothly over the ice.

Solid ice.

And the only sound he could hear was the throaty roar of his Peterbilt as he kept his foot hard on the gas.

He raced up the incline toward the road without slowing.

When he reached the road, he got off the gas, but still had plenty of momentum, not to mention weight, behind him.

Too much of both, it seemed.

He pulled gently on the rear brake lever, but found that his tires had little grip on the snow-covered road. His rear wheels locked up and began sliding out from behind.

He turned the wheel, but it was no use.

He closed his eyes and braced himself for the rig to topple onto its side.

He waited and waited for the crash . . .

But it never came.

Suddenly all was quiet except for the calming rattle of the Peterbilt's diesel engine at idle.

Rick opened his eyes.

He breathed hard as he looked around to get his bearings.

He was horizontal across the highway, pointed in the direction he'd come.

He looked north out the passenger side window and saw the puffing smokestacks of MacKenzie, and smiled.

He'd made it.

Made it across the bridge.

The moment of celebration was sweet, but short-lived . . .

Cut off by the loud cry of a gas horn, splitting the air like a scream.

He turned to look south down the highway.

Harry Heskith's rig had just crested the hill and was heading straight for him.

Rick threw the Peterbilt into gear, stomped on the gas and popped the clutch.

The rig lurched forward, but he was too slow and too late.

All of Heskith's rear wheels were locked and sliding over the snow like skis. Heskith was turning his front wheels frantically left and right even though it was doing nothing to change the direction he was headed.

And then as he got closer, Rick could clearly see Heskith's face. What surprised Rick most was the realization that the old man was shaking his fist at him.

Shaking his fist, as if to say he was a crazy fool for taking the bridge.

But as the two trucks came together, all Rick could think of was how *he'd* been right all along.

The dangers of the ice bridge had been a cakewalk compared to —

The Prize in the Pack

William Bankier

Bill is one the finest writers of short crime fiction Canada has ever produced. His first story, "What Happened in Act One," appeared in *Ellery Queen's Mystery Magazine* in 1963. Since then, he has produced hundreds more, appearing primarily in both *Ellery Queen's* and *Alfred Hitchcock's Mystery Magazines*. He has been frequently anthologized. In 1968, he was a finalist for the Edgar Award for Best Short Story (the year the award was won by fellow CWC member Ed Hoch), and he has been nominated numerous times for the Arthur Ellis Award. In 1992, the Crime Writers of Canada honoured Bill with the Derrick Murdoch Award. *Fear is a Killer*, a collection of Bill's finest stories, was published in 1995 by Mosaic Press. "The Prize in the Pack" is one of Bill's long series of loosely connected stories set in Baytown. Based on his own hometown of Belleville, Ontario, Baytown first appeared on the map of the crime world in 1965. "Prize" also features one of Bill's powerful recurring themes: the destructive power of the family and the dark potential of human relationships.

Here was Casey Dolan trying to prepare his six o'clock sports broadcast and there was Carmen's big brother Alvin, waiting for her to finish work and giving Dolan the evil eye from the outer office.

Clement Foy's sonorous voice poured out of the monitor speaker. "A reminder that in fifteen minutes the old catcher will be along with your early-evening sports show. In the meantime, more rolling-home music here on CBAY, the voice of Baytown, as Les Brown and the Band of Renown offer some musical reassurance, 'I've Got My Love To Keep Me Warm.' "

Foy was stuck in the big-band era, which Dolan could stand. At forty-eight, he was five years older than the program director and he liked the bouncy sound. His two-finger typing of tonight's script rattled along almost in time with the rhythm. The age problem, if he had one, was in relation to Carmen Hopkins, who was only nineteen. This was a gap that had seemed unbridgeable six months ago when she came on staff. Now that they had made love, there turned out to be no gap. Dolan had been surprised and gratified but soon learned he was exchanging the fear of inadequacy for that of an early death at the hands of big brother Alvin. He had always suspected there was a trace of Indian in the Hopkins genetic pool. Now those Iroquois eyes watched him from beyond the front desk. Did Alvin know? How could he know? Should Dolan give him a smile?

"I'm on my way," Carmen said, leaving her desk at the back of the room, passing Dolan's chair, letting her fingers brush the back of his neck. "Any problems with continuity, talk to my lawyer." That was a laugh. In six months, she had mastered the job better than anybody the radio station had ever employed. She was good. Too good for such routine work, Dolan kept telling her. "You take it easy now, young lady," he said in an avuncular tone. It was the voice he had used when he was catching for the Redmen and a young pitcher needed reassurance out there on the mound.

"I always try," she said, riveting him with her mischievous stare, "though I don't always succeed." She swaggered away to join her brother. Dolan feasted his eyes on her. She still carried some babyfat he had discovered. Heart-shaped face, lips a bit on the heavy side but perfectly shaped, cheeks forever blushing. Her hair was glossy toffee, tied in twin braids with green ribbons. She had skin that drove Dolan mad, arms, legs, shoulders — she was packaged in this slightly textured, almost café-au-lait material and keeping his hands off it was for the over-the-hill but lately reborn athlete a severe exercise in self-discipline.

"Let's go, Carmen," Alvin said as he opened the door, towering over her, pretending to be out of patience with her instead of her slave, as even Dolan with his deteriorating vision could see. "I want to pick up some beer before the store closes."

"If you're getting drunk tonight," she said, "I'm going out."

Dolan got the message and the typewriter keys jammed. His heart was still pounding like a teenager's when he went on the air ten minutes later. "Good evening, sports fans. First place changed hands last night in the Baytown Fastball League as — "

# # #

After he signed off, Dolan drove home and showered and washed what was left of his hair. He was still using Anna's shampoo. A few drops was all he needed, so three months after his wife's departure for Centralia the big plastic bottle was holding out. The smell still reminded him of her. So did the bath itself, oddly and sadly. In early years, when David was still a baby, they sometimes performed what seemed in those days an adventurous act — they got into the shower together. Soaping each other, they laughed a lot and he called her his seal. Now — it seemed no more than a few weeks later — David was in charge of the science department at Centralia Polytechnic while his mother had opened a shop in the same city selling coordinated paints and wallpapers. And Dad was making it on his own.

Dolan rubbed himself dry with a rough towel. He faced the mirror at an angle that showed the least paunch, the fewest veins. Carmen seemed to like him. Mind you, it was always lights off and after a couple of drinks. He got dressed in the coordinated green-and-grey outfit, a modified track suit. The store manager had said he looked twenty years younger. Anna would laugh. She had forever been after Dolan to smarten himself up, buy new clothes. All she had to do to get her wish was leave him.

She hasn't really left me, Dolan said to himself, as he pocketed money and keys and went outside into a balmy summer night. After twenty-six years together, we're trying it apart. A little freedom, room to move.

He knew he'd find Carmen in the back lounge of the Coronet Hotel. It was her idea to conduct their meetings in the public eye. "If we sneak around and drive out to The Cedars like you're suggesting, somebody is bound to see us and say those two are up to something. But here in the heart of town, how bad can it be? We're fellow employees having a drink together."

"My problem will be keeping my hands off you," he said.

"I have the cure. Think of you touching me, and then Alvin walking in."

The blind jazz pianist was at the keyboard when Dolan entered the lounge. His dog lay at his feet, head down, barely tolerant of what was going on. Jack Danforth, owner of the Coronet, sat at the end of the bar. Dolan placed himself at a corner table, distributed a few waves, and ordered a large brandy and soda. He was halfway through it when Carmen appeared, spotted him, hugged the wall on her way to the table, and slipped furtively onto a chair.

"Are you all right?" he asked her.

"Do I look all right?"

He studied her face. It might have been called a swelling on the jaw. "There's no light in here. Have you been hit?"

The music climaxed, lots of applause, end of set. Pianist and seeing-eye dog filed out behind Danforth to sit in his office. Carmen was at her most rebellious, a sailor on leave. "I came so close to putting a knife in him, Casey — "

"Tell me."

"It's one thing when he nags me. That's what a big brother is for. But when he started in on Peter, I went for him."

"Calm down."

"All right. All right. Get me a beer."

He ordered a Molson and another brandy. The drinks came and they started in on them but she was still taking deep breaths through her nostrils. In this mood, she was more attractive than ever to Dolan.

"Did he know you were coming out to meet me?"

"No. I don't know. I don't care. Do you care?"

"I don't care."

"Stop worrying about my brother. I'm over eighteen, I can do whatever I want. There's not a damn thing Alvin can do about it."

Dolan tried to put from his mind thoughts of Alvin Hopkins doing something about it and then being punished for it by a life sentence, with Dolan no longer around to appreciate justice being done. "What made you so mad?" he asked.

"He said I'm not a responsible person. Without him to look after me, I'd go down the drain. He thinks I should still be at university."

Dolan thought so, too, but knew better than to tell the headstrong girl. She was a classic under-achiever. Born with brains to spare and limitless energy, she refused ever to do more than just enough to get by. In Baytown High School, she got top grades while hardly cracking a book. Her brother Alvin, with no encouragement from Carmen, borrowed the money to pay for her first year in an arts course at Queen's University in Kingston, sixty miles down the road, past Centralia. He bullied her into registering and moving there and attending some lectures. But she only stayed three weeks, arriving back home on the bus, her trunk showing up, rail freight, a few days later.

The debacle cost Alvin a good part of the money he paid. And when his clever little sister got a job selling dresses at Artistic Ladies Wear, it was almost more than he could bear. The new job writing continuity (whatever that was) at CBAY was an improvement. But still she seemed more interested in going through the motions and having fun than in getting ahead. For a man who used all his limited ability to work his way up through the yards to a job behind a ticket window at the CN station, Carmen's behaviour was calculated to drive him up the wall.

Dolan said to her, "What did he say about Pete?" Carmen Hopkins' other brother Peter, known to his friends as Hophead, had killed himself two years ago in a road accident involving his pickup truck and a steel power pylon.

"He said I'm not just bad for myself, I'm a bad influence on other people. That's a laugh. Pete was drunk when he showed up that night."

"I know."

The Prize in the Pack

"I couldn't ask him to stay. It was a girls' party. And he kept grabbing hold of people, it wasn't funny. Vera didn't like him and he kept grabbing hold of Vera."

Dolan had heard the story before. "So you ordered him out," he said gloomily.

"I whacked him and pushed him out the door and locked it. Then when I went after him, it was too late. He was driving away."

Dolan stared into the battered-baby eyes, hoping it was over. "Carmen," he said softly, "it was not your fault."

After a minute or so, she became calm. "You've had a normal life, eh, Case?" she said. "Good family. Lots of success."

"Yeah, sure." He gave her the grin that usually worked. "The only reason the Redmen kept old Casey Dolan behind the plate was I didn't mind being hit by bouncing baseballs." He took a drink. "And with our pitching we had a lot of bouncing baseballs." He showed her his collection of broken fingers.

"It explains a lot," he said.

They went off for a drive later, across the Bay Bridge and into the country. The windows were down and there was a lot of clover in the air. On the radio, Clem Foy was doing his night show, ignoring the musical tastes of his audience, playing a selection of 78s from his own library. He thanked Lionel Hampton for rendering "Midnight Sun," then introduced Louis singing "A Kiss To Build a Dream On."

As they approached the coloured lights of a roadhouse, Carmen said she was hungry. Dolan drove in and parked in darkness on the farthest patch of gravel and went inside to get take-out, leaving her in the car.

"That really cheeses me off," she said when he came back with hamburgers and shakes. He could feel the vibrations, so he switched on and got rolling again, heading farther into farmland. "You won't even take me inside," she complained with her mouth full. "I feel like some kind of cheap whore."

Half an hour later, he parked off the road on a headland with a view of the bay where it becomes part of Lake Ontario. Her mood was sweet again. Dolan kissed her, and his advancing years faded, leaving him feeling strong, not worried for the moment about anything. He knew it was only nature trying to get him to propagate the race, but he didn't care. Her mouth was soft, she smelled of soap and lipstick.

On the way home, she was buoyant. Her window was down, her eyes narrowed against the rush of air. "If you and I were married, there'd be no problem," she said. "Alvin would have to shut up."

"I'm already married. Did you forget?"

"She's left you. Get a divorce."

"What's the rush to get married? You're a kid, you've got your whole life. You're a talented girl, you can write up a storm. I'm just a stupid ball player but I can recognize what you've got."

"Here we go."

"You sit at that desk bashing out promotion announcements and program scripts with one brain tied behind your back. Work, damn it. Write." He glanced at her face, saw the down-turned mouth. "Develop the talent God gave you."

"Who asked Him?" she said. Then after half a mile of slipstream, she said, "Would you marry me if I said I was pregnant? I'm not, but if I told you I was?" She was smiling now. "You wouldn't believe me, would you?"

"Not in the nineteen-eighties." He shrugged. "I believed it in the fifties."

Carmen passed Dolan's desk one afternoon in the following week and dropped a sheaf of folded typewritten pages in front of him. "Read it and weep," she said and wandered away. He glanced at page one, saw "Nor Iron Bars by Carmen Hopkins." He was so excited by the manuscript, he couldn't get on with his work. He took it to the washroom and read it in the privacy of a cubicle.

She had written a story about a young girl in love with an older man. They both worked in a small town radio station. There was practically no invention in it, the plot was his experience and hers, but it read like a house afire. At the end, the sports announcer was still with his wife and the girl was floating face-down in the bay.

He emerged into the office and went to her desk, where she was elaborately turning the pages of a newspaper. "Come for coffee," he said, handing her the manuscript.

"You like?" It was the only time she had appeared nervous in front of him.

"Come for coffee."

They went around the corner to the Paragon Café, where he ordered two coffees and the slab of cream pie she asked for. A kid. "Your story is brilliant," he said. "Exactly what I wanted you to do. Keep it up."

"What for?"

"Because you can."

"I tried it and now I know how easy it is. Big deal."

"You want to be infuriating, don't you? Who are you trying to provoke, your father?"

"The great prospector?" She laughed. "All he ever did was search for uranium that wasn't there and come back once in a while to get my mother pregnant."

"Succeed for yourself," Dolan pontificated. "Not for anyone else."

Carmen finished her pie, gave him the mischievous smile with her mouth half full. "I forget," she said. "Did you promise the other night to marry me if you got me pregnant?"

He knew she was teasing him, but his heart turned over anyway. "One of these days, kid — over my knee."

"Ready when you are," she said.

# # #

The Redmen were batting in the bottom of the third against the Napanee Oilers. The sun was settling behind the canning factory. Seated at the microphone in the press box under the grandstand roof, Dolan called the balls and strikes and kept up a flow of anecdote and description. He was feeling at peace with the world, almost smug, hoping Management never discovered that he would broadcast baseball for nothing. In the bleachers, several hundred fans in shirtsleeves watched and ate and drank and yelled at the players and the umpires.

Around eight o'clock, Carmen made her way up the ladder and took a seat not far from Dolan. Perhaps to make her entry legal, she had put on her CBAY T-shirt. She was munching caramel corn from the famous narrow red box. When they cut back to the studio for a commercial she extended the package in his direction.

"Thanks, I can't. Gets in my throat."

"Is it all right for me to be here?"

He looked at the scrubbed healthy face, the glistening braids, the ripe body in a shirt one size too small. "It is absolutely perfect for you to be here." Then, encouraged by her glow, and just before his cue from the engineer, he said to her, "Carmen dear, life is a box of Cracker Jacks and you are the prize in the pack."

She stirred the air above her head with a finger. "Hoopdedoo!" she said.

After the game, they walked to his car in the parking lot behind the dance pavilion. The Clem Foy Five was playing inside, and through screened windows coloured lights glowed behind the movement of dancing couples. They watched in silence holding hands. It was a big regret for Dolan that he couldn't take the girl inside and hold her for a while to music. Now he drew her to him. She must have been reading his mind because she angled her cheek against his shoulder, rested her hand on his collar, pressed herself against him, and moving hardly at all, unsteady on gravel, they danced part of the chorus of "Moonglow."

"Come here often?" she said to lighten the atmosphere. He said nothing, unlocked the car, let her in, slammed the door, and strode around to the driver's side. As he switched on, backed away, gunned a ferocious turn, and raced out of the fair grounds, she said, "You can come home with me tonight."

He said, "What?"

"Alvin has gone away for a few days. A friend of his called and asked him to go up to Montreal for some stag thing. A guy they know is getting married. He got on the train this afternoon."

Dolan drove on in silence.

"On the other hand, if you don't want to — I just thought it would be nice to get in bed and not have to worry about rushing off."

He thought of what she had written. A young girl dead by her own hand. The possessive brother. The old athlete trying to squeeze a few more drops of flavour out of a desiccated life. She called it "Nor Iron Bars." "I want to," he said as he made the turn to take them down the hill toward Station Street. "I just can't believe my luck." In his mind, cutting through the confusion, Dolan heard a sound that was not hard to identify. If was the door of a cage slamming shut behind him —

Her house reminded Dolan of vacation cottages he had inhabited in wilderness country. It was of frame construction, ramshackle, okay in summer as long as it didn't rain. The furnishings were lightweight, carpets worn through, woodwork covered in paint faded years since to the colour of an ancient keyboard. The telephone (only once had Dolan dared speak to her on this vulnerable line) hung on the kitchen wall. For a yard around it, the wallpaper was peppered with a buckshot explosion of scrawled numbers and messages.

She found a bottle of gin and gave him a drink he did not want. "Relax," she said, bouncing into place beside him on the sprung settee, tucking a leg under her where he could not miss seeing the plump, shiny curve where calf met thigh.

She surveyed him with delight. "You're among friends, Casey. Don't look so mournful."

She gave him butterfly kisses with her eyelashes. He let his hand rest on that smooth leg. His anxiety evaporated and he began to share her excitement. The feeling reminded him of a time when he and some of the kids went into Woolworth's on Front Street and lifted a few lead soldiers. It was wrong and he knew he would hate himself later, but the urge had been irresistible.

Her bedroom was through a curtained doorway off the sitting room. She said, "Give me a minute," and went in there. Dolan sat, glass in both hands, elbows on knees, staring at the floor. Strange, he thought. The room smelled of decay, it showed no evidence of maintenance and yet he sensed there was a stability about the place as if it would still be here, sheltering the Hopkins tribe in a hundred years, long after his tidy bungalow had been bulldozed and built over.

"Ready!"

He went to her in the silent bedroom, saw a small cot with the covers turned back, inviting in pink light from a tiny lamp. She was naked under a flimsy gown, torn at the hip. He embraced her and was so overpowered that he lost his balance and they did a struggling dance, laughing at themselves. "You'd better lie down," she said, "before you fall down."

The front door opened, then closed with a slam. Alvin's voice was bored. "Carmen? You home?"

Dolan went ice cold. He stepped away from her and faced the curtain. Footsteps in the other room. The brother's boots showed in the light at the hem of the curtain. "You decent, kid?"

"Yes," she said in a tone of great weariness.

"What is it?"

"You might as well come in."

Alvin drew the curtain aside. He saw Dolan, saw his sister sitting on the edge of the bed. "What the hell?" He stayed where he was but raised his arm and pointed a finger at Dolan's face. "You bastard!"

"Alvin, calm down. He's here because I asked him. I work. I bring in money — "

"Shut your mouth."

"You don't own me!"

"Shut up!" Alvin's voice rose. He moved toward Dolan.

"Listen! Listen to me!" Carmen ran at her brother, grabbed his arm, and used her strength to turn him. "You touch him, you lay a hand on him — " her finger was in his face now " — and I'll be gone so far from here you'll never see me again!"

Dolan felt as if he had been tied hand and foot and set on fire. He was due to die horribly and could do nothing about it. Shock numbed him. "I don't want any trouble," he said lamely, able to feel embarrassment through his panic at the weakness of his response.

"Just go, Casey." Carmen put her back against her brother, making way for Dolan's departure. "Don't say anything, get out. I'll take care of this." As he fled, she told him, "I'll talk to you tomorrow."

Seated in his car where he had parked it on the next street, Dolan had to wait a good minute before his fingers could fit the key to the ignition lock. As he drove away, he assured himself of one good thing emerging from the debacle — he would certainly not be spending any more time with that dangerous little bitch.

# # #

Carmen was waiting for Dolan in the Coronet lounge. She had telephoned in sick to the radio station, taking a day's leave. At four in the afternoon, with his evening broadcast mostly prepared, he had responded to her call and come down to see her. She was halfway through a beer. Soon due on the air, Dolan ordered a coffee.

"Can you believe it?" she opened. "That whole business about the stag in Montreal was a put-on. He suspected us. He set it up to catch you with me."

Dolan could believe anything of Alvin and he said so.

"You don't have to worry," she said. "I'm sorry I put you through it."

"Not your fault," he said bleakly. But he thought it was — why couldn't she just leave him alone? He was old enough to be her father. Why all the provocative attention?

"We talked for a long time after you left. Alvin can be sweet when you approach him the right way. At first he didn't want to know but I kept on and finally he understood. We love each other."

"Carmen, did you see his face?"

"He was all right later. I told him you wanted to marry me."

"Carmen — "

"Don't you? Are you just in this for what you can get?"

"You know better."

"Well?"

He tried to be patient with this stubborn child. "I have a wife."

"You talk as if you've got cancer. Millions of men get cured of wives. It's called divorce."

"It takes two to get a divorce."

"Have you asked her? She doesn't even live with you. She's over in Centralia having a ball running her store. She's probably waiting for you to bring up the subject."

It was all so complicated. What had happened to the quiet life he used to think was boring? A divorce would cost money. A wedding would cost money. Carmen would get pregnant. Babies cost money. He would be the oldest daddy in Baytown — laughter in the beverage rooms, to say the least.

William Bankier

He drank his coffee doggedly, aware that she was watching him across her beer.

"Okay," he said at last. "I'll drive over to Centralia and put the question to her."

. # #

Dolan waited until Sunday when he had no program to do and then drove down the Bayshore Road and through a region of dairy farms and acres of half-grown corn, reaching the concrete towers of Centralia at five o'clock in the afternoon.

He had always hated the big city. Years ago, the Redmen had come up against Centralia in a sudden-death semifinal leading to the Southern Ontario Baseball League championship. Baytown lost the game eleven to four and Dolan, besides going hitless, had allowed the ball to get past him twice and each time a run scored while he was scrambling around twenty feet behind homeplate, trying to find the handle.

Warned by his telephone call the day before, Anna was waiting for him in the back garden when he walked around the side of the house. It was bigger than his place back home but she was only renting it, furnished. Reclining in a folding chair, an empty one beside her, she raised her sunglasses and studied him as he shambled across the grass.

"You've lost weight," she said.

"Pining away without you."

"You look younger." Her voice and her frown conveyed suspicion. "What's her name?"

There was a pitcher of lemonade and a couple of glasses on a table between the chairs. He poured himself a splash and sat down. "You're a mindreader."

"Why else would you ask to come and see me?"

"Maybe I miss you."

"Maybe, but you don't." She had not taken her eyes from his face. "Don't look so pathetic. I wrote us off a long time ago."

"I hate it when you say that."

"Stop clinging to a finished thing. Move on, Case."

He set down his empty glass on the tin table. It rang like the signal for the start of round one. "Funny you should say that, Annie. I need a divorce."

"So. What's her name?"

"Carmen Hopkins."

Anna turned her head.

"Is that the fat little teenager I met the last time I came into the station? You must be joking."

"She's a clever young woman."

"She's a bloody genius if she's trapped you." Her face was pale, she looked her age. "Is she pregnant?"

"Not that I've heard."

"She's saving her trump card. Casey, listen to me, I'm about to do you a favour."

"I'm listening."

"No way will I ever grant you a divorce to marry that carnivorous high school dropout. If you were to come to me with some mature, intelligent, decent woman — " She watched his face for a few minutes while he counted blooms on hollyhocks. Then she got up and carried the pitcher and her glass to the house. "Crazy," she threw back at him. "Out of sight."

Dolan came in a few minutes later and heard the shower drumming. He wandered through rooms he had seen only once before. He used to believe, like a kid, that he and Anna in the house in Baytown were permanent because nothing else could ever contain their relationship. He was wrong. There was always another way.

She joined him as he was exploring the bedroom. It was a new robe, soft towelling in a shade of blue he liked, and she smelled of the lilac soap she had brought into his life decades ago. She stood beside him; there was no place for his arm except across her hip. They slipped easily into a familiar embrace. As they kissed, she whispered, "I was hoping you hadn't driven all this way just to argue."

"Seems I didn't," he said.

In the next hour, the light in the room diminished slowly as afternoon became evening. Casey lay at ease with Anna tucked close against his side. The occasional things she said buzzed against his ear. He was falling asleep. The trip had solved nothing. All it proved was that he and Anna could still get it on, but that had never been in doubt. They could not live together, and she would never, clearly, release him to marry Carmen.

"No divorce?"

"No divorce."

"You're a bitch," he said.

"I'm the best friend you ever had."

They ate something at nine o'clock. By then, he was outside unlocking the car, making his escape from boredom, the nagging that was beginning to emerge — not all hers, he was dishing out his share. The car smelled strange inside, but he cranked down the window, switched on, and began to roll. Then Alvin Hopkins got up off the floor behind the driver's seat and put a knife against his neck.

"Hey!" The car swerved before Casey got control and stepped on the brake, easing to a stop fifty yards from Anna's house.

"Keep driving."

"How the hell did you get in here?"

"You shouldn't have given Carmen your spare key. She doesn't even have a license."

"She told me she does."

"She tells you lots of things. Like I was going to Montreal for a friend's wedding."

"She made that up?"

"That's right. My sister is crazy, don't you know that? After Pete crashed his truck and died, she went out of the house one night and put her head on the mainline track, waiting for the Toronto express. I think she knew I'd find her and bring her back but I'm not sure."

"So the whole story about she'd be alone in the house for a couple of days was to get me found there by you."

"She likes excitement."

They drove slowly in silence, down empty streets. At last Dolan said, "Where are we going?"

"I'm going back to Baytown. By bus, the way I came."

Dolan felt, at last, the cold tide of fear. It filled his gut, loosened his muscles, his foot relaxed on the accelerator.

"Don't do anything crazy."

"Keep driving. Turn left at the corner."

They drove into an area with trees and shrubs on either side of the road. Street lamps cast pools of brilliance which only emphasized the black distances beyond.

"Slow down. Pull off over there, between the lights. Here."

Dolan switched off and sat, trembling, sweating ice-water. "If you want me to stay away from Carmen, you've got it. I was just with my wife — we're planning on getting back together."

"It's Carmen staying away from you. She'll never do it, no matter what I tell her. She's a bad little girl. It's vital that I prevent her having her own way. The kid is spoiled rotten." Alvin leaned forward. "Now look at this. I want you to see something." He held the knife blade in front of Dolan's face. The thick fist, the muscular wrist formed an unbreakable grip that trembled slightly. The blade itself gleamed — at least seven inches long, a streak of oil on the honed edge. "If you yell. If you run. If you do anything but as I say, this goes into your gut and I turn it."

"Oh, Jesus," Dolan whimpered. "Jesus."

"Get out of the car. Slowly."

Hopkins was out and waiting for him on the pavement, took his arm as he slammed the door and led the old ballplayer away from the light and down a pathway smelling of ripe earth. Furtive movement occurred at intervals in the shadows. "This is where the gays hang out," Alvin said. "We're not alone."

They came to a silent clearing. Dolan could make out the surroundings, could see the shape of Alvin Hopkins as he was forced around to face him. "You'll be robbed and stabbed a lot. They have these crazy killings here all the time. But you've behaved, so I'm not going to hurt you. This blade is razor-sharp. I'll cut your throat — you won't even feel it. Then I'll do the rest. Believe me, it won't hurt."

Casey Dolan found the desperate courage to raise his voice. "Not going to hurt me?" he screamed. "Bloody hell, you're killing me."

Alvin moved swiftly, turned Dolan, lifted his chin, and swung the knife. And he was right about that important thing — Dolan didn't feel a thing.

# # #

Six months passed, during which Carmen Hopkins stayed late every night at the radio station. She told her brother she was writing a novel. He didn't believe her, he thought she was messing around with Dolan's replacement. But try as he would, however often he popped in unexpectedly, he always found her at the old typewriter, knocking hell out of the keys.

Then it was finished and she began coming home after work, eating whatever he put in front of her, then watching television until signoff. It was agreeable in a way, a nice routine which Alvin appreciated. But she was putting on weight and had stopped doing anything with her hair, which gave him an uneasy feeling. In fact, by the end of the year she was looking more like a fat sloven than his sexy little sister.

"You should take a look at yourself in the mirror," he said to her one evening.

"You should burn in hell," was her calm response.

The letter from Toronto came one Saturday morning while Carmen was still in bed. She received little mail, but whatever arrived with her name on it, Alvin opened and read. This one was first-class, typewritten envelope, a company name in the corner — Tandem Publishing Ltd. The letter was brief. It said:

Dear Miss Hopkins:

Thank you for letting us see your novel, *Hey, Don't You Remember?* It needs a bit of tightening but it is a powerful work and we would like to publish it. Is it autobiographical? The character of the psychopathic bother, Al, is particularly well drawn while the doomed love affair between the young girl and the broadcaster is poignant, to say the least.

Can you come to Toronto and talk to us? I'll look forward to an early reply —

Holding letter and envelope in one hand, Alvin shuffled across the room in his broken slippers, drew back the curtain, and went through into the musty cave where Carmen lay asleep on her cot. She was breathing slowly, a hand resting below her chin, wrinkled thumb not far from her open mouth. When it used to be his job to watch her as a child, Alvin had repeatedly dragged the wet thumb free, trying to break her of the habit. Another failure.

Now he had a new problem. His little sister was going to become a published author. She would be rich and famous and a guest on TV chat shows, where she would discuss the background of her book. Or not. It was up to him and he would have to make up his mind soon.

Counting her shallow breaths, eyeing the pillow on the floor beside the cot, Alvin smiled with deep affection. "Carmen, Carmen," he said softly. "What in the world am I going to do with you?"

Sister Companion

Therese Greenwood

A freelance writer living in Kingston, Ontario, Therese has worked as a reporter, editor and journalism professor. She is also a regular correspondent for both CBC Radio and an online mystery magazine. Her family has lived in Kingston since 1812 and her great-great-grandfather Maxime Boisvert, who drove the stage from Ottawa to Kingston, was once held up and robbed by a "notorious pirate." Both that incident and her intimate connection with Canadian history are in full evidence in the evocative sense of time and place exhibited in "Sister Companion."

The snow had turned to icy beads that should have stung my face but I could scarce distinguish them from the tears flowing down my cheeks. The white garniture designed to modestly cover my head hung in a sodden mass about my neck, my hair was plastered to my head, and my thick woollen cloak hung heavily about me like a great black blanket as I lashed the lines against the horses to urge them to greater speed.

Surely the others were as cold and frightened as I, but they gave no sign. Behind me Mother Anthony worked calmly to cushion Mr. Toomey against the bumping of the sleigh. Mr. Toomey mumbled curses — words he might have roared in front of anyone but two nuns — and tried to make little of the shotgun wound to his shoulder.

"A scratch," he said. "Don't need no woman driving."

"Nonsense," said Mother Anthony in the gentle but firm tone she usually reserved for novices and the bishop. "Sister Mary is perfectly capable of driving the horses."

"I drove a team of four after the boys left the farm," I said heartily over my shoulder, hoping they would not notice my tears amid the snowdrops.

Mr. Toomey struggled to push off the bulky travelling blanket but Mother Anthony, a substantial woman who outweighed him by a good fifty pounds, forcefully tucked him back in. "You must keep still to stem the bleeding," she chided him. "It will be some time before we reach a doctor."

"No doctor," Mr. Toomey said. "Been in worse spots. Lived to tell it."

Certainly his appearance gave that credence, for it looked as if he had lived every one of his forty-odd years. A nasty scar dashed up the left side of his misshapen face, ending in a patch that would have been black had it not been dirty grey. He had lost the eye when a horse kicked him during a shoeing — and that was almost all we knew of him, for Mr. Toomey was a reserved man who never spoke of himself or his people. We were sure, however, that the Lord sent him to us for a reason.

We had waited till after the fall harvest to begin begging alms for the residence for the aged that Toronto needed so desperately. Despite the size of our diocese, we had soon exhausted the financial prospects of our parishes and were forced to travel far afield to gather funds. Several men had then petitioned to drive Mother Anthony and I, her sister companion, on the collecting tour that would take us hundreds of cold miles from home.

While rough in appearance, Mr. Toomey stood out from the others in the test Mother Anthony had devised. She asked all to run the horses up the lane behind our Motherhouse, a finely appointed building somewhat off the Kingston Road on the outskirts of the city. They were to stop on the bluff from which we could see the big lake. The others had come as close to the bluff's edge as possible to show their skill in managing the horses. Mr. Toomey, however, had pulled up several yards away, mindful of the safety of his would-be passengers. I was not surprised he was chosen to accompany us on our journey.

As our journey progressed it became clear Mother Anthony was a good judge of character. We had ranged far, south into Buffalo and through the United States, then back into Canada and north to Ottawa, the new capital. Throughout our travels Mr. Toomey had shown great fortitude, particularly when our sleigh crashed through the ice as we passed through the Thousand Islands. I had thought all was lost but, in the blink of an eye, Mr. Toomey had cut the horses from the traces, saving both passengers and beasts. He had spent the next day begging, in his taciturn way, and the result was a sleigh better than the one we had lost.

Indeed, he was a man of many resources and had kept our horses steady while Mother Anthony had kept faith in our mission. Bit by bit Providence had prevailed through their labour and we had sent some hard-won money home.

The final few days of our expedition, however, had seen little success. As we returned through the north we found no friends in such Methodist hamlets as Fisherville, Newtonbrook and Willowdale and even the inhabitants of O'Sullivan's Corners proved to be staunch supporters of the Orange Lodge. We had just about given up hope when we met with a final, unexpected success.

It being Sunday we had stopped for Mass at St. Columbine's, just a few hours from our Motherhouse, and found the congregation had not been idle in our absence. In full support of our cause, they had held a raffle raising the princely sum of $800. With much thanks Mother Anthony had gathered it to her purse, giving no thought to carrying such a sum with our final destination so close at hand.

Disaster had struck as we were passing a sharp bend at the Don Forks. A cut-throat, a flour sack over his head and an ugly weapon in his hand, stood up in the snow.

"Throw down your purse," he ordered, casually aiming a shot gun like my brother Earl had used on the farm. Later I found all I could remember of his appearance was that he handled the weapon with a maddening composure.

"Steal from the church and from women of God!" Mother Anthony said sternly, no fear in her voice. "You should be ashamed."

"Shame don't enter into it," replied the cut-throat, making a trifling motion with the gun barrel. "Throw it down."

"Can't reason with such a one," Mr. Toomey said in the sharp, raspy voice I had heard frighten a hostler who tried to cheat us in Ottawa. "Give up."

"That's right, friend," said the bandit. "Let the good Sister throw down her money."

"You shall not have it!" Mother Anthony said. "There are eleven infirm men in our wards who need this money to die in some peace and comfort."

"Those men will die poor with or without that money," said the cut-throat. "Throw it down."

"You're a terrible sinner," Mother Anthony said, and it seemed she was pulling her purse from her pocket. But, with a quickness astonishing in a woman of her proportions, she grabbed the whip that sat upright next to Mr. Toomey and snapped it at the bandit.

As the whip cracked Mr. Toomey threw himself in front of us. The blast from the gun caught him in the shoulder, propelling him back into our laps, and the spooked horses took off at a gallop. Mr. Toomey held to the lines with one hand to keep them from running free under the sleigh as Mother Anthony swiftly attempted to wrest them from him, shouting for me to scramble into the driver's seat.

It seemed an impossible task and I directed my prayers to St. Jude as I tumbled into place, my skirts a muddle on the snow-slick bench. I was barely upright before Mother Anthony gave the lines over to me and I began to pull back.

"No! Faster!" shouted Mother Anthony. "We must flee!"

I had not thought of the bandit's pursuit, only of stopping the horses before we overturned. Now I lashed at the team, calling to them as I had heard my brothers shout when they raced father's best pair at the fall exhibition. But our horses were a working pair, not bred for speed, and as I looked behind me I saw a dark figure gaining despite the slippery purchase.

I lashed again at the beasts, already trying their best to slither up a hill, when there was a yell from Mr. Toomey. I turned to glimpse him flinging Mother Anthony's purse onto the road.

"Stop! Whoa!" shouted Mother Anthony.

"G'up!" yelled Mr. Toomey and the horses began to pull even harder at the sound of his voice. When I was able to turn back a second time the bandit had disappeared.

"You should not have done that," Mother Anthony said angrily. "You had no authority."

"Must see you home safe."

"The Lord would have protected us!"

"He did," said Mr. Toomey, and that set Mother Anthony back. After months of using her wit and skill to do the Lord's work, she saw the sense of it.

"We may get it back," she said finally. "The police will soon catch the bandit."

"No police," said Mr. Toomey.

"Surely you do not expect such a crime to go unreported!"

"I tossed the money. They'll wonder 'bout me," said Mr. Toomey, who knew the ways of men well enough. "Won't do."

The next few miles were anxious and it was with great relief that I pulled up the nearly spent team in front of the Motherhouse. I was young in those days, little more than a girl, and it was nothing for me to make an undignified leap from the seat. I skittered forward in the icy road, my skirt gathered in my hand, to steady the team as Mother Anthony helped Mr. Toomey from the sleigh. He was a small man, just two inches taller than my own five feet two, and slim and wiry. Now he looked runty beside the queenly proportions of our black-cloaked superior.

Our arrival home would have caused a stir in any event and it was no surprise to see our Sisters come running to greet us. Their looks of joy turned quickly to concern, but it was a time for action, not explanation.

"We met with trouble on the road," said Mother Anthony. "Sister Mary must be warmed up and dressed in a fresh habit, and do not plague her with questions."

I left the care of the horses, who had done a mighty job, to two Sisters who had also been raised on the farm. Then I hurried gratefully towards warm water and a clean habit. The Sisters were bursting to query me but obeyed Mother Anthony's instructions and, indeed, I was too exhausted to speak. As I waited for the water to heat, I knelt to thank God for guiding my hands on the lines and asked him to keep Mr. Toomey safe from his wounds.

I had only the one habit and so was fastening my rosary to borrowed garments when I was summoned to our front parlour. It was the first time I was to sit in the good parlour, although as a novice I had spent some hours cleaning the marble fireplace. There I found Mr. Toomey and Mother Anthony with Constable O'Reilly.

I was not surprised to see the young policeman. Toronto was a much smaller place in those days and someone must have seen our wild race through the snow and felt it merited the attention of the officials.

"The damn — , oddest thing," Mr. Toomey was saying. "Had Bess's hoof in hand hundred times a'fore."

Mr. Toomey looked even smaller without his snow-covered muffler, great coat, and cap. His blue jeans, a bit too long, were turned up to reveal the cuffs of a rather good pair of wool trousers which he wore to Mass on Sundays. His shoulder was bound and, though he must have been in great pain, his funny rasp of a voice never quaked.

"Come in, Sister Mary," said Mother Anthony, looking up from the silver tea service which the bishop's sister had bequeathed to us. "Mr. Toomey has been telling the constable how he injured himself."

Puzzling over her uncharitable description of what could be described as rash behaviour on her part but certainly not Mr. Toomey's, I sat on the embroidered chair they had left for me near the fire.

"Good afternoon, Sister Mary," said Constable O'Reilly, balancing one of our best china cups on his knee. "I understand you have had quite a fright."

"Fright does not describe it," I said.

"Indeed," Mother Anthony took over. "To think we travelled so far without incident and then had such an accident close to home. And that so much could come of a horse throwing a shoe! Thanks be to God we arrived here safely."

I was astonished at her words but kept chastity of my eyes, staring down into the teacup she had presented me.

"You may have been very fortunate, Sisters," Constable O'Reilly said. "There have been several robberies on the Kingston Road these past few months."

"Alas, we had nothing to steal," said Mother Anthony. "Our travels have not given us the bounty we were seeking. We were returning empty-handed."

Mindful of my vow of obedience I mutely sipped my tea, hoping Mother Anthony's meaning would be made clear. Did she fear others would think Mr. Toomey had tossed our money at the bandit as a conspirator? Perhaps the constable sensed my discomfort, for he certainly did not suspect Mother Anthony of deception. He was from a fine church-going family and could not conceive of a Sister telling an untruth. And truly, when he inquired how I felt, I replied honestly.

"I thank the Lord I did not overturn the sleigh," I said.

"It seems you have some talent as a driver," Constable O'Reilly said. "Perhaps you will be able to give Mr. Toomey some tips."

Mother Anthony gave a small laugh at his joke and more polite talk was exchanged, but the constable was a busy man and he soon finished up his tea and left. He was barely out the door when Mr. Toomey slumped forward, allowing the strain to appear on his pale face. He seemed to weigh almost nothing as Mother Anthony and I carried him to her office, where a bowl of hot water and some clean cloths sat waiting on her desk.

"I need assistance cleaning Mr. Toomey's wound," said Mother Anthony. "I trust that what you see and hear shall remain between the three of us and God."

"Of course, Mother Anthony," I said.

"Sister Mary." Mr. Toomey's squeak was now thin with pain. "Hear my story."

"There's no need," I said. "I am sure that you have always been a good Christian gentleman."

"No," he said with a small laugh, the only one I ever heard him give. "Born on farm, like you. Hard work, but always food and such. Was twelve when Pa lost the farm."

It was a long speech for him, but he continued. "Too proud for poorhouse. Went to town. No work. Much handsomer creature then. Might've took bad ways."

I was unsure of his meaning. I knew of grinding poverty and the poor nameless babes who showed up at our door. But I had not yet seen all the evil that Satan can work and that a boy could be used so foully did not occur to me.

"Liked horses," he went on. "Work 'em ways others cain't. Worked lots of places. Like it here. Don't want to move on."

The bell that guided the Motherhouse through the day rang for the evening prayer and Mr. Toomey took it as a signal to end his story. I was more confused than ever as I stood by Mother Anthony and prepared to help clean shot and bits of wool shirt from the nasty wound.

People think we Sisters lead sheltered lives but our cloister is the world and as we nurse its sick and dying we see much of its mortification. Still, I was unprepared as Mother Anthony pulled Mr. Toomey's shirt from his back. My hands started involuntarily, nearly knocking the water basin to the floor.

"Steady, Sister Mary," Mother Anthony said.

Those were the last words we ever spoke on the subject.

I kept Mr. Toomey's secret until his death causes me to share it with you, your Grace. You have often encountered Mr. Toomey, as I find I still refer to him, as he drove us about, even in these late days when the Lord has seen fit for me to assume the role of Mother Superior. I believe he has even driven you when your man was indisposed.

Now we find he has left his savings to our home for the aged, after already paying us many times over for the $800 Mother Anthony sacrificed for him. But truly, it was no sacrifice. Of course he would have been cleared by an inquiry but appearances would have dictated he no longer serve the Lord with us at the Motherhouse, and he has been a good and faithful servant.

And what safer place was there for such a person than a convent? There was no sin in the fact that Mr. Toomey was a woman. I'm sure there is no reason he — I must learn to say she — cannot lie in consecrated ground.

Keller's Therapy

Lawrence Block

Lawrence is one of the most respected names in contemporary crime fiction. He has garnered countless honours — including multiple Edgar and Shamus Awards — over a professional career that continues unabated after forty years. His frequently dark and brooding novels about Matthew Scudder the recovering alcoholic, unlicensed private eye are among the finest of modern American detective stories. On the other hand, his novels about Bernie Rhodenbarr, the thief cum used book dealer, offer deft caper plotting and delightful whimsy. He has also created series characters Chip Harrison and Evan Tanner, as well as producing dozens of powerful short stories. Born in Buffalo, New York, Lawrence is a frequent guest at mystery and writers' conventions the world over — from the US to Ireland to Australia. He has also written extensively on the subject of writing, producing books and a series of magazine articles offering sound guidance for aspiring authors. "Keller's Therapy" is one of a series of connected stories (published in the book *Hit Man* in 1997) about a uniquely businesslike, philosophical and compassionate hired assassin.

"I had this dream," Keller said. "Matter of fact, I wrote it down, as you suggested."

"Good."

Before getting on the couch, Keller had removed his jacket and hung it on the back of a chair. He moved from the couch to retrieve his notebook from the jacket's inside breast pocket, then sat on the couch and found the page with the dream on it. He read through his notes rapidly, closed the book, and sat there, uncertain of how to proceed.

"As you prefer," said Breen. "Sitting up or lying down, whichever is more comfortable."

"It doesn't matter?"

"Not to me."

And which was more comfortable? A seated posture seemed natural for conversation, while lying down on the couch had the weight of tradition on its side. Keller, who felt driven to give this his best shot, decided to go with tradition. He stretched out, put his feet up.

He said, "I'm living in a house, except it's almost like a castle. Endless passageways and dozens of rooms."

"Is it your house?"

"No, I just live here. In fact, I'm a kind of servant for the family that owns the house. They're almost like royalty."

"And you are a servant."

"Except I have very little to do and I'm treated like an equal. I play tennis with members of the family. There's this tennis court in the back."

"And this is your job? To play tennis?"

"No, that's an example of how they treat me as an equal. I eat at the same table with them, instead of with the servants. My job is the mice."

"The mice?"

"The house is infested with mice. I'm having dinner with the family, I've got a plate piled high with good food, and a waiter in black tie comes in and presents a covered dish. I lift the cover and there's a note on it, and it says, 'Mice'."

"Just the single word?"

"That's all. I get up from the table and follow the waiter down a long hallway, and I wind up in an unfinished room in the attic. There are tiny mice all over the room — there must be twenty or thirty of them — and I have to kill them."

"How?"

"By crushing them underfoot. That's the quickest and most humane way, but it bothers me and I don't want to do it. But the sooner I finish, the sooner I can get back to my dinner, and I'm hungry."

"So you kill the mice?"

"Yes," Keller said. "One almost gets away, but I stomp on it just as it's running out the door. And then I'm back at the dinner table and everybody's eating and drinking and laughing, and my plate's been cleared away. Then there's a big fuss, and finally they bring back my plate from the kitchen, but it's not the same food as before. It's — "

"Yes?"

"Mice," Keller said. "They're skinned and cooked, but it's a plateful of mice."

"And you eat them?"

"That's when I woke up," Keller said. "And not a moment too soon, I'd say."

"Ah," Breen said. He was a tall man, long-limbed and gawky, wearing chinos, a dark green shirt, and a brown corduroy jacket. He looked to Keller like someone who had been a nerd in high school and who now managed to look distinguished in an eccentric sort of way. He said "Ah" again, folded his hands, and asked Keller what he thought the dream meant.

"You're the doctor," Keller said.

"You think it means I'm the doctor?"

"No, I think you're the one who can say what it means. Maybe it just means I shouldn't eat Rocky Road ice cream right before I go to bed."

"Tell me what you think the dream means."

"Maybe I see myself as a cat."

"Or as an exterminator?"

Keller didn't say anything.

"Let's work with this dream on a superficial level," Breen said. "You're employed as a corporate troubleshooter, except that you use another word for it."

"They tend to call us expediters," Keller said, "but troubleshooter is what it amounts to."

"Most of the time there is nothing for you to do. You have considerable opportunity for recreation, for living the good life. For tennis, as it were, and for nourishing yourself at the table of the rich and powerful. Then mice are discovered, and it is at once clear that you are a servant with a job to do."

"I get it," Keller said.

"Go on, then. Explain it to me."

"Well, it's obvious, isn't it? There's a problem and I'm called in and I have to drop what I'm doing and go and deal with it. I have to take abrupt, arbitrary action, and that can involve firing people and closing out entire departments. I have to do it, but it's like stepping on mice. And when I'm back at the table and I want my food — I suppose that's my salary?"

"Your compensation, yes."

"And I get a plate of mice." Keller made a face. "In other words, what? My compensation comes from the destruction of the people I have to cut adrift. My sustenance comes at their expense. So it's a guilt dream?"

"What do you think?"

"I think it's guilt. My profit derives from the misfortunes of others, from the grief I bring to others. That's it, isn't it?"

"On the surface, yes. When we go deeper, perhaps we will begin to discover other connections. With your having chosen this job in the first place, perhaps, and with some aspects of your childhood." He interlaced his fingers and sat back in his chair. "Everything is of a piece, you know. Nothing exists alone and nothing is accidental. Not even your name."

"My name?"

"Peter Stone. Think about it, why don't you, between now and our next session."

"Think about my name?"

"About your name and how it suits you. And" — a reflexive glance at this wristwatch — "I'm afraid our hour is up."

# # #

Jerrold Breen's office was on Central Park West at Ninety-fourth Street. Keller walked to Columbus Avenue, rode a bus five blocks, crossed the street, and hailed a taxi. He had the driver go through Central Park, and by the time he got out of the cab at Fiftieth Street, he was reasonably certain he hadn't been followed. He bought coffee in a deli and stood on the sidewalk, keeping an eye open while he drank it. Then he walked to the building where he lived, on First Avenue between Forty-eighth and Forty-ninth. It was a prewar high-rise with an art deco lobby and an attended elevator. "Ah, Mr. Keller," the attendant said. "A beautiful day, yes?"

"Beautiful," Keller agreed.

Keller had a one-bedroom apartment on the nineteenth floor. He could look out his window and see the UN building, the East River, the borough of Queens. On the first Sunday in November he could watch the runners streaming across the Queensboro Bridge, just a couple of miles past the midpoint of the New York Marathon.

It was a spectacle Keller tried not to miss. He would sit at his window for hours while thousands of them passed through his field of vision, first the world-class runners, then the middle-of-the-pack plodders, and finally the slowest of the slow, some walking, some hobbling. They started in Staten Island and finished in Central Park, and all he saw was a few hundred yards of their ordeal as they made their way over the bridge and into Manhattan. The sight always moved him to tears, though he could not have said why.

Maybe it was something to talk about with Breen.

It was a woman who had led him to the therapist's couch, an aerobics instructor named Donna. Keller had met her at the gym. They'd had a couple of dates and had been to bed a couple of times, enough to establish their sexual incompatibility. Keller still went to the same gym two or three times a week to raise and lower heavy metal objects, and when he ran into her, they were friendly.

One time, just back from a trip somewhere, he must have rattled on about what a nice town it was. "Keller," she said, "if there was ever a born New Yorker, you're it. You know that, don't you?"

"I suppose so."

"But you always have this fantasy of living the good life in Elephant, Montana. Every place you go, you dream up a whole life to go with it."

"Is that bad?"

"Who's saying it's bad? But I bet you could have fun with it in therapy."

"You think I need to be in therapy?"

"I think you'd get a lot out of therapy," she said. "Look, you come here, right? You climb the stair monster, you use the Nautilus."

"Mostly free weights."

"Whatever. You don't do this because you're a physical wreck."

"I do it to stay in shape. So?"

"So I see you as closed in and trying to reach out," she said. "Going all over the country, getting real estate agents to show you houses that you're not going to buy."

"That was only a couple of times. And what's so bad about it, anyway? It passes the time."

"You do these things and don't know why," she said. "You know what therapy is? It's an adventure, it's a voyage of discovery. And it's like going to the gym. Look, forget it. The whole thing's pointless unless you're interested."

"Maybe I'm interested," he said.

Donna, not surprisingly, was in therapy herself. But her therapist was a woman, and they agreed that he'd be more comfortable working with a man. Her ex-husband had been very fond of his therapist, a West Side psychologist named Breen. Donna had never met the man, and she wasn't on the best of terms with her ex, but —

"That's all right," Keller said. "I'll call him myself."

He'd called Breen, using Donna's ex-husband's name as a reference. "I doubt that he even knows me by name," Keller said. "We got to talking a while back at a party and I haven't seen him since. But something he said struck a chord with me and, well, I thought I ought to explore it."

"Intuition is always a powerful teacher," Breen said.

Keller made an appointment, giving his name as Peter Stone. In his first session he talked about his work for a large and unnamed conglomerate. "They're a little old-fashioned when it comes to psychotherapy," he told Breen.

"So I'm not going to give you an address or telephone number, and I'll pay for each session in cash."

"Your life is filled with secrets," Breen said.

"I'm afraid it is. My work demands it."

"This is a place where you can be honest and open. The idea is to uncover the secrets you've been keeping from yourself. Here you are protected by the sanctity of the confessional, but it's not my task to grant you absolution. Ultimately, you absolve yourself."

"Well," Keller said.

"Meanwhile, you have secrets to keep. I respect that. I won't need your address or telephone number unless I'm forced to cancel an appointment. I suggest you call to confirm your sessions an hour or two ahead of time, or you can take the chance of an occasional wasted trip. If you have to cancel an appointment, be sure to give twenty-four hours notice. Or I'll have to charge you for the missed session."

"That's fair," Keller said.

He went twice a week, Mondays and Thursdays at two in the afternoon. It was hard to tell what they were accomplishing. Sometimes Keller relaxed completely on the sofa, talking freely and honestly about his childhood. Other times he experienced the fifty-minute session as a balancing act: he yearned to tell everything and was compelled to keep it all a secret.

No one knew he was doing this. Once, when he ran into Donna, she asked if he'd ever given the shrink a call, and he'd shrugged sheepishly and said he hadn't. "I thought about it," he said, "but then somebody told me about this masseuse — she does a combination of Swedish and shiatsu — and I have to tell you, I think it does me more good than somebody poking and probing at the inside of my head."

"Oh, Keller," she'd said, not without affection. "Don't ever change."

# # #

It was on a Monday that he recounted the dream about the mice. Wednesday morning his phone rang, and it was Dot. "He wants to see you," she said.

"Be right out," he said.

He put on a tie and jacket and caught a cab to Grand Central and a train to White Plains. There he caught another cab and told the driver to head out Washington Boulevard and to let him off at the corner of Norwalk. After the cab drove off, he walked up Norwalk to Taunton Place and turned left. The second house on the right was an old Victorian with a wraparound porch. He rang the bell and Dot let him in.

"The upstairs den, Keller," she said. "He's expecting you."

He went upstairs, and forty minutes later he came down again. A young man named Louis drove him back to the station, and on the way they chatted about a recent boxing match they'd both seen on ESPN. "What I wish," Louis said, "is that they had, like, a mute button on the remote, except what it would do is mute the announcers but you'd still hear the crowd noise and the punches landing. What you wouldn't have is the constant yammer-yammer-yammer in your ear." Keller wondered if they could do that. "I don't see why not," Louis said. "They can do everything else. If you can put a man on the moon, you ought to be able to shut up Al Bernstein."

Keller took a train back to New York and walked to his apartment. He made a couple of phone calls and packed a bag. At three thirty he went downstairs, walked half a block, hailed a cab for JFK, and picked up his boarding pass for American's five fifty-five flight to Tucson.

In the departure lounge he remembered his appointment with Breen. He called to cancel the Thursday session. Since it was less than twenty-four hours away, Breen said he'd have to charge him for the missed session, unless he was able to book someone else into the slot.

"Don't worry about it," Keller told him. "I hope I'll be back in time for my Monday appointment, but it's always hard to know how long these things are going to take. If I can't make it, I should at least be able to give you the twenty-four hours notice."

He changed planes in Dallas and got to Tucson shortly before midnight. He had no luggage aside from the piece he was carrying, but he went to the baggage-claim area anyway. A rail-thin man with a broad-brimmed straw hat held a hand-lettered sign that read NOSCAASI. Keller watched the man for a few minutes and observed that no one else was watching him. He went up to him and said, "You know, I was figuring it out the whole way to Dallas. What I came up with, it's Isaacson spelled backwards."

"That's it," the man said. "That's exactly it." He seemed impressed, as if Keller had cracked the Japanese naval code. He said, "You didn't check a bag, did you? I didn't think so. The car's this way."

In the car the man showed Keller three photographs, all of the same man, heavyset, dark, with glossy black hair and a greedy pig face. Bushy mustache, bushy eyebrows and enlarged pores on his nose.

"That's Rollie Vasquez," the man said. "Son of a bitch wouldn't exactly win a beauty contest, would he?"

"I guess not."

"Let's go," the man said. "Show you where he lives, where he eats, where he gets his ashes hauled. Rollie Vasquez, this is your life."

Two hours later the man dropped Keller at a Ramada Inn and gave him a room key and a car key. "You're all checked in," he said. "Car's parked at the foot of the staircase closest to your room. She's a Mitsubishi Eclipse, pretty decent transportation. Colour's supposed to be silver-blue, but she says grey on the papers. Registration's in the glove compartment."

"There was supposed to be something else."

"That's in the glove compartment, too. Locked, of course, but the one key fits the ignition and the glove compartment. And the doors and the trunk, too. And if you turn the key upside down, it'll still fit, because there's no up or down to it. You really got to hand it to those Japs."

"What'll they think of next?"

"Well, it may not seem like much," the man said, "but all the time you waste making sure you got the right key, then making sure you got it right side up..."

"It adds up."

"It does," the man said. "Now you have a full tank of gas. It takes regular, but what's in there's enough to take you upward of four hundred miles."

"How're the tires? Never mind. Just a joke."

"And a good one," the man said. "'How're the tires?' I like that."

# # #

The car was where it was supposed to be, and the glove compartment held the registration and a semiautomatic pistol, a .22-calibre Horstmann Sun Dog, loaded, with a spare clip lying alongside it. Keller slipped the gun and the spare clip into his carry-on, locked the car, and went to his room without passing the front desk.

After a shower, he sat down and put his feet up on the coffee table. It was all arranged, and that made it simpler, but sometimes he liked it better the other way, when all he had was a name and address and no one to smooth the way for him. This was simple, all right, but who knew what traces were being left? Who knew what kind of history the gun had, or what the string bean with the NOSCAASI sign would say if the police picked him up and shook him?

All the more reason to do it quickly. He watched enough of an old movie on cable to ready him for sleep. When he woke up, he went out to the car and took his bag with him. He expected to return to the room, but if he didn't, he would be leaving nothing behind, not even a fingerprint.

He stopped at Denny's for breakfast. Around one he had lunch at a Mexican place on Figueroa. In the late afternoon he drove into the foothills north of the city, and he was still there when the sun went down. Then he drove back to the Ramada.

That was Thursday. Friday morning the phone rang while he was shaving. He let it ring. It rang again as he was showering. He let it ring. It rang again just as he was ready to leave. He didn't answer it this time, either, but he went around wiping surfaces a second time with a hand towel. Then he went out to the car.

At two that afternoon he followed Rolando Vasquez into the men's room of the Saguaro Lanes bowling alley and shot him three times in the head. The little gun didn't make much noise, not even in the confines of the tiled lavatory. Earlier he had fashioned an improvised suppressor by wrapping the barrel of the gun with a space-age insulating material that muffled the gun's report without adding much weight or bulk. If you could do that, he thought, you ought to be able to shut up Al Bernstein.

He left Vasquez propped in a stall, left the gun in a storm drain half a mile away, left the car in the long-term lot at the airport. Flying home, he wondered why they had needed him in the first place. They'd supplied the car and the gun and the finger man. Why not do it themselves? Did they really need to bring him all the way from New York to step on the mouse?

# # #

"You said to think about my name," he told Breen. "The significance of it. But I don't see how it could have any significance. It's not as if I chose it."

"Let me suggest something," Breen said. "There is a metaphysical principle which holds that we choose everything about our lives, that we select the parents we are born to, that everything which happens in our lives is a manifestation of our wills. Thus, there are no accidents, no coincidences."

"I don't know if I believe that."

"You don't have to. We'll just take it as a postulate. So assuming that you chose the name Peter Stone, what does your choice tell us?"

Keller, stretched full length upon the couch, was not enjoying this. "Well, a peter's a penis," he said reluctantly. "A stone peter would be an erection, wouldn't it?"

"Would it?"

"So I suppose a guy who decides to call himself Peter Stone would have something to prove. Anxiety about his virility. Is that what you want me to say?"

"I want you to say whatever you wish," Breen said. "Are you anxious about your virility?"

"I never thought I was," Keller said. "Of course, it's hard to say how much anxiety I might have had back before I was born, around the time I was picking my parents and deciding what name they should choose for me. At that age I probably had a certain amount of difficulty maintaining an erection, so I guess I had a lot to be anxious about."

"And now?"

"I don't have a performance problem, if that's the question. I'm not the way I was in my teens, ready to go three or four times a night, but then, who in his right mind would want to? I can generally get the job done."

"You get the job done."

"Right."

"You perform."

"Is there something wrong with that?"

"What do you think?"

"Don't do that," Keller said. "Don't answer a question with a question. If I ask a question and you don't want to respond, just leave it alone. But don't turn it back on me. It's irritating."

Breen said, "You perform, you get the job done. But what do you feel, Mr. Peter Stone?"

"Feel?"

"It is unquestionably true that peter is a colloquialism for the penis, but is has an earlier meaning. Do you recall Christ's words to Peter? 'Thou art Peter, and upon this rock I shall build my church.' Because Peter *means* rock. Our Lord was making a pun. So your first name means rock and your last name is Stone. What does that give us? Rock and stone. Hard, unyielding, obdurate. Insensitive. Unfeeling . . ."

"Stop," Keller said.

"In the dream, when you kill the mice, what do you feel?"

"Nothing. I just want to get the job done."

"Do you feel their pain? Do you feel pride in your accomplishment, satisfaction in a job well done? Do you feel a thrill, a sexual pleasure, in their deaths?"

"Nothing," Keller said. "I feel nothing. Could we stop for a moment?"

"What do you feel right now?"

"I'm just a little sick to my stomach, that's all."

"Do you want to use the bathroom? Shall I get you a glass of water?"

"No, I'm all right. It's better when I sit up. It'll pass. It's passing already."

# # #

Sitting at his window, watching not marathoners but cars streaming over the Queensboro Bridge, Keller thought about names. What was particularly annoying, he thought, was that he didn't need to be under the care of a board-certified metaphysician to acknowledge the implications of the name Peter Stone. He had chosen it, but not in the matter of a soul deciding what parents to be born to and planting names in their heads. He had picked the name when he called to make his initial appointment with Jerrold Breen. "Name?" Breen had demanded. "Stone," he had replied. "Peter Stone."

Thing is, he wasn't stupid. Cold, unyielding, insensitive, but not stupid. If you wanted to play the name game, you didn't have to limit yourself to the alias he had selected. You could have plenty of fun with the name he'd had all his life.

His full name was John Paul Keller, but no one called him anything but Keller, and few people even knew his first and middle names. His apartment lease and most of the cards in his wallet showed his name as J. P. Keller. Just plain Keller was what people called him, men and women alike. ("The upstairs den, Keller. He's expecting you." "Oh Keller, don't ever change." "I don't know how to say this, Keller, but I'm simply not getting my needs met in this relationship.")

Keller. In German it meant cellar, or tavern. But the hell with that. You didn't need to know what it meant in a foreign language. Change a vowel. Killer.

Clear enough, wasn't it?

# # #

On the couch, eyes closed, Keller said, "I guess the therapy's working."

"Why do you say that?"

"I met this girl last night, bought her a couple of drinks, and went home with her. We went to bed and I couldn't do anything."

"You couldn't do anything?"

"Well, if you want to be technical, there were other things I could have done. I could have typed a letter or sent out for pizza. I could have sung 'Melancholy Baby.' But I couldn't do what we'd both been hoping for, which was to have sex."

"You were impotent?"

"You know, you're very sharp. You never miss a trick."

"You blame me for your impotence," Breen said.

"Do I? I don't know about that. I'm not sure I even blame myself. To tell you the truth, I was more amused than devastated. And she wasn't upset, perhaps out of relief that I wasn't upset. But just so nothing like that happens again, I've decided to change my name to Dick Hardin."

"What was your father's name?"

"My father," Keller said. "Jesus, what a question. Where did that come from?"

Breen didn't say anything.

Neither, for several minutes, did Keller. Then, eyes closed, he said, "I never knew my father. He was a soldier. He was killed in action before I was born. Or he was shipped overseas before I was born and killed when I was just a few months old. Or possibly he was home when I was born or came home on leave when I was small, and he held me on his knee and told me he was proud of me."

"You have such a memory?"

"No," Keller said. "The only memory I have is of my mother telling me about him, and that's the source of the confusion, because she told me different things at different times. Either he was killed before I was born or shortly after, and either he died without seeing me, or he saw me one time and sat me on his knee. She was a good woman, but she was vague about a lot of things. The one thing she was completely clear on was that he was a soldier. And he was killed over there."

"And his name?"

Was Keller, he thought. "Same as mine," he said. "But forget the name, this is more important then the name. Listen to this. She had a picture of him. A head-and-shoulders shot, this good-looking young soldier in a uniform and wearing a cap, the kind that folds flat when you take it off. The picture was in a gold frame on her dresser when I was a little kid."

"And then one day the picture wasn't there anymore. 'It's gone,' she said. And that was all she would say on the subject. I was older then, I must have been seven or eight years old

"Couple of years later I got a dog. I named him Soldier, after my father. Years after that, two things occurred to me. One, Soldier's a funny thing to call a dog. Two, who ever heard of naming a dog after his father? But at the time it didn't seem the least bit unusual to me."

"What happened to the dog?"

"He became impotent. Shut up, will you? What I'm getting to is a lot more important than the dog. When I was fourteen, fifteen years old, I used to work after school helping out this guy who did odd jobs in the neighbourhood. Cleaning out basements and attics, hauling trash, that sort of thing. One time this notions store went out of business, the owner must have died, and we were cleaning out the basement for the new tenant. Boxes of junk were all over the place, and we had to go through everything, because part of how this guy made his money was selling off the stuff he got paid to haul. But you couldn't go through all this crap too thoroughly or you were wasting your time.

"I was checking out this one box, and what do I pull out but a framed picture of my father. The very same one that sat on my mother's dresser, him in his uniform and military cap, the picture that had disappeared, it's even in the same frame, and what's it doing here?"

Not a word from Breen.

"I can still remember how I felt. Stunned, like *Twilight Zone* time. Then I reach back into the box and pull out the first thing I touch, and it's the same picture in the same frame.

"The box is full of framed pictures. About half of them are the soldier, and the others are a fresh-faced blonde with her hair in a pageboy and a big smile on her face. It was in a box of frames. They used to package inexpensive frames that way, with photos in them for display. For all I know they still do. My mother must have bought a frame in a five-and-dime and told me it was my father. Then when I got a little older, she got rid of it.

"I took one of the framed photos home with me. I didn't say anything to her, I didn't show it to her, but I kept it around for a while. I found out the photo dated from World War Two. In other words, it couldn't have been a picture of my father, because he would have been wearing a different uniform.

"By this time I think I already knew that the story she told me was, well, a story. I don't believe she knew who my father was. I think she got drunk and went with somebody, or maybe there were several different men. What difference does it make? She moved to another town, she told people that she was married, that her husband was in the service or that he was dead, whatever she told them."

"How do you feel about it?"

"How do I feel about it?" Keller shook his head. "If I slammed my hand in a car door you'd ask me how I felt about it."

"And you'd be stuck for an answer," Breen said. "Here's a question for you: Who was your father?"

"I just told you."

"But *someone* fathered you. Whether or not you knew him, whether or not your mother knew who he was, there was a particular man who planted the seed that grew into you. Unless you believe yourself to be the second coming of Christ."

"No," Keller said. "That's one delusion I've been spared."

"So tell me who he was, this man who spawned you. Not on the basis of what you were told or what you've managed to figure out. I'm not asking the part of you that thinks and reasons. I'm asking the part of you that simply knows. Who was your father? What was your father?"

"He was a soldier," Keller said.

# # #

Keller, walking uptown on Second Avenue, found himself standing in front of a pet shop, watching a couple of puppies cavorting in the window.

He went inside. One wall was given over to stacked cages of puppies and kittens. Keller felt his spirits sink as he looked into the cages. Waves of sadness rocked him.

He turned away and looked at the other pets. Birds in cages, gerbils and snakes in dry aquariums, tanks of tropical fish. He felt all right about them; it was the puppies he couldn't bear to look at.

He left the store. The next day he went to an animal shelter and walked past cages of dogs waiting to be adopted. This time the sadness was overwhelming, and he felt its physical pressure against his chest. Something must have shown on his face, because the young women in charge asked him if he was all right.

"Just a dizzy spell," he said.

In the office she told him that they could probably accommodate him if he was especially interested in a particular breed. They could keep his name on file, and when a specimen of that breed became available —

"I don't think that I can have a pet," he said. "I travel too much. I can't handle the responsibility." The women didn't respond, and Keller's words echoed in her silence. "But I want to make a donation," he said. "I want to support the work you do."

He got out his wallet, pulled out bills from it, handed them to her without counting them. "An anonymous donation," he said. "I don't want a receipt. I'm sorry for taking your time. I'm sorry I can't adopt a dog. Thank you. Thank you very much."

She was saying something, but he didn't listen. He hurried out of there.

# # #

"'I want to support the work you do.' That's what I told her, and then rushed out of there because I didn't want her thanking me. Or asking questions."

"What would she ask?"

"I don't know," Keller said. He rolled over on the couch, facing away from Breen, facing the wall. "'I want to support the work you do.' But I don't know what their work is. They find homes for some animals, and what do they do with the others? Put them to sleep?"

"Perhaps."

"What do I want to support? The placement or the killing?"

"You tell me."

"I tell you too much as it is," Keller said.

"Or not enough."

Keller didn't say anything.

"Why did it sadden you to see the dogs in their cages?"

"I felt their sadness."

"One feels only one's own sadness. Why is it sad to you, a dog in a cage? Are you in a cage?"

"No."

"Your dog, Soldier. Tell me about him."

"All right," Keller said. "I guess I could do that."

# # #

A session or two later, Breen said, "You have never been married?"

"No."

"I was married."

"Oh?"

"For eight years. She was my receptionist. She booked my appointments, showed clients to the waiting room. Now I have no receptionist. A machine answers the phone. I check the machine between appointments and take and return calls at that time. If I had the machine in the first place, I'd have been spared a lot of agony."

"It wasn't a good marriage?"

Breen didn't seem to have heard the question. "I wanted children. She had three abortions in eight years and never told me. Never said a word. Then one day she threw it in my face. I'd been to a doctor, I'd had tests and all indications were that I was fertile, with a high sperm count and extremely motile sperm. So I wanted her to see a doctor. 'You fool. I've killed three of your babies already, so why don't you leave me alone?' I told her I wanted a divorce. She said it would cost me."

"And?"

"We've been divorced for nine years. Every month I write an alimony check and put it in the mail. If it were up to me, I'd burn the money."

Breen fell silent. After a moment Keller said, "Why are you telling me all this?"

"No reason."

"Is it supposed to relate to something in my psyche? Am I supposed to make a connection, clap my hand to my forehead and say, 'Of course, of course! I've been so blind!' "

"You confide in me," Breen said. "It seems only fitting that I confide in you."

# # #

Dot called a couple of days later. Keller took a train to White Plains, where Louis met him at the station and drove him to the house on Taunton Place. Later, Louis drove him back to the train station and he returned to the city. He timed his call to Breen so that he got the man's machine. "This is Peter Stone," he said. "I'm flying to San Diego on business. I'll have to miss my next appointment and possibly the one after that. I'll try to let you know."

He hung up, packed a bag, and rode the Amtrak to Philadelphia. No one met his train. The man in White Plains had shown him a photograph and given him a slip of paper with a name and address on it. The man in question managed an adult bookstore a few blocks from Independence Hall. There was a tavern across the street, a perfect vantage point, but one look inside made it clear to Keller that he couldn't spend time there without calling attention to himself, not unless he first got rid of his tie and jacket and spent twenty minutes rolling around in the gutter.

Down the street Keller found a diner, and if he sat at the far end he could keep an eye on the bookstore's mirrored front windows. He had a cup of coffee, then walked across the street to the bookstore, where two men were on duty. One was a sad-eyed youth from India or Pakistan, the other the jowly, slightly exophthalmic fellow in the photo Keller had seen in White Plains.

Keller walked past a wall of videocassettes and leafed through a display of magazines. He had been there for about fifteen minutes when the kid said he was going for his dinner. The older man said, "Oh, it's that time already, huh? Okay, but make sure you're back at seven for a change, will you?"

Keller looked at his watch. It was six o'clock. The only other customers were closeted in video booths in the back. Still, the kid had a look at him, and what was the big hurry anyway? He grabbed a couple of magazines and paid for them. The jowly man bagged them and sealed the bag with a strip of tape. Keller stowed his purchase in his carry-on and went to find a hotel.

The next day he went to a museum and a movie and arrived at the bookstore at ten minutes after six. The young clerk was gone, presumably having a plate of curry somewhere. The jowly man was behind the counter and there were three customers in the store, two checking video selections, one looking at magazines.

Keller browsed, hoping they would clear out. At one point he was standing in front of a wall of videos and it turned into a wall of caged puppies. It was momentary, and he couldn't tell if it was a genuine hallucination or just some sort of flashback. Whatever it was, he didn't like it.

One customer left, but the other two lingered, and then someone new came in off the street. The Indian kid was due back in half an hour, and who knew if he would take his full hour, anyway?

Keller approached the counter, trying to look a little more nervous than he felt. Shifty eyes, furtive glances. Pitching his voice low, he said, "Talk to you in private?"

"About what?"

Eyes down, shoulders drawn in, he said, "Something special."

"If it's got to do with little kids," the man said, "no disrespect intended, but I don't know nothing about it, I don't want to know nothing about it, and I wouldn't even know where to steer you."

"Nothing like that," Keller said.

They went into a room in back. The jowly man closed the door, and as he was turning around, Keller hit him with the edge of his hand at the juncture of his neck and shoulder. The man's knees buckled, and in an instant Keller had a loop of wire around his neck. In another minute, he was out the door, and within an hour he was on the northbound Metroliner.

When he got home he realized he still had the magazines in his bag. That was sloppy. He should have discarded them the previous night, but he had simply forgotten and never even unsealed the package.

Nor could he find a reason to unseal it now. He carried it down the hall and dropped it into the incinerator. Back in his apartment, he fixed himself a weak scotch and water and watched a documentary on the Discovery Channel. The vanishing rain forest. One more goddamned thing to worry about.

# # #

"Oedipus," Jerrold Breen said, holding his hands in front of his chest, his fingertips pressed together. "I presume you know the story. He killed his father and married his mother."

"Two pitfalls I've thus far managed to avoid."

"Indeed," Breen said. "But have you? When you fly off somewhere in your official capacity as corporate expediter, when you shoot trouble, as it were, what exactly are you doing? You fire people, you cashier divisions, close plants, rearrange lives, is that a fair description?"

"I suppose so."

"There's an implied violence. Firing a man, terminating his career, is the symbolic equivalent to killing him. And he's a stranger, and I shouldn't doubt that the more important of these men are more often than not older than you, isn't that so?"

"What's the point?"

"When you do what you do, it's as if you are seeking out and killing your unknown father."

"I don't know," Keller said. "Isn't that a little farfetched?"

"And your relationships with women," Breen went on, "have a strong Oedipal component. Your mother was a vague and unfocused woman, incompletely present in your life, incapable of connecting with others. Your own relationships with women are likewise out of focus. Your problems with impotence —"

"Once!"

"— are a natural consequence of this confusion. Your mother is dead now, isn't that so?"

"Yes."

"And your father is not to be found, and almost certainly deceased. What's called for, Peter, is an act specifically designed to reverse this pattern on a symbolic level."

"I don't follow you."

"It's a subtle point," Breen admitted. He crossed his legs, propped an elbow on a knee, extended his thumb, and rested his bony chin on it. Keller thought, for the first time, that Breen must have been a stork in a prior life. "If there were a male figure in your life," Breen went on, "preferably at least a few years your senior, someone playing a parental role vis-à-vis yourself, someone to whom you turn for advice for direction."

Keller thought of the man in White Plains.

"Instead of killing this man," Breen said, "symbolically, I am speaking symbolically throughout, but instead of killing him as you have done with father figures in the past, you might do something to *nourish* this man."

Cook a meal for the man in White Plains? Buy him a hamburger? Toss him a salad?

"Perhaps you could think of a way to use your talents to this man's benefit instead of to his detriment," Breen went on. He drew a handkerchief from his pocket and mopped his forehead. "Perhaps there is a woman in his life — your mother, symbolically — and perhaps she is a source of great pain to your father. So, instead of making love to her and slaying him, like Oedipus, you might reverse the usual course of things by, uh, showing love to him and slaying her."

"Oh," Keller said.

"Symbolically, that is to say."

"Symbolically," Keller said.

# # #

A week later Breen handed Keller a photograph. "This is called the thematic apperception test," Breen said. "You look at the photograph and make up a story about it."

"What kind of story?"

"Any kind at all," Breen said. "This is an exercise in imagination. You look at the subject of the photograph and imagine what sort of woman she is and what she is doing."

The photo was in colour and showed a rather elegant brunette dressed in tailored clothing. She had a dog on a leash. The dog was medium-sized, with a chunky body and an alert expression. It was the colour that dog people called blue and that everyone else calls grey.

"It's a woman and a dog," Keller said.

"Very good."

Keller took a breath. "The dog can talk," he said, "but he doesn't do it in front of other people. The woman made a fool of herself once when she tried to show him off. Now she knows better. When they're alone, he talks a blue streak, and the son of a bitch has an opinion on everything from the real cause of the Thirty Years' War to the best recipe for lasagna."

"He's quite a dog," Breen said.

"Yes, and now the woman doesn't want people to know he can talk, because she's afraid they might take him away from her. In this picture they're in a park. It looks like Central Park."

"Or perhaps Washington Square."

"It could be Washington Square," Keller agreed. "The woman is crazy about the dog. The dog's not so sure about the woman."

"And what do you think about the woman?"

"She's attractive," Keller said.

"On the surface," Breen said. "Underneath, it's another story, believe me. Where do you suppose she lives?"

Keller gave it some thought. "Cleveland," he said.

"Cleveland? Why Cleveland for God's sake?"

"Everybody's got to be someplace."

"If I were taking this test," Breen said, "I'd probably imagine the woman living at the foot of Fifth Avenue, at Washington Square. I'd have her living at Number One Fifth Avenue, perhaps because I'm familiar with the building. You see, I once lived there."

"Oh?"

"In a spacious apartment on a high floor. And once a month," he continued, "I write an enormous check and mail it to that address, which used to be mine. So it's only natural that I would have this particular building in mind, especially when I look at this particular photo." His eyes met Keller's. "You have a question, don't you? Go ahead and ask it."

"What breed is the dog?"

"As it happens," Breen said, "it's an Australian cattle dog. Looks like a mongrel, doesn't it? Believe me, it doesn't talk. But why don't you hang on to that photograph?"

"All right."

"You're making really fine progress in therapy," Breen said. "I want to acknowledge the work you're doing. And I just know you'll do the right thing."

# # #

A few days later, Keller was sitting on a bench in Washington Square. He folded his newspaper and walked over to a dark haired woman wearing a blazer and a beret. "Excuse me," he said, "but isn't that an Australian cattle dog?"

"That's right," she said.

"It's a handsome animal," he said. "You don't see many of them."

"Most people think he's a mutt. It's such an esoteric breed. Do you own one yourself?"

"I did. My ex-wife got custody."

"How sad for you."

"Sadder still for the dog. His name was Soldier. Is Soldier, unless she's changed it."

"This fellow's name is Nelson. That's his call name. Of course, the name on the papers is a real mouthful."

"Do you show him?"

"He's seen it all," she said. "You can't show him a thing."

# # #

"I went down to the Village last week," Keller said, "and the damnedest thing happened. I met a woman in the park."

"Is that the damnedest thing?"

"Well, it's unusual for me. I meet women at bars and parties, or someone introduces us. But we met and talked, and then I ran into her the following morning. I bought her a cappuccino."

"You just happened to run into her on two successive days?"

"Yes."

"In the Village?"

"It's where I live."

Breen frowned. "You shouldn't be seen with her, should you?"

"Why not?"

"Don't you think it's dangerous?"

"All it's cost me so far," Keller said, "is the price of a cappuccino."

"I thought we had an understanding."

"An understanding?"

"You don't live in the Village," Breen said. "I know where you live. Don't look surprised. The first time you left here I watched you from the window. You behaved as if you were trying to avoid being followed. So I took my time, and when you stopped taking precautions, I followed you. It wasn't that difficult."

"Why follow me?"

"To find out who you are. Your name is Keller, you live at Eight-six-five First Avenue. I already knew what you were. Anybody might have known just from listening to your dreams. And paying in cash, and the sudden business trips. I still don't know who employs you, crime bosses or the government, but what difference does it make? Have you been to bed with my wife?"

"Your ex-wife?"

"Answer the question."

"Yes, I have."

"Jesus Christ. And you were able to perform?"

"Yes."

"Why the smile?"

"I was just thinking," Keller said, "that it was quite a performance."

Breen was silent for a long moment. His eyes fixed above and to the right of Keller's shoulder. Then he said, "This is profoundly disappointing. I hoped you would find the strength to transcend the Oedipal myth, not merely re-enact it. You've had fun, haven't you? What a naughty boy you've been. What a triumph you've scored over your symbolic father. You've taken this woman to bed. No doubt you've had visions of getting her pregnant, so that she can give you what she cruelly denied him. Eh?"

"Never occurred to me."

"It would, sooner or later." Breen leaned forward, concern showing on his face. "I hate to see you sabotaging your therapeutic progress this way," he said. "You were doing so *well*."

#

From the bedroom window you could look down on Washington Square Park. There were plenty of dogs there now, but none were Australian cattle dogs.

"Some view," Keller said. "Some apartment."

"Believe me," she said, "I earned it. You're getting dressed. Are you going somewhere?"

"Just feeling a little restless. Okay if I take Nelson for a walk?"

"You're spoiling him," she said. "You're spoiling both of us."

#

On a Wednesday morning, Keller took a cab to La Guardia and a plane to St. Louis. He had a cup of coffee with an associate of the man in White Plains and caught an evening flight back to New York. He took another cab directly to the apartment building at the foot of Fifth Avenue.

"I'm Peter Stone," he said to the doorman. "Mrs. Breen is expecting me."

The doorman stared.

"Mrs. Breen," Keller said. "In Seventeen-J."

"Jesus."

"Is something the matter?"

"I guess you haven't heard," the doorman said. "I wish it wasn't me who had to tell you."

# # #

"You killed her," he said.

"That's ridiculous," Breen told Keller. "She killed herself. She threw herself out the window. If you want my professional opinion, she was suffering from depression."

"If you want *my* professional opinion," Keller said, "she had help."

"I wouldn't advance that argument if I were you," Breen said. "If the police were to look for a murderer, they might look long and hard at Mr. Stone-hyphen-Keller, the stone killer. And I might have to tell them how the unusual process of transference went awry, how you became obsessed with me and my personal life, how I couldn't dissuade you from some insane plan to reverse the Oedipus complex. And then they might ask you why you employ an alias and just how you make your living. Do you see why it might be best to let sleeping dogs lie?"

As if on cue, Nelson stepped out from behind the desk. He caught sight of Keller and his tail began to wag.

"Sit," Breen said. "You see? He's well trained. You might take a seat yourself."

"I'll stand. You killed her and then walked off with the dog."

Breen sighed. "The police found the dog in the apartment, whimpering in front of the open window. After I identified the body, and told them of her previous suicide attempts, I volunteered to take the dog home with me. There was no one else to look after him."

"I would have taken him," Keller said.

"But that won't be necessary, will it? You won't be called upon to walk my dog or make love to my wife or bed down in my apartment. Your services are no longer required." Breen seemed to recoil at the harshness of his own words. His face softened. "You'll be able to get back to the far more important business of therapy. In fact," he indicated to the couch, " why not stretch out right now?"

"That's not a bad idea. First though, could you put the dog in the other room?"

"Not afraid he'll interrupt, are you? Just a little joke. He can wait in the outer office. There you go Nelson. Good dog — oh, no. How *dare* you bring a gun. Put that down immediately."

"I don't think so."

"For God's sake, why kill me? I'm not your father, I'm your therapist. It makes no sense to kill me. You have nothing to gain and everything to lose. It's completely irrational. It's worse than that, it's neurotically self-destructive."

"I guess I'm not cured yet."

"What's that, gallows humour? It happens to be true. You're a long way from being cured, my friend. As a matter of fact, I would say you're approaching a psychotherapeutic crisis. How will you get through it if you shoot me?"

Keller went to the window, flung it wide open. "I'm not going to shoot you," he said.

"I've never been the least bit suicidal," Breen said, pressing his back against a wall of bookshelves. "Never."

"You've grown despondent over the death of your ex-wife."

"That's sickening, just sickening. And who would believe it?"

"We'll see," Keller told him. "As far as the therapeutic crisis is concerned, well, we'll see about that too. I'll think of something."

# # #

The woman at the animal shelter said, "Talk about coincidence. One day you come in and put your name down for an Australian cattle dog. You know, that's quite an uncommon breed in this country."

"You don't see many of them."

"And what came in this morning? A perfectly lovely Australian cattle dog. You could have knocked me over with a sledgehammer. Isn't he a beauty?"

"He certainly is."

"He's been whimpering ever since he got here. It's very sad. His owner died and there was nobody to keep him. My goodness, look how he went right to you. I think he likes you."

"I'd say we were made for each other."

"I believe it. His name is Nelson, but you can change it of course."

"Nelson," he said. The dog's ears perked up. Keller reached to give him a scratch. "No, I don't think I'll have to change it. Who is Nelson anyway? Some kind of English hero, wasn't he? A famous general or something?"

"I think an admiral. Commander of the British fleet, if I remember correctly. Remember? The Battle of Trafalgar Square?"

"It rings a muted bell," he said. "Not a soldier but a sailor. Well, that's close enough, wouldn't you say? Now I suppose there's an adoption fee and some papers to fill out."

When they handled all that part she said, "I still can't get over it. The coincidence and all."

"I knew a man once," Keller said, "who insisted that there was no such thing as a coincidence or an accident."

"Well, I wonder how he'd explain this."

"I'd like to see him try," Keller said. "Let's go Nelson. Good boy."